THE
SHARK
RIDER

TRISTAN HUNT AND
THE SEA GUARDIANS

BY
ELLEN PRAGER

WITH ILLUSTRATIONS BY
ANTONIO JAVIER CAPARO

mighty media JUNIOR READERS

MINNEAPOLIS, MINNESOTA

The Lexile Framework for Reading® Lexile measure® 740L
LEXILE®, LEXILE FRAMEWORK®, LEXILE ANALYZER®, and the LEXILE® logo are trademarks of MetaMetrics, Inc., and are registered in the United States and abroad. The trademarks and names of other companies and products mentioned herein are the property of their respective owners.
Copyright © 2011 MetaMetrics, Inc. All rights reserved.

Illustrations: Antonio Javier Caparo
Design by Mighty Media, Inc., Minneapolis, Minnesota
Interior: Chris Long · Cover: Anders Hanson
Editor: Karen Latchana Kenney

Library of Congress Cataloging-in-Publication Data
Prager, Ellen J.
The shark rider / by Ellen Prager ; illustrated by Antonio Javier Caparo.
      pages   cm. — (Tristan Hunt and the Sea Guardians; book 2)
Summary: "Tristan Hunt is having trouble keeping his newfound underwater talents a secret. And if undercover spies and a mysterious illness threatening to expose his special summer camp in the Florida Keys weren't enough, reports of dying fish and disappearing sponge in the Caribbean call Tristan and his friends back into action" —Provided by publisher.
ISBN 978-1-938063-51-0 (trade paper) — ISBN 978-1-938063-52-7 (ebook)
[1. Camps—Fiction. 2. Ability—Fiction. 3. Marine animals—Fiction. 4. Wildlife conservation—Fiction. 5. Florida Keys (Fla.)—Fiction.]
I. Caparó, Antonio Javier, illustrator. II. Title.
PZ7.P88642Sg 2015 [Fic]—dc23

                                                                    2014043985

Manufactured in the United States of America
Distributed by Publishers Group West

To all my finned friends and those who love them too.

TABLE OF CONTENTS

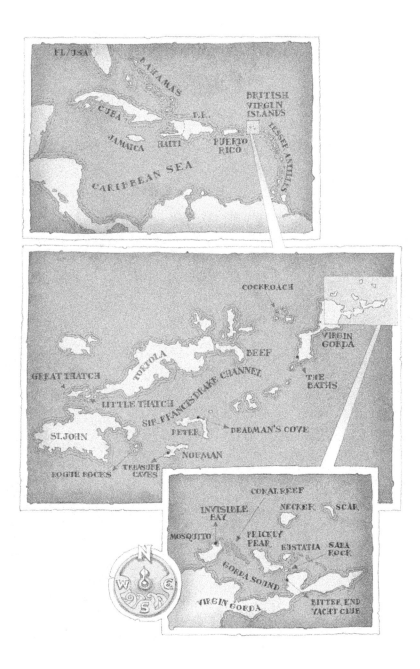

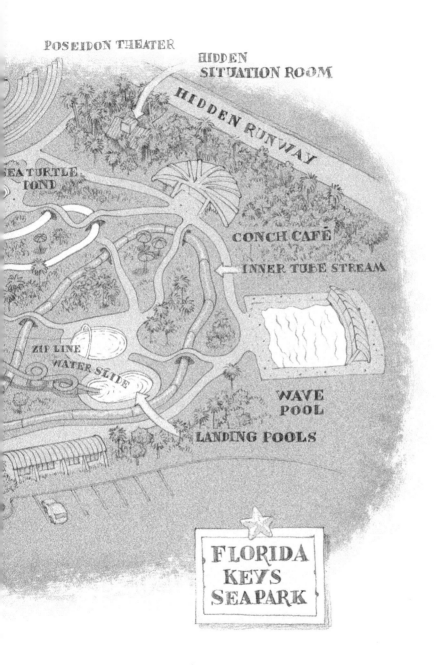

POSEIDON THEATER

HIDDEN
SITUATION ROOM

HIDDEN RUNWAY

SEA TURTLE
POND

CONCH CAFÉ

INNER TUBE STREAM

ZIP LINE
WATER SLIDE

WAVE
POOL

LANDING POOLS

FLORIDA
KEYS
SEAPARK

1

A DAY AT THE BEACH

IF ONLY HE HADN'T ACTED SO RASHLY. BUT THEY were going to murder the shark. Tristan sat on his bed and stared at the aquarium. The tropical fish stared back knowingly, shaking their heads—just like his dad had. Sea Camp was going to start in a week. No way his parents would let him go back now.

Tristan's foot thumped nervously on the floor as he waited for their decision. He thought about his science teacher, Mrs. Hawk, and when she announced they were going on a field trip to the beach. He'd been so excited. Tristan hadn't been near the ocean for months. His parents were still kind of freaked out about the whole Sea Camp thing. They acted like he'd turn into a mutant seaweed monster if he went anywhere near seawater. Now he'd probably be banned from going close to the ocean until he was really old, like thirty or something. Looking back, the day started off only slightly horrible, basically like normal.

The bus arrived at the beach parking lot mid-morning. As soon as it stopped, most of the students jumped up, anxious to get off. Tristan remained seated, trying to get a glimpse of the ocean. He knew that technically it wasn't called the ocean. Since Sarasota was on the west coast of Florida, it was actually the Gulf of Mexico. But he still thought of it as the ocean, not really sure what the difference was anyway. Stretching his neck giraffe-like, Tristan searched for the water from where he sat. Just the thought of the ocean made him long for his days at Sea Camp. Sitting in the classroom throughout the school year had been torture. Not to mention all the exams they had to take. Tristan wondered if grown-ups took so many tests. At career day, no one talked about the importance of being an expert at multiple choice or fill-in-the-blank questions.

When it was finally his turn to get up and file down the aisle, Tristan was still trying to get a glimpse of the sea. He was so distracted he didn't hear the group of hulky boys in back snickering or see the foot shoved out into the aisle in front of him.

At thirteen, Tristan Hunt was still an outsider at school. With his gangly limbs and habitual klutziness he'd always been an easy mark for practical jokes and a target for bullying. Last fall, things had been different, better—for a while. With the confidence he gained during the summer at Sea Camp, he was less apt to trip

over his own feet or stumble in whatever athletic tor-
ment was that day's gym class. He was still a klutz, just
a little bit less of one. Tristan's improved self-esteem,
however, came with a new, but sort of old and recur-
ring problem. He was ever more frequently the victim
of blurt mouth—an affliction that caused words to
spew from his mouth without any prior thought or
consideration of the consequences. His rapid-fire
remarks had gotten him grounded more times than
he could count.

At school, his biting comebacks incited his school-
mates' wrath and inspired them to find new ways to
make him look and feel like an idiot. Two boys loos-
ened the screws of the chair Tristan always sat in for
math class. It wobbled noisily and then dumped him
gawkily onto the floor in front of his classmates. At
lunch, if he didn't spill his drink or splatter himself
with something, someone else always seemed at the
ready to make sure Tristan left the cafeteria wearing
more food than he managed to consume.

Tristan tried to ignore the pranks and name-
calling by thinking of last summer and his friends at
Sea Camp. But having to keep all the cool stuff that
happened a secret made him feel even more isolated
and alone than ever. He e-mailed and texted his best
friends from camp, Sam Marten and Hugh Haverford.
But it wasn't the same as seeing them in person or
being together. Besides, they had to be careful about
what they wrote. Things had a way of getting out on
the Internet.

Tristan walked distractedly down the aisle of the school bus. Almost immediately, one of his long spindly legs caught on the outstretched foot. He careened headfirst into the line of students in front of him. Like teenage dominoes they went down, one on top of another. Howls of laughter erupted from the brawny football players waiting to be the last off.

Avoiding the angry glares and shoves of the students he just plowed into, Tristan stared back at the bulky boy who tripped him. "What *is* your problem?"

"I just don't like your face," the teen scoffed.

"Yeah, well you're no Prince Charming."

An instant later, Tristan regretted his all-too-quick retort. If he was a twig, the other boy was a giant redwood. Tristan was undoubtedly about to be pummeled into a pancake on the chewing-gum-caked, filth-covered bus floor or flung out the window like a human Frisbee.

"What did you say to me?"

Just then, the rather large bus driver stepped in. He grabbed Tristan's shoulder and shoved him like a matchstick toward the door. "That's enough. There will be no fighting on my bus."

Tristan fell out of the bus onto the pavement. His heart raced and his legs were all wobbly. He wished that just once he could control what came out of his mouth. Why couldn't he just walk away, knowing that they were just jerks? He jogged on rubbery legs to catch up with the rest of the class.

Mrs. Hawk was talking when he arrived. "Okay, students. See how the grass was planted on the dunes to prevent erosion? Please stay on the boardwalk."

Tristan looked back. The group of football players was stepping purposely off the wooden boardwalk and squashing the grass. They glared at him, daring him to say something.

"Everyone gather around," Mrs. Hawk instructed.

Tristan's teacher was in her late thirties and looked as if she just escaped a time machine from the 1960s. She had straggly brown hair that fell to her waist, and a scrawny, abnormally pale, and bird-like face. Like most days, she wore a wrinkled ankle-length cotton skirt, a tie-dyed T-shirt, and a long necklace she called her "love beads." One of the girls in Tristan's class said it was supposed to be hippie-chic or something. He just thought she was weird.

"Everyone have your gloves, clipboards, data sheets, pencils, and collection bags?" she asked.

"Yeah," the students muttered.

Mrs. Hawk told the teens to work their way down the beach, collecting trash. They were to record what each piece was on their data sheets. She also reminded them to put the trash in their bags.

"Duh!" one of the hefty boys in back shouted. "Yeah, this is why I go to school. I wanna be a garbage collector."

Ignoring the boy's remark, the teacher continued, "Once we're done, we'll collate and analyze the data back in the classroom. Remember the questions we're trying to answer. What's the most abundant type of trash? Where is it coming from? And is there something that can be done to reduce litter on the beach? We'll send our results to local officials and maybe they can use the information to prevent garbage from getting on the beach in the first place. You know, it only takes a strong wind or some rain and that trash can end up in the ocean where it may harm marine life."

When they first walked onto the beach, Tristan was sure his flaky teacher was going to make them sit in a circle, hold hands, and sing "Kumbayah." But after hearing her concern for marine life, he decided maybe she wasn't so bad after all.

The students spread out. Most split up into pairs or threesomes to pick up trash and record the information on their data sheets. Tristan stayed by himself, making sure he was a safe distance away from the group of cocky jocks. It was sunny and there was a slight onshore breeze. He inhaled the salty air, thinking how good it was to be near the sea again. Tristan walked to the water's edge and stared out over the murky brown water. Small waves rolled toward shore. He wondered what sort of sea creatures lived there, wishing he could dive in to find out.

Tristan thought again of last summer. He and the other Seasquirts had been the newest recruits at Sea Camp. Finding out why they'd been invited to attend had been a shock, to say the least. Sea Camp wasn't just an ocean-themed summer camp like they thought. It was actually a training program for teens with special— no, make that bizarre and totally amazing—abilities in the ocean. It had something to do with ancient genes still left in humans from when animals first adapted to life in the sea. And if they drank Sea Camp's slightly pink algae water before going in the ocean, they got Aquaman webbing between their fingers and toes.

Sometimes Tristan wondered if it was all just a really awesome dream. Then he remembered what it felt like to zoom through the water with his just-add-seawater duck feet. Rubbing his head, he also remembered crashing into the dock—a lot. He was fast, but not so good with control. He thought about his other talent, communicating with sharks and rays. Tristan wondered if his friend Snaggle-Tooth was still recuperating in the camp's giant tank in Shark Alley. He then thought about Hugh and Sam. Hugh could change the color of his skin in the ocean and was especially adept at conversing with octopuses and other sea creatures. Sam could talk to dolphins and whales, and had the rare ability to echolocate. She had her own underwater sonar. If all that wasn't cool enough, senior campers went on secret missions to help marine life and investigate problems in the ocean. Tristan got excited just thinking about it. But not being able to talk about camp or what they did there made him feel like a can of soda, shaken and ready to explode.

Glancing down the beach, Tristan noticed a guy fishing. The man was standing in waist-deep water just offshore, holding a long black rod. He cast out into the waves and then reeled the line in. He cast again. Tristan continued walking. He stepped on something hard and looked down. It was a seashell partly buried in the sand. Thin brown lines curled around the spiraling, orangey-yellow shell. He bent down to pick it up. Suddenly, there was a loud buzzing sound as if he was being dive-bombed by the world's largest bee. Tristan jerked around and swatted the air near his head. He then promptly tripped over his feet and flopped awkwardly onto the sand.

Once Tristan realized there was no mutant bee attacking him, he glanced around self-consciously to see if anyone had seen him fall. No one seemed to have noticed. They were all staring at the fisherman's rod. It was bent so far over it looked about to snap in half, and the line was spooling out crazily fast. That's what was making the buzzing sound.

"Got a big one on," the man yelled to a buddy a little way down the beach.

The students ran over, gathering to watch as the man backed out of the water. He struggled to reel the line in, and his face was turning an alarming shade of red. Beads of sweat poured down the man's forehead, and the veins on his muscular arms looked as if they were about to pop.

Just offshore, a triangular gray fin broke the surface.

"Shark!" yelled one of the students.

The other fisherman threw down his pole and ran over to help. Together, the two men fought to reel the creature in. But the shark wasn't giving up easily. It was fighting just as hard to get away. It swam to the right and then tacked back left. The fishermen gripped the pole, leaned back, and tried to prevent its escape. The shark changed direction. It headed out to sea, but again the men fought to pull it back. The shark then jumped straight up into the air; its head twisted grotesquely back due to the hook embedded in its mouth.

Tristan watched in horror, especially when the shark was finally dragged, writhing, out of the water and onto the sand. It was a broad gray beast about six feet long.

"Bull shark," one of the fishermen announced. "Definite man-eater."

The other students got closer to see the monster, but not too close. Tristan shook his shaggy-haired head. It was as if he could feel the shark's pain—like the hook had pierced his own lips and he'd been dragged out of the life-giving sea. The shark thrashed on the sand, its head whipping from side to side.

Then, in his head, Tristan heard the shark say: *Yo, you want a piece of me? Come closer; I'll show you. You no good, rotten, air-breathing, land-waddling human. Yeah, that's it, just a little closer.*

The hook became embedded even more deeply in the shark's mouth. Blood streamed out.

"Cut it loose," one of the fishermen said.

"Shoot it," shouted one of the football players.

"Nah, just bash it over the head," another boy suggested.

"No, stop it! You're hurting it," Tristan yelled. Then, without even a slight pause, he sprinted to the shark, silently telling it: *Stop moving. I can help you.* Tristan couldn't tell if it understood. It had been a while since he chatted with a shark.

"Oh my god," Mrs. Hawk shouted. "Tristan, stop! Get back."

But Tristan didn't stop. Instead, he jumped right onto the shark's back, like a bull-rider at a rodeo. He wrapped his legs around the shark's fat belly and put his hands on top of its wide head to hold it steady. The shark's sandpapery skin felt scratchy against Tristan's legs. Its powerful muscles flexed beneath him.

C'mon, stop moving. I can help you, Tristan thought.

Then, before anyone could stop him, Tristan reached into the shark's flesh-tearing teeth-filled mouth. He grabbed hold of the hook, thinking: *Sorry, this is gonna sting.* And as quickly as he could, he pulled the hook out.

Realizing what he'd done, Tristan looked at his hand. He still had a hand and all ten fingers, but blood was smeared across his skin. He held up his hand to get a closer look. He had nicked his knuckles on the shark's teeth, but it was only a minor scratch. The blood wasn't his—it was the shark's. The shark's silvery eyes looked up at him.

Thanks, kid! Now get the heck off me. Don't want my buddies to see me like this. Could you also get me back into the water? I can't breathe.

Tristan got off the shark and grabbed its tail. He tried to pull it back into the water, but the shark was too heavy.

"C'mon, help me," he yelled to the others.

They all backed away, shook their heads, and looked at Tristan like he was totally insane—except for one person. Mrs. Hawk kicked off her Birkenstocks and grabbed hold with Tristan. Then the two of them hauled the shark into the water. They'd barely gone a few feet out when the shark flexed its tail, turned, and swam off. Tristan heard the shark say: *Guess not all humans are such schmucks. Thanks, man.*

Mrs. Hawk stood staring in amazement. Not so much at the shark, but at Tristan. The other students and the fishermen were looking at him as well, their mouths hanging open. Even the tough-guy jocks were staring at Tristan with something almost like respect. One girl had her cell phone out. Her gaze wasn't fixed on Tristan, but on the photo she'd just taken. It showed a boy straddling a shark with his hand inside the huge gray monster's mouth.

By the time Tristan got home, the photo had gone viral. The image of Tristan atop the shark was plastered across the Internet. Reporters started calling local hospitals to see if the boy in the photo had lost his hand or worse. They also called the Hunts' house; a few even knocked on their front door. Tristan's parents closed all the curtains and shut off the lights to make it look like nobody was home. Tristan's older sister was sent out the back door to a friend's house and told not to talk to anyone else about the photo. She'd already told several reporters that her brother was obsessed with sharks and just loony enough to try to ride one. She didn't know the truth about Tristan or Sea Camp. His father made one last call before unplugging and shutting off their phones.

Tristan was sitting on his bed, still staring at the fish in his aquarium, and waiting for his parents' decision. He knew he acted recklessly, without thinking how it would look. But he just couldn't help it. They were going to kill the shark.

His parents walked into the room.

"We've spoken to Director Davis," his father said sternly.

Tristan held his breath.

"Given the circumstances, he suggested you go to camp a little early. Pack your bag. We're leaving first thing in the morning for the Keys."

"You mean I still get to go back?"

"What were you thinking, Tristan?" his mother scolded. "We've kept this whole shark thing a secret all year, and here you go and jump on one and *then* stick your hand in its mouth. You could have lost that hand. Besides, didn't you think that would seem rather *unusual*?"

"I know, I know," Tristan said. "I just did it. You should have seen what they were doing to the shark. They wanted to shoot it or bash it over the head. And it was in pain."

"Well, we can't turn back the clock. What's done

is done," his father said, shaking his head. "But you have got to be more careful, especially out in public, if you want to continue training at Sea Camp and go on their so-called missions. This is not the way to gain our confidence. We'll see how things go, but any more *incidents* like this and that'll be it. No more Sea Camp. And no missions."

Before Tristan could say anything else, his parents were out the door, still mumbling about his irresponsible and rash behavior. Tristan continued to gaze at the aquarium—so much for making his father proud. The confidence and pride he felt after last summer were gone. All his insecurities about being clumsy and not living up to his father's expectations came rushing back. Tristan could just imagine what Director Davis would say. Coach Fred would probably make him swim a gazillion laps around the lagoon or scrub out all of the aquariums in the Rehab Center.

Tristan got out his Sea Camp backpack, a duffle bag, and his T-shirt with the camp's shark and wave logo on it. It read "SNAPPER" on the back. At least he was going back. He wondered if Coach Fred would demote him to Seasquirt because of his day at the beach.

2
STRANGER AT
THE WALL

THE ENTRANCE TO THE FLORIDA KEYS SEA PARK was just as Tristan remembered it. Water spouted from the blowholes of three stone dolphins at the center of a fountain. Behind it was a white stucco arch draped with bright pink and purple bougainvillea blooms. And just like his first time there, he heard laughter and screeches of joy as kids and their parents rode down the park's winding streams and snorkeled in its clear blue pools.

Director Davis was at the entrance when they arrived. He was wearing an impossibly clean, bright white polo shirt with the camp's logo and khaki shorts. His sandy hair was shorter than last year. Tristan noted a distinct scowl on the man's rugged, pockmarked face.

"Mr. and Mrs. Hunt, good to see you again," he said and then eyed Tristan.

Tristan let his hair fall over his eyes and stared down at the man's sneakers, one blue and one red.

"Thank you for letting Tristan come early," his father said.

"We really appreciate it, given what happened," his mother added. "We just didn't know what to do. He could have lost a hand or been killed. And then all those reporters knocking on the door and the phone calls, and the photo of Tristan on the shark and what it . . ."

Director Davis took Mrs. Hunt's hand, interrupting her. "It's not a problem. You did the right thing." He glanced at Tristan. "We're just glad it didn't get out of hand and that Tristan is here."

Tristan looked up, his bright green eyes filled with hope. "I'm really sorry, but they were going to murder the shark."

The director acknowledged Tristan's apology with just the slightest of nods and then turned to his parents. "Since you're here, I assume you're okay with your son's continued involvement and training with us?"

Tristan's parents exchanged anxious glances. His mother appeared ready to grab her son and bolt.

"It's all he's talked about the entire year," his father answered. "Probably would have run off down here on his own if we'd said no."

Tristan shrugged and smiled innocently at the camp director.

His father looked sternly at him. "We're not completely sold on the idea or sure that he should be here, given what happened. We'll see how things go. Maybe you can teach him to *think* before he acts."

"Excellent!" Director Davis said. He grabbed Tristan's duffle bag, shook his parents' hands, and assured them he'd look after their son.

Tristan thought his parents seemed uncertain, expecting further discussion or something. Before they could change their minds, he thanked his father awkwardly, hugged his mother, and said good-bye. He then ran to catch up with the director as the man walked quickly into the Florida Keys Sea Park.

As they walked, Tristan prepared himself for the lecture that was about to come. But Director Davis said nothing. That almost made it worse. They walked in deafening silence for several more minutes.

"Head over to the Snapper bungalow to unpack, and then why don't you visit the Rehab Center. They've got some new patients and could probably use your help with at least one of them."

Tristan stared at the man dumbfounded. "Okay."

He waited for the director to yell or say something about how reckless he'd been or how his actions could have put the camp at risk. But the man just waved his hand in the direction of the bungalows. "Get a move on."

Tristan turned and sprinted down the path, still thinking about the reaming-out that was sure to come. He nearly ran straight into one of the park's meandering streams. Stopping short and teetering at the water's edge, he watched as twenty small golden cownose rays swam by like a flock of underwater birds. Each ray gracefully waved its velvety fins up and down. A school of fish trailed behind. It was a menagerie of color and size. There were several large turquoise parrotfish, a few smaller blue and yellow surgeonfish, and lots of skinny two-inch-long multicolored striped fish.

Everything in the park seemed somehow bigger and better than before. The streams, fish, and lush tropical plants were all larger, fuller, and more vibrant than he remembered. Or maybe it just looked that way because he was so happy to be there.

When Tristan came to the jungle wall, he thought about Jade. She was the one who showed him the secret way to pass through. It had been her last summer at camp. Jade was eighteen now, and, like most teens that age, her ocean talents had begun to fade. The director said it had something to do with changing hormones.

Tristan stood staring at the wall. The tangle of thick green thorny vines and smooth gray tree trunks was so dense it appeared almost solid. He now understood why they used the jungle wall to keep the park's regular visitors out of the campers' more private areas. After a few minutes of searching, Tristan found the sea turtle–shaped stone. He was about to jump onto it when, out of the corner of his eye, he saw someone approaching. He turned to the stranger.

"Excuse me," the man said a little too quickly. "Could you tell me where the, uh, Wave Pool is? I was on my way there with my daughter and seem to have gotten turned around. Can't find her or the pool."

Tristan stared at the man. He wasn't anywhere near the Wave Pool. He was about Tristan's parents' age and wore a T-shirt that read *I "heart" Dolphins* along with a pair of flowered, poop-brown shorts. Other than his truly ugly sportswear, there wasn't anything abnormal about his appearance. But for some reason, something just seemed off about the guy, and Tristan didn't like the way he was looking at him. Besides, he didn't seem very upset about losing his daughter. Tristan's mother would already have called in the FBI.

Tristan pointed down the path. "The Wave Pool is back that way on the other side of the park. Look for the signposts with colored arrows on them. The Wave Pool is the light blue one."

"Oh, must have missed that. Thanks."

The stranger hesitated and peered suspiciously at Tristan and the jungle wall. He then abruptly turned and went the way Tristan suggested.

Tristan watched the man go. Feeling uneasy, instead of going through the jungle wall he took a trail that paralleled it. After a few minutes, he doubled back and scanned the area. The man was nowhere in sight. Tristan swiveled around one more time to be sure he was gone and then hopped onto the sea turtle rock. The wall's interlocking vines began to wiggle and squirm. Like big green snakes, they withdrew into the wall, revealing a shadowy entrance. He leapt onto the fish and then the whale-shaped stone. Soon he forgot about the stranger looking for the Wave Pool. The dim light and odd glow inside the jungle wall made Tristan's skin appear eerily zombie green. The ground was a checkerboard of grass and rocks. Tristan leapt carefully to the next sea creature rock, thinking about last year when he fell off. He had no desire to face another grab grass attack.

Once past the jungle wall, Tristan stood transfixed in front of Sea Camp's wide lagoon. It was just as beautiful as he remembered, like a commercial for a perfect tropical island getaway. He couldn't wait to dive into the clear blue water. After a few more minutes admiring the lagoon, Tristan made his way past the Seasquirts' raised bungalow to the next one along the sandy shore. It was for second-year campers—the Snappers. Tristan climbed the short flight of stairs and opened the bamboo door. Inside was a large open room with a high ceiling, dark wood beams, scattered overstuffed couches, a table, and some comfortable-looking chairs. Floor-to-ceiling windows provided a spectacular view of the sparkling lagoon. Tristan noticed a small refrigerator and opened the door. Stacked inside were bottles of slightly pink water. He grabbed one, twisted off the cap, and took a long swig. The tart flavor puckered his lips, but was also strangely comforting. It reminded him of Hugh and Sam and all the fun they had when they were together. Tristan put the bottle in the outside pocket of his backpack.

There were two bunkrooms connected to the main room. Tristan went into the one on the left. He smiled and placed his things on a bed. Being at camp early came with at least one big advantage—a bottom bunk. He wouldn't constantly step on Hugh's head climbing into bed or regularly crash-land on the floor when just getting up in the morning. This summer was sure to be more bruise-free.

After unpacking a few things, Tristan grabbed his backpack and headed for the Rehab Center. He hoped his palm print would still open the door at the side entrance and wondered if the trees there still had funky gray flowers that smelled like mashed potatoes.

3

SHARK CHOW

When Tristan arrived at the Rehab Center, he saw Director Davis standing with Ms. Sanchez. She was Sea Camp's communication and camouflage expert. They were talking with Mark, the guy he met last summer who was in charge of the park's seawater system. As Tristan approached, the conversation stopped abruptly.

In his typically clashing plaid shorts, striped shirt, and yellow rubber boots, Mark nodded to Tristan and turned to the others. "It's not a problem—*yet*."

Tristan wondered what he was talking about. He looked to the director and Ms. Sanchez, but they made no effort to explain. Ms Sanchez appeared unchanged since last year. She was short, thin, and had gray-white spiky hair. The reflection from her tight blue clothes tinted her spiked hair and the slightly shaded square glasses she wore. It suddenly struck Tristan as a little funny because she resembled a giant skinny Smurf.

Director Davis headed for the door. "Tristan, after you're done here, come to my office if you would."

"Okay," Tristan replied, figuring that's when he'd get the lecture about the whole shark thing.

"Nice to have you back," Ms. Sanchez told him.

"Thanks."

"And I hear your shark communication skills are still working quite well."

Tristan shrugged self-consciously and gazed at the floor. "Yeah, I guess you heard what happened."

Ms. Sanchez put an arm around him. "I hope I would have done the same thing. Glad you were there."

"Really?" he said, looking up.

"Of course. No harm seems to have come from it, and you saved that shark. Maybe you even got people thinking about the morality of killing such a magnificent animal."

"Guess I never thought of it that way. I just thought it was another one of my screw-ups, like my parents thought. Hey, is Snaggle-Tooth still around?"

"Once he got used to his new teeth, we released Snaggle-Tooth into the lagoon," Ms. Sanchez answered. "But he does like to come back now and then to visit and show off his pearly whites." She smiled and stepped onto the mat to decontaminate her sandals, leading Tristan into the room full of aquariums.

Ms. Sanchez walked swiftly through the room.

Tristan looked around to see if any of the patients from last summer were still there—the diva scallop who demanded a blue shell to match her eyes, or Hugh's buddy, Old Jack, the six-armed octopus.

"We can visit the patients in here in a bit," Ms. Sanchez told him as they walked to a large, open, garage-like door. Going outside, they came to several small, round pools spread out and shaded under a plastic tarp.

Doc Jordan, the park's slightly chubby veterinarian, was standing next to one of the pools. She wore a pair of thin Lycra leggings and a camp T-shirt. Her frizzy, dark hair appeared to be trying to escape from the thick headband she used to hold it back. With her hands on her hips, the veterinarian stood staring into the tank. Her kind, round face was scrunched up in a puzzled look. "Hey there, Tristan. Heard you were back early. Good timing, given our new patient here."

Tristan got an odd but now recognizable feeling. He peered curiously into the pool. Something thin and silvery gray cruised slowly by. It was about two feet long. He leaned down to get a closer look. "What is it?"

He heard a faint voice in his head: *What is it? I'm not a what. I'm a she, obviously.*

Sorry 'bout that, he thought.

Doc Jordan climbed into the tank. "It's a young shark, a female blacktip. Her friends brought her in a few days ago. Dragged her here, really. We don't think she was very happy about coming."

"What's wrong with her?" Tristan asked.

Sugar, nothing's wrong with me. I'm gorgeous.

"Not sure. She's very thin and obviously weak," Doc Jordan answered. "Maybe you could come in here and ask her what's wrong."

Tristan took a swig of the Sea Camp water he'd brought along, thinking it might strengthen his communication skills. He took off his sandals and stepped into a nearby rinse bucket. He then climbed into the tank. The small silvery gray shark slowly swam by. When her black-tipped dorsal fin broke the surface it wobbled from side to side.

"Ask her what she ate before she arrived," Doc Jordan said. "Might be that she had something toxic or bad. She's refused everything we've tried to feed her so far."

In his head, Tristan said hello and asked the shark about her diet.

She replied weakly. *Let's see. The other day I had some lovely green algae with grassy overtones and some nice crunchy Sargassum. Ooh—just love those little balls filled with air. They pop in your mouth.*

Tristan turned to Doc Jordan. "She says she's been eating green algae and Sargassum. Whatever that is."

"It's a brown algae. Any fish, like barracuda? They can carry ciguatera poisoning."

Tristan asked the shark if she'd had barracuda lately or some other fish.

Heavens, no, honey. I'm a vegan.

"She says no. She's a vegan," Tristan told her. "What's a vegan?"

"Aha," Doc Jordan exclaimed. "A vegan is a very

strict vegetarian. That could be the problem. Sharks are not herbivores; they eat meat. If she's only been eating algae, her stomach is probably a mess. And she must not be getting enough protein or minerals."

Tristan explained to the shark why they thought that being vegan might not be so good for a shark.

The young blacktip paused for a moment and then told him: *But sweetheart, I don't like the taste of meat or blood. Just the sight of it makes me feel faint.*

Tristan chuckled thinking of a shark that faints at the sight of blood. The small blacktip swam next to him and smacked his leg with her tail. *Hey, it's not nice to laugh at me just because I'm different from others of my kind.*

Tristan silently said he was sorry and that he knew how she felt. "She doesn't like the taste of meat and especially blood. Makes her feel faint."

"Oh, well that could be a problem," Doc Jordan said, stroking her chin quizzically. "Hold on, I've got an idea. I'll be back in just a minute." She hurried off into the aquarium room.

Minutes later, the veterinarian returned carrying a metal bucket filled with brown pellets. "Tristan, see if you can convince her to try one of these yummy *shark treats* we just happen to have on hand." She winked at him, adding, "They're soy-based. We feed them to some of the other fish. Just tell her they are definitely vegan-friendly and very tasty. And we've added some vitamins that will make her feel better."

Doc Jordan gave a few of the brown pellets to

Tristan, suggesting he feed them to her by hand. Tristan thought back to last year when he fed Snaggle-Tooth with a squeeze bottle. Even though the shark didn't have any teeth, his hand still quivered like a jiggling piece of Jell-O.

He heard the shark say: *Honey, I'm not going to bite you. Remember, I don't like blood—especially human. It's disgusting! I'm getting woozy just thinking about it.*

Tristan looked at the pellets. They reminded him of dog chow. He lowered his trembling hand into the water. The shark swam slowly around the pool and then approached Tristan's hand cautiously. She took two pellets, munched on them and then took a few more. It reminded Tristan of feeding goats at the petting zoo when he was little.

Goats? I'm no goat! Now I really feel faint. Imagine, me being compared to a goat.

Tristan forgot that sharks and rays could essentially read his mind. This shark was not only a vegan, but also clearly very sensitive and not just to the smell of blood. He'd have to be more careful. *Sorry. That's not what I meant. You don't look anything like a goat.*

Heavens me, I should think not.

As the small blacktip continued to chew her food, Tristan listened intently. *Not bad, not bad, tastes a bit like fresh sargassum, a little crunchy and kind of tart. Do they have this stuff in sea grass flavor?*

Tristan asked Doc Jordan.

"Not sure. But I guess we can try to make it sea grass flavored. We need to fatten her up and get her stronger. She probably has a body image problem as well. We'll have to work on that. Thanks so much for your help, Tristan. It would be great if you could stop by now and then."

"Sure," Tristan replied, thinking how good it was to be back at camp, to feel useful and like he was good at something.

"Want to see some of our other new patients?" Ms. Sanchez asked as she walked to another of the large round tanks. Tristan got out of the shark's tank, said good-bye, and followed eagerly.

There were two sea turtles in the tank. He watched as one swam slowly up to a large bucket affixed to the side of the pool. It put its front flippers and head over the edge of the bucket. The sea turtle then coughed, spitting up some yellowish liquid along with several bits of blue. It coughed again and puked out a scrunched up ball of tan plastic. Now Tristan was the one who felt queasy. It reminded him of when he had the stomach flu and spent several super nasty hours hugging the toilet.

"I can hardly watch," Ms. Sanchez noted. "We've been getting a lot of marine life in like this. It's all that plastic pollution in the ocean. The animals ingest it and it clogs up their throats, stomachs, and intestines."

She picked up a brown bottle from a table nearby. "It induces vomiting. Not very pleasant for them, though. But if we can get the animals to spit up most of the plastic, they have a pretty good chance of survival. Unfortunately, many creatures don't make it. Sea turtles are particularly vulnerable. They think those thin plastic bags so many stores use look like jellyfish, one of their favorite foods. They gobble them right up."

Tristan vowed to get his mother to use cloth bags at the grocery store from then on.

From there they went back into the room filled with aquariums. The first tank they came to was about three feet long. The glass was unusually thick, like a double-hulled tanker, and, strangely, the lower six inches of each inner wall was covered in plastic bubble wrap. Inside, a small pile of rocks sat on the sandy bottom. There was also something stuck in the sand near the rocks. Tristan bent down to get a better view. It was a puffy, six-inch-tall red doll, like a miniature version of those padded dummies he'd seen people use to practice karate or boxing.

He must have had a puzzled look on his face, because even before he could ask what was in the tank, Ms. Sanchez said, "Ever seen a stomatopod? It's also called a mantis shrimp."

"Uh, no." Tristan shook his head.

"Amazing creatures. Let's see if we can lure Hammer out of his burrow."

Ms. Sanchez rinsed her hand with seawater and took a small snail out of a bucket sitting nearby. She placed it inside the tank. "Okay, now watch closely. If you blink, you might miss it."

Tristan had no idea what to expect. Seconds later, one of the weirdest, strangest, most bizarre animals he'd ever seen scurried out from under the rocks. It sort of resembled a shrimp—a mega mutant shrimp. Or maybe it was a miniature messed-up lobster without big claws or spines. It was about five inches in length and had a long, segmented, shelled body; a square head; two big, round, half-blue, half-pink eyes on stalks; and a whole lot of legs. The odd creature made a beeline for the snail; its numerous short legs moved surprisingly fast. It waved two small antennae over the snail's round shell and then paused to look around. Then the mantis shrimp attacked. But it was so fast that Tristan wasn't sure exactly what happened. The snail's shell, however, now lay in pieces, decimated, as if blown up by mini underwater explosives. Astonished, Tristan watched as the stomatopod picked up the limp, lifeless body of the snail and sauntered proudly back to its lair.

"Just amazing," Ms. Sanchez said. "They have one of the fastest, most powerful strikes in the animal kingdom. Want to see that again?"

Tristan nodded, at a loss for words.

"Okay, this time look closely at the shape of the stomatopod's second pair of legs. Then watch how Hammer attacks the snail." She placed another unsuspecting victim into the tank.

The mantis shrimp reappeared, hesitated for a moment, and then scurried over to the snail. Tristan leaned down. His eyes were wide and his straight, narrow nose was mashed up against the tank. The creature's second leg was funny looking, kind of like a hinged club. The stomatopod again waved his antennae deceptively gently over the snail. Then, lightning-quick, Hammer whacked the snail. Over and over, he struck with his clubbed leg. The snail's shell was once again totally destroyed. And with another tasty treat in claw, the stomatopod returned to his burrow.

"Whoa! It hit it wicked fast."

"Exactly," Ms. Sanchez said. "For quite obvious reasons, this type of stomatopod is called a smasher. They use their club-shaped second legs to literally smash their prey to bits. Some stomatopods have legs shaped like spears instead of clubs. They're called spearers and thrust out their legs like swords to impale their prey."

"Cool," Tristan said. "What's the bubble wrap around the tank for? And that doll thing?"

Before Ms. Sanchez could answer, Hammer, the club-wielding attack shrimp, came out of his burrow. The creature stood up on his middle legs and rotated his freaky half-blue, half-pink eyeballs around. The stomatopod then crawled to the tank's bubble-wrapped front wall and struck with such ferocity that Tristan leapt backwards, thinking the glass would shatter. Before disappearing back into his sandy burrow, Hammer took a moment to also smack the miniature fighting dummy over the head.

"There's your answer. I don't think Hammer likes us watching him eat, and besides, he has a serious anger management issue. It's why he's here. The residents of the reef where he lives were sick of him destroying the neighborhood and attacking other creatures. They asked if we could do something. It was sort of an undersea intervention. We sent a team in to work with his neighbors and lure him out of his burrow. They convinced Hammer to come here for help. We need to figure out why he's so mad and find other ways for him to deal with his anger. But so far, the only thing that's happened is that he's destroyed three of those fighting dummies and cracked two aquariums. We're hoping he'll take a shine to someone soon and open up about his problems."

"Hey," Tristan said. "Maybe Hugh can help. He's pretty good with the communication thing."

"Maybe," Ms. Sanchez replied. "I really don't want to lose any more tanks." She moved on to another aquarium nearby. It was larger than the first and half-filled with rubble, some corals, and a cluster of sea anemones that resembled flat, multicolored flowers.

Tristan peered into the tank. He didn't see anything all that unusual. He recognized a cute, two-inch-long pufferfish. It was brown with white, crisscrossing lines, had a skinny little snout, and had a barely-there tail. There was also a tiny, bright yellow, coin-shaped fish and a few skinny ones with stripes like he'd seen in the stream earlier.

"See the fish in the corner with the big black eyes? The silvery one with the pinkish-red, horizontal stripes?"

"Yeah, that one." Tristan pointed to a fish about three inches long.

"That's a juvenile squirrelfish. They're nocturnal. They hide in the reef during the day and then come out at night to hunt. That's why they've got those big eyes—for night vision."

"But it's daytime, and it's out swimming around."

Ms. Sanchez nodded. "Exactly. That's the problem. Sandy here is afraid of the dark. We've been putting a nightlight in the tank after dark with some food to entice her out. We're trying to get her to feed regularly at night and then wean her off the light."

They moved on to the condo complex of aquariums that was Old Jack's home—the camp's resident elderly octopus. Like last year, there was a collection of pickle jars, some rocks, seaweed, and a variety of plastic play toys in the tanks. A Rubik's Cube sat in one aquarium. It looked dingy. It was covered with a thin film of algae, as if it hadn't been played with in a long time.

"Is he still in there?" Tristan asked, thinking that Hugh would be really bummed if Old Jack had died.

"Oh, he's in there. But he's been coming out of his hiding spots less and less often, and he's moving more slowly. We're not sure how much time Old Jack has left."

After searching unsuccessfully for the elderly octopus, they moved on. Ms. Sanchez showed Tristan a spiny lobster whose long front spines had been torn off by a careless diver. The lobster had been fitted with prosthetic spines and was walking tentatively around the tank feeling things, like a blind person using a cane for the first time.

Ms. Sanchez looked at her watch. "Look at the time. You'd better get over to the director's office. Thanks for the help with the blacktip."

"Sure," Tristan said. On his way out he noticed a door he didn't remember seeing before. "Where does that go?"

"That's the entrance to the new chemistry lab. It used to be the old algae grow room for the Sea Camp water. Thanks partly to you, Tristan, and, shall we say, a boatload of new funding, we've been able to expand and renovate the area. And we've brought in an expert chemist to do some exciting research."

Tristan headed for the director's office, thinking: *What sort of research did they need a new chemist for*?

4

THE SECRET
ASSIGNMENT

The door to Director Davis's office was ajar. As he approached, Tristan could hear the camp's leader talking. It sounded like he was on the phone.

"Yes, we'll do that. So far nothing definite, but we've never had so many power problems. Since Rickerton wasn't able to hack into the system, we've been waiting to see if he would try something else. This might be it."

Tristan had been about to knock. He hesitated. Had he heard right? Did the director just say that crazy, evil billionaire guy, Rickerton, tried to hack into Sea Camp's computers and might be messing with the power?

"The added security should help on that end. I'll be in touch."

Tristan peeked around the door.

"Tristan, c'mon in. How'd it go at the Rehab Center?"

"Good."

"Glad to hear it. Have a seat."

Tristan's mind was racing. J.P. Rickerton was the guy whose yacht they sank in the Bahamas last summer. He killed a bunch of sharks for their fins and kidnapped three campers. Had he found out about camp and what they'd done? Tristan didn't want to ask the director straight off. That would make it seem like he'd been eavesdropping. He sat on one of the simple wooden chairs in front of the director's desk and glanced uncomfortably around the room. A photo of Jade, Rusty, and Rory on the lagoon dock with their arms around each other had been added to the wall of campers' pictures. On a table nearby sat the elaborate LEGO model of an undersea community. He still couldn't believe the detail in the domed structures, underwater vehicles, and marine life all built out of interlocking, multicolored pieces of plastic. On the opposite wall was the map of the world's oceans. It was color-coded for depth and had little flags over the locations of organizations and facilities that partnered with the camp. Something new sat beside a flag over the Bahamas. Tristan looked closer. It was a miniature model of a tall sailing ship.

"Oh, I see you've noticed the latest addition to the wall," the director said proudly. "I thought it only fitting to recognize the final resting place of the *Santa Viento*. After all, since the discovery of the shipwreck, thanks in part to you, we'll have sufficient funding for years to come."

Tristan thought of the gold coin he found last summer. "Did they find more gold?"

"We're still exploring the wreck and photographing and documenting the site. But yes, they found more gold and silver as well; also some jewelry and numerous other artifacts. The marine archeologist we brought in is thrilled. She thinks the wreck will reveal a lot about how people lived and traded back in about the seventeenth century. We don't know the total value yet, but it could be in the hundreds of millions, maybe even billions."

"Awesome. Did that guy, uh, Rickerton, try to get the wreck or find his yacht?"

Director Davis's expression turned more serious, and he paused noticeably before speaking. "Mr. Rickerton seems to be a rather persistent man. Once we made a claim on the shipwreck, though, he had no rights or access to it. He has, however, recovered his yacht from the Tongue of the Ocean, and it must have cost him a pretty penny. But let's not talk about him. I have a favor to ask, since you're here early."

"Really?" Tristan said. "I just thought you were going to yell at me about, you know, the shark thing."

"I see no reason to discuss it any further, Tristan. I suspect you now better understand why we have to think before we act out in public."

"Yeah, I got that."

"But, given your parents' reaction, better be extra

careful this summer. Now for that favor—over the past several months, we've noticed a few visitors in the park behaving rather oddly. They seem out of place and a little too inquisitive. We're afraid they might be trying to learn what goes on here, behind the scenes."

Tristan thought again of Rickerton as well as the man who asked about the Wave Pool earlier. He had to ask. "Do you think Rickerton found out about us and what we did in the Bahamas?"

"No, no, I doubt it," the director responded quickly. "I've asked a couple of the older campers to return early and hang out in the park to keep an eye out for people acting suspiciously. Luckily, with our newly improved finances, we can afford to beef up security. But things aren't in place just yet. I was hoping you would help out with the other campers for a day or two."

"Sure. What do I have to do?"

The director handed Tristan what looked like a thick black pen that had "Sea Camp" written on the side. "Here. All you need to do is pretend to be enjoying the park, and if you see someone acting oddly, just let us know. Press the top button on the pen and speak into it. It will buzz myself or Coach Fred, and we'll be able to hear you. If you point the pen and press the button on the side, it will take a photograph of whatever you're pointing at and transfer the image to us. There's also a small speaker on the pen. You should be able to hear one of us talking back to you. But Tristan, if you do see someone acting strangely—just report it. Do nothing else. Got it?"

"Yes, sir."

"Excellent. Are you all set in the Snapper bungalow?"

"Uh-huh."

"Okay, then. I'll meet you at the Conch Café tomorrow morning at eight for a briefing before the park opens. And Tristan, please remember, campers are not allowed to swim in the lagoon by themselves. I know it will be tempting to go in before the other Snappers arrive, but no going in alone."

"Okay," Tristan mumbled disappointedly. He had hoped to go for a swim in the lagoon as soon as possible. Maybe one of the other campers would go in with him before Hugh or Sam arrived. That is, assuming they were coming back. He was pretty sure Hugh would be there. Sam was more of a question. Tristan assumed her father still thought the camp was some kind of eco-cult.

"See you tomorrow," the director said.

"Bye," Tristan replied, walking out the door.

With the park closed, it was very quiet and now nearly dark. Tristan glanced around nervously. Were people really trying to spy on them? Were they Rickerton's goons? He thought back to last summer. Rickerton's armed men had chased after Tristan and the other Seasquirts. What if he really had found out about them?

The next morning, Tristan stumbled out of bed—literally. When he woke up, he forgot where he was and sat up too fast. He smacked his head on the bottom of the upper bunk and sprawled onto the floor. Thankfully, no one was there to see.

He threw on a swimsuit and his Snapper T-shirt, and then made his way through the jungle wall onto the minefield path. As usual, the walkway was strewn with way too many potentially head-smashing, ankle-turning coconuts. Tristan was so focused on avoiding the coconuts he tripped over a ladder leaned up against one of the palm trees at the side of the path.

"Hey, kid, watch it down there," shouted a man high up on the ladder, wavering badly. He grabbed onto some palm fronds to steady himself.

"Sorry," Tristan said sheepishly.

A coconut tumbled down from the tree. Tristan leapt out of the way and jogged out of the target zone. Soon he came to one of the park's arched bridges. There was another stranger standing in the underlying stream. She was securing something to the underside of the bridge. He glanced into the water around the woman's feet. A school of yellow fish circled her legs. Every time she moved, they shifted in perfect synchrony. She nodded to Tristan as he walked by.

Just past the rainforest area, Tristan stopped again and stared ahead, this time in surprise. The stone walkway was gone. In its stead was a raised boardwalk made of orangey wood planks. It circled the now expanded sea turtle pond, which also had three new and extremely large residents. They were sunning themselves on the sand. A new sign read: "Stay on the trail. And please don't feed the crocodiles."

Each of the pond's new residents was dark gray, at least eight feet long, and covered with raised, spiky ridges. Their thick skin reminded Tristan of a medieval knight's armor—one with a reptilian sense of fashion. The crocodiles' long teeth poked out around the outside of their blunt snouts. Tristan decided not even the best braces could fix that overbite. A small flock of flamingoes still resided on the island at the pond's center. Each stood on one leg with the other tucked neatly under its orange-fuchsia feathers. He hoped flamingoes and sea turtles weren't considered fine dining for crocodiles.

When Tristan arrived at the Conch Café, there were already two other teenagers there. They were campers he recognized from last summer, though he didn't know them very well. Since they were Sharks before, he figured they were now in the most senior bungalow—Dolphins. One camper was a girl with short, jet-black hair. The other was a boy who had been long and lean, much like Tristan. Over the school year, however, he seemed to have bulked up and gone completely bald. As Tristan got breakfast, he tried hard not to stare at the boy's shiny cue-ball head.

"You can sit over here if you want," the girl said.

Tristan walked over. "Thanks."

"Saw your photo on the Internet," the boy noted. "Cool move on that shark."

The girl kicked him under the table. "Yeah, except everyone saw it. We're not supposed to bring attention to ourselves."

"I know, I know," Tristan said, shaking his head. "Stupid."

"Yeah, but still pretty awesome," the boy added.

"By the way, my name's Mia, and he's Luis."

"I'm Tristan."

Luis grinned. "We know who you are—shark boy."

The director and Coach Fred entered the Conch Café. They were both wearing white shirts with the camp logo and khaki shorts. Coach Fred was still stocky and built like an ox. As usual, his dark hair was slicked back into a short ponytail. He confidently strutted forward with a military air about him. Tristan chuckled quietly, thinking about how he dressed at camp shows, where he liked to pair camouflage with sparkly sequins.

The men got their breakfasts and joined the campers at the table.

"Glad to see you're up and ready to go," Director Davis said.

Coach Fred just nodded, eyeing the teens like he was inspecting them for defects.

"So what sea creature goes well with peanut butter?" the director asked, smiling.

Tristan and the other two campers shook their heads.

"The jellyfish of course!"

The campers rolled their eyes and continued eating.

"Must be too early for you to appreciate one of my

new jokes. I'll just have to try it out on the other campers when they arrive."

Coach Fred and the campers looked at the director,
again shaking their heads.

"Well, no worries. Lots more where that came
from. Now to the task at hand. We want to be sure you
understand your job. As you may have noticed, the
new security cameras are being installed as we speak."

"May I?" Coach Fred asked the director, picking up
a conch shell from the table. He turned the spiraling
shiny pink shell over. It was at least eight inches long.
From inside, he pulled out a small lipstick camera. He
then pointed to a pinprick hole in the top whorl of the
shell. "Here's an example of the new cameras that will
be scattered throughout the park."

Coach continued, "Security here is serious business.
We need you to focus for the next two days. Spend your
time in the park as inconspicuously as possible. That
means no drinking Sea Camp water, sprouting webbed
feet, and going for a swim in the Wave Pool or snorkeling streams while visitors are present."

"We're not idiots," Mia groaned.

Coach raised his eyebrows and stared at her with an
expression that clearly said, *I'm not so sure.*

"Just keep your eyes open for anyone acting
strangely or who looks like they don't belong in the
park," Director Davis told them.

"Who do you think it is?" Mia asked.

Tristan waited to see what the director would say.

He hesitated. "We're not sure, Mia. It could be
someone from the government trying to come up

with a reason to shut us down. With our new source of funds, we've been able to cut our ties with one agency, and they're not very happy about it. Luckily, we have other more helpful and supportive partners both in and outside of the government."

Or it could be Rickerton's thugs, Tristan thought silently.

"And just so we're clear," Director Davis added. "If you do see someone suspicious, you are not to talk to them or engage them in any way. Is that understood?"

They nodded.

Coach Fred showed them a little black box hooked onto the top of his shorts. A wire ran from it, up beneath his shirt, and into his ear like a secret service agent. "We'll be listening for you throughout the day. Everyone have a Sea Camp communicator pen?"

Again they nodded.

"Okay then," the director said. "Have a good day out there. And when you get a chance, stop by my office to let me know how it's going."

After the director and Coach Fred left, Mia said, "It's almost like a mission."

"Yeah, a mission inside the park," Luis noted, rubbing his smooth-shaven, shiny head. "That can't be good."

Tristan nodded in agreement. His gaze lingered on the boy's head.

"Like it?" Luis asked smiling, again rubbing his hand over his smooth pate. "Just shaved it. Now I'm bound to be faster in the water."

Tristan ran a hand through his mop-like brown hair. As usual, several long strands sprang back over his eyes. Would he swim faster if he shaved it all off? Showers would be quicker. Plus, major savings on shampoo and haircuts. Luis did look kinda cool, but Tristan decided he wasn't ready to give up his shaggy locks. Besides, he liked the way his hair hung over his eyes. It gave him a way to hide where he was looking.

Tristan, Mia, and Luis joined the visitors enjoying the day at the Florida Keys Sea Park and watched for people acting strangely. They didn't drink any Sea Camp water and, to blend in, even wore masks and fins while snorkeling in the park's streams. Tristan was nervous, thinking that some of Rickerton's men might be there. He wondered if he should tell Luis and Mia. Then again, why freak them out? Besides, they were probably safe in the park with so many people around.

The morning passed without incident, and Tristan began to feel less anxious. After lunch, he decided to check out the sea turtles, wondering if any had been chomped on by their new neighbors. He walked by the park's zip line. A boy zoomed past him toward the landing pool, screaming. Tristan couldn't decide if the kid was having fun or wailing out of sheer terror. He then noticed a man nearby also watching the boy. He was wearing a hard-shelled tan hat like people wore in old jungle safari movies and was dressed in khaki from head to toe. On top of his khaki shirt and overlapping his khaki shorts, he had on a long khaki vest laden with khaki pockets. Tristan decided to nickname him "Jungle Joe."

Unlike the other adults in the park, Jungle Joe appeared to be alone. He wasn't pensively watching as his kids raced down the water slide or floated down a stream. He wasn't chasing them around until the brink of exhaustion or laughing as they pointed to fish and made funny faces in their snorkeling masks. He was walking slowly around by himself, peering at the fish in the streams and pools, looking behind plants along the trails, and staring intently at what the visitors and park employees were doing. It seemed peculiar.

Tristan decided to follow Jungle Joe. He walked casually behind the man. When Jungle Joe suddenly stopped, Tristan ducked behind a low palm tree with long, vertical green fronds splayed out like a gigantic Japanese fan. Tristan peeked out from behind the tree. Jungle Joe was snapping photos with a pocket-sized camera. The man glanced around nervously. Tristan ducked back behind the tree. He let about thirty seconds go by and then peeked out again. Jungle Joe was gone. Tristan stepped out from behind the tree and swiveled around, looking for the man. He saw a flash of khaki. Jungle Joe had gone down the path toward the sea turtle pond. Tristan went after him.

When Tristan found Jungle Joe, he was peering through a pair of miniature binoculars at the flamingoes on the island at the center of the pond. Tristan stopped before getting too close. Jungle Joe then began slowly turning, scanning the area.

Tristan searched for a place to hide. But he was on the new raised wooden walkway. There was only one choice. He ducked under the railing and jumped down, sliding on his butt in the sand behind a bush with clusters of yellow, bell-shaped flowers.

As quietly as possible, Tristan then crawled to his knees and peeked out from around the bush. Jungle Joe was staring his way. Tristan ducked back down, thinking the man must have heard his rear end smack the ground. He sure felt it. Tristan rubbed his butt cheek and looked out again. Jungle Joe had turned back toward the pond. Tristan breathed a sigh of relief. The man took out his camera and began taking more photos. Tristan pulled out his Sea Camp communicator pen, aimed it at Jungle Joe, and pushed the button on the side. He clicked the top, whispering, "This is Tristan. I've got a guy acting weird and taking photos."

He looked at the pen, not sure if anyone had heard him or if the photo went through.

Then, for just a moment, he thought he heard chuckling. A quiet voice came from the pen. "Got it, Tristan. Thanks. That's just our old friend, Harold Strangman, from the water park in Ft. Lauderdale. He comes down here every year. Slinks around taking photos like he's doing industrial espionage. He's harmless. But good job spotting him."

Tristan stood up, thinking, *So much for Tristan the spy.* He turned to climb up onto the boardwalk and then noticed one of the pond's new residents. It was just ten feet away and staring right at him. The huge crocodile was eyeing him like a tasty boy burger—best when eaten rare. Tristan froze.

"I'd get a move on, if I were you," a voice called out. "Need a hand?"

Tristan glanced briefly up at the walkway, not wanting to take his eyes off the undoubtedly drooling crocodile. It was Harold, alias Jungle Joe. His hand was extended out under the railing. Tristan's gaze returned to the crocodile. Was it closer than before? He didn't want to hang around to find out. Grabbing the man's hand, Tristan leapt off the sand and was pulled up onto the raised walkway.

"Thanks," he said, his pulse pounding in his ears.

"Best not to tempt the crocs," Harold told him. "I'm sure they're well fed. But you never know. That was a little too close."

"You're telling me."

Tristan watched as the crocodile closed its eyes, now clearly disinterested in his meaty presence.

"But they are a nice addition to the pond," the man noted. "Hmm, bet you could attract a crowd when feeding them." He walked away, muttering something about wondering where he could get one. Tristan looked once more at the lengthy, boy-deprived reptile and decided to continue his lookout duties elsewhere, preferably someplace crocodile free.

By Friday night, after two days of looking for spies, Tristan was exhausted. It didn't help that he kept thinking about Rickerton and what the man might do if he found out about them. And that any more *incidents* like the shark thing, and his parents would pull him from camp. It was a lot to worry about, especially without Hugh and Sam there to talk to.

They hadn't discovered any truly dangerous intruders. Mia did rescue a kid who jumped into the snorkeling stream to pet the rays but couldn't swim. Tristan and Luis helped identify two representatives of an extremist animal welfare group trying to catch and smuggle marine life out of the park so they could release the animals into the wild. Of course, most of the wildlife in the Florida Keys Sea Park had either been rescued or born in captivity. They would probably die if released. Tristan didn't understand what these people were thinking. He was glad when they were promptly escorted to the exit. With the exception of Jungle Joe, no other suspicious characters were spotted. If Rickerton had been sending his men into the park, maybe he knew they were now watching for them.

Lying in his bunk, Tristan could barely keep his eyes open. He'd been so busy he hadn't even had a chance to convince Mia or Luis to go for a swim in the lagoon. Nor had he spent much time in his favorite place—Shark Alley. He went there once. But it wasn't a great place for him to be inconspicuous. As soon as he entered the see-through viewing tube in the enormous aquarium, nearly all of the sharks and rays in the tank swam over. They hovered by the glass, stared at him, and jostled for a better position in front to say hello. He tried to tell them to act natural. But they trailed after him like a bunch of lovesick puppies. Kids started pointing and shouting to their parents. Tristan said a hasty good-bye and ran for the exit.

As his eyes closed, he thought about how quiet the empty bungalow was. He could hardly wait for tomorrow when the rest of the campers would arrive, hopefully including both Hugh and Sam.

5

TEETH MADE FOR CHEWING

THE NEXT MORNING, TRISTAN TRIED TO STAY BUSY while he waited for the others to arrive. He visited the vegan blacktip shark at the Rehab Center and went back to Shark Alley to apologize for his rude behavior earlier in the week. He started to worry as the morning wore on and there was still no sign of Hugh or Sam. Cell phones were useless in the park, so he had no way of knowing when or even if they would arrive.

Other campers began to show up. Tristan noticed Anthony Price walking toward the jungle wall. He was a short, skinny boy with a pug nose and small, pouty lips. He was one year ahead of Tristan. The guy was a pretty good swimmer and could communicate with fish, but he always seemed to give Tristan dirty looks. As Tristan wondered if he'd done something to make the other teen mad, he saw Brianna arrive. He couldn't help but notice her. She was also in the Squids' bungalow. Just looking at her made Tristan blush. She had smooth, light mocha-colored skin, curly dark hair that fell in ringlets to her shoulders, and soft, brown eyes. Not only that, she had a really cool ocean skill. Brianna could suck in air and blow up like a puffer or balloonfish. Tristan wasn't sure what it was good for, but being self-inflatable was a seriously wicked talent. He seemed to get all tongue-tied and especially klutzy whenever she was around.

At lunch, Tristan sat alone at the Snapper table and stared unhappily at his bowl of split-pea soup. He eyed a nice crispy bacon floater and scooped it up. Just as he put the spoonful of soup into his mouth, someone smacked him hard on the back. Tristan spewed pea soup out over the table and some dribbled down his chin. The other campers stared his way and laughed. Tristan turned bright red. Wiping the green gunk off his face, he turned to see who'd caused him to lose his peas and pig.

"Hey, dude! Like, how's it going?" Ryder laughed as he walked by, heading toward a group of older campers.

Tristan was about to say something extremely rude when he saw Hugh. He'd been right behind Ryder.

"Hi," Hugh said, smiling. Just like the day they first met, he seemed particularly well groomed and very neatly dressed. His short, dark hair was tidily combed and smooth, coming to just above his ears. And his monogrammed, dark blue polo shirt was well ironed and matched the smartly creased plaid shorts that went to his knees.

Hugh saw Tristan looking him over. He glanced down at his clothes. "Mom. Made me wear it. Got my Snapper shirt right here." He held up his Sea Camp backpack.

Tristan smiled. "It's not *that* bad."

Hugh looked at Tristan like he just said his favorite color was pink and he liked to wear bunny suits.

"Okay, it's pretty bad."

Hugh put his backpack down and headed for the buffet. Tristan happily finished his pea soup and started on a grilled cheese sandwich. He refilled his glass with pink-tinged water from a pitcher on the table and filled one for Hugh.

"Thanks," Hugh said. He had a heaping plate of non-seafood food. He was a little taller than last year, but still shorter than Tristan and definitely still on the pudgy side.

"Nice photo," Hugh noted as he bit into a hamburger. Ketchup and pickles popped out the back.

Tristan looked at him. "What photo?"

"Duh, the one of you on the shark with your hand in its mouth."

Tristan had been so distracted over the last few days, he'd actually forgotten about the photo. "Oh, *that* photo."

Realizing that others might have seen it too, he looked around. Some of the other campers were glancing his way and whispering.

"Stupid move, I know," he said.

"Hey, I didn't say that. No way I would have done it, though."

"Yeah, my parents didn't like it very much. They're not sure I should be here. One more *incident* and I'm history."

"No way. It's not your fault you could tell what an about-to-be-murdered shark was thinking."

"Yeah, that's what I said."

"Hey, have you seen Sam yet? Is she here?" Hugh asked.

"Not yet," Tristan said, glancing around hopefully. He then filled Hugh in about overhearing that Rickerton tried to hack into Sea Camp, and that the director thought there might be spies in the park.

"Oh, man," Hugh said. "Maybe, uh, it's not him? Maybe it's someone from the government, like the director said."

"Maybe."

After lunch they went to the Snapper bungalow so Hugh could change. Stepping through the bamboo door, they ran smack into two girls coming out. The timing was perfectly bad and resulted in a multiple, head-on camper collision. Hugh remained standing while Tristan tumbled down the short flight of stairs they just climbed. The two girls were sprawled out on the shiny wood floor in front of Hugh.

"Hey, just like when we first met," Hugh laughed.

"You think that was funny, pudge pot?" Rosina snarled from the ground. Her hair was still straggly and dishwater brown, but at least it looked like it had been combed within the last week or so. She had on her navy blue camp T-shirt and a pair of well-worn cutoff jeans.

"Uh, sorry," Hugh said, giving her a helping hand up. He then reached over to assist Sam.

"No broken bones, I guess," Rosina said a little less sourly.

"Hi, Hugh." Sam gave him a hug. "Where's Tristan?"

"Down here," Tristan called out, sitting in the sand, brushing it out of his hair and off his clothes.

"Things never change." Sam laughed as she ran down the steps to help Tristan up. She gave him a hug, her gray-blue eyes twinkling with delight. Sam's wheat-colored hair was in a ponytail, and she, too, was wearing her camp T-shirt.

"Just got here. Dad's finally coming around—said it was okay for me to come back. Have you been to the Rehab Center? What about the lagoon? Saw that photo, Tristan—what were you thinking? What . . ."

"Yup, things don't change, do they," Tristan said, interrupting. Sam still had a habit of speed talking whenever she was nervous or excited.

"Have you seen Ryder or the twins?" Sam asked.

"Ran into Ryder at lunch. No sign of the twins," Tristan told her.

They had several hours before the camp welcome dinner. Tristan eagerly suggested they go for a swim in the lagoon.

As they walked, Tristan told Sam about the new security cameras in the park and about the last two days spent watching for spies, possibly some of Rickerton's men. He also described the lengthy new reptiles in the sea turtle pond, though he neglected to mention his near face-to-face introduction to one. Rosina walked slightly behind and snapped at them whenever they tried to talk to her or include her in the conversation.

"What's her problem, anyway?" Hugh said quietly to Tristan and Sam.

Sam whispered, "Not sure. Maybe she's nervous. She was never a great swimmer. I'm kinda nervous too. Just hope my webbing comes back and I haven't forgotten anything from last year."

"You forgot to mention this whole evil rich guy possibly coming after us thing," Hugh said sarcastically. "Nervous? Who's nervous?"

"Look, it may not even be him," Tristan said. "And Hugh, you're not still freaked out about swimming in the lagoon are you?"

Hugh shrugged.

"But you did great last year," Sam told him. "Remember the octopus, fish, and squid in the Bahamas? You were a star. I thought you got over all that."

"That seems like a long time ago," Hugh mumbled, dragging his feet as they arrived at the dock.

For as much as Hugh was hesitant, Tristan was equally, if not more, excited. He loved swimming in the lagoon, going fast and looking for sea creatures. Tristan whipped off his T-shirt and took a long swig of the pink Sea Camp water they'd brought along.

"Hope the stuff in here still works," Tristan said, just before he dove into the lagoon and sped away underwater.

Sam jumped in next and chased after Tristan. Hugh sat down on the dock, staring into the water below. Rosina sat next to him. A large bird suddenly swooped down, grazing the tops of their heads. Both teens ducked so quickly they nearly fell into the water. The pelican landed and waddled over to them.

Rosina's face lit up. "Hi, Henry."

A small flock of white birds flew low over their heads, again causing the teens to duck.

"I wish they'd stop doing that," Hugh groaned.

The winged newcomers landed nearby and began milling about. The six white birds were smaller than Henry, each with a long, curved, reddish-pink bill. When they walked, the birds' heads bobbed back and forth like they were doing the funky chicken dance.

"What type of birds are those?" Hugh asked curiously.

"Henry says they're ibis. Not the smartest birds in the sky."

The ibis took no notice of the teens. They were busy plucking small insects out of the dock's wooden planks. Two of the birds collided and got their long bills twisted together. Another ibis was backing up while feeding and fell off the dock.

Henry shook his head at the other birds and then hopped closer to Hugh. The pelican reached out with his nearly two-foot-long bill to poke him.

"Hey, watch it," Hugh said.

"He says the water's warm. You should go in."

Henry poked Hugh again. Only this time it was more of a shove, and Hugh tumbled off the dock into the water.

Rosina laughed. "Good one, Henry."

Hugh popped up, grabbed Rosina's feet, and pulled her into the lagoon.

Tristan and Sam swam over just in time to see Rosina stand up and move toward Hugh. Fire blazed in her eyes.

"C'mon, it was just a joke," Hugh said, backing away. "Look, you're in the water now, just like me."

She stopped and looked at her hands. The others gazed at theirs. Sure enough, there was a thin film of skin between their fingers.

Rosina stepped next to Hugh. She patted him encouragingly on the arm. "How's it going, Hugh?"

The others were shocked until Hugh said, "That's disgusting." Slimy mucus ran down his arm.

"I still got it," Rosina bragged. She raised her hands out of the water. Strands of transparent slime hung from her fingers.

"Yup, looks like your mucus deployment skills are working alright," Sam noted.

"How about your echolocation?" Tristan asked.

"I don't know. Let me give it a try."

Sam ducked underwater and made a clicking noise. She popped back up, swam to where it was a little deeper, and went under.

"Kind of hard to tell," Sam told them after swimming back. "I'm a little rusty. But I think we have a visitor."

Hugh looked at her nervously. "A dolphin? Scarface or Toosha?"

"No, I don't think so." Sam pointed to a large gray dorsal fin at the surface about thirty feet away. It was moving toward them, fast.

Hugh scrambled behind Tristan.

Tristan ducked underwater. He saw the upturned snout of a large shark heading directly for them. And it wasn't slowing down. Tristan's heart beat faster, and he began backing up. He bumped into Hugh, and they got all tangled up. Just before the shark crashed into them, it swerved sharply, like a snowboarder coming to a quick stop. A wave of water washed over the teens. In his head, Tristan heard the shark say: *Did I scare you? How 'bout your friends?*

Tristan relaxed, laughed, and thought: O*h yes, Snaggle-Tooth, very scary. We were terrified, too scared to move.*

Hey, how'd you know it was me?

I recognized you. How are the teeth?

Tristan turned to the others. "Don't worry. It's just Snaggle-Tooth. He wants to show you his teeth."

Sam ducked underwater to look at the shark. Hugh and Rosina put their faces in the water more hesitantly. When they were all looking below the surface, Snaggle-Tooth opened his mouth and smiled, exposing a set of perfectly aligned, pointy white teeth.

Sam popped back up. "Very nice."

Hugh and Rosina just nodded uncomfortably, smiling awkwardly. They both looked about ready to run for it.

Tristan told the shark how impressed they were with his teeth.

Not as good as my old ones for catching fish, but much better for chewing and grabbing onto things. The shark swam near Hugh's leg. *Want to see?*

No, no, that's okay, Tristan responded quickly.

Hugh was frozen still, his eyes the size of baseballs.

Okay, maybe another time. Heard what you did for that bull shark. Nice work. Hey, did you hear about the fish and stuff dying? Sounds bad. You guys going to investigate?

Tristan told the shark that they just arrived and hadn't heard anything about any fish dying. He then told the others what Snaggle-Tooth had said.

"Ask him where," Sam suggested.

Tristan conversed with Snaggle-Tooth for a few more minutes before the shark swam away.

"He wants to go find some other people to show his teeth to," Tristan told them.

"Hope he doesn't run into any new campers or, like, normal people," Hugh said. "Talk about freaking out. Would've scared me out of the water *forever.*"

"So what about the fish dying? Where is it?" Sam asked.

"Snaggle-Tooth said he doesn't know much, but it's near some island named Virgin Gorda. Never heard of it."

"Well, we should probably tell the director," Sam suggested.

"We can tell him at dinner," Tristan said, and the others nodded.

"Hey, Hugh, want to try to find a seahorse or something to see if you can still do the camouflage thing with your skin?" Sam asked.

"No, that's okay. Maybe tomorrow."

Just then, a thin, dark brown bird popped up nearby. Something small and tan was wiggling in its short, yellow bill. Tristan looked closer. The bird had an orange face, and in the afternoon sun its eyes resembled glowing emeralds. He'd seen similar birds diving in the lagoon last year.

As Tristan and the others watched, the cormorant shook its head, trying to find a way to swallow its squirming catch. Eating got a whole lot harder when a seagull homed in on the cormorant's prize. The gull swooped down and pecked at the bird's bill to dislodge its wriggling meal. The cormorant paddled away, trying to dodge its attacker.

Tristan felt bad for the bird. He knew how it felt to be bullied. Then things then got even worse for the poor cormorant. The seagull landed right on top of its head. The cormorant shook itself to dislodge the seagull, but the bird stayed put, wavering like someone trying to balance on a tightrope. To get rid of its feathery headdress, the cormorant then whipped its head back. The seagull took flight, but the cormorant's catch also went flying, straight into Rosina's face.

"Aargh!" she shouted, stepping back and swatting the air by her face. The bird's wiggling catch was now floating in the water in front of her.

Sam jumped in to prevent Rosina from flinging it away. "Wait, what is it?"

Tristan looked down. It was soft, speckled, and about the size of a golf ball.

"Octopus," Hugh said. "A baby, I think. Still alive, but hurt."

"Let's take it to the Rehab Center," Sam suggested.

The seagull hovered nearby. It squawked loudly at them, while the cormorant silently eyed the teens like they just stole the last very best meal of its life.

"What about the birds?" Rosina said. "They say they're hungry and that's a seriously good treat."

"Oh, there's plenty more for them to eat," Sam replied. "Look how cute this little guy is. I bet Doc Jordan can help him—or her."

"Well, pick it up," Tristan said to Hugh.

"You pick it up," Hugh snapped back.

"*Boys,*" Sam said as she carefully scooped up the creature and ran from the shallow water to the beach. "Grab my stuff."

Tristan and Hugh followed her.

"Wait for me," Rosina shouted. "I have to apologize to the birds since you guys are all a bunch of wimpy do-gooders."

"Tell them we'll bring a few scraps from dinner instead," Tristan shouted back.

Rosina waved to the birds. "I'll be back with take-out."

6

SURF'S UP

AFTER DROPPING OFF THE BABY OCTOPUS AT THE Rehab Center, the teens changed and made their way to the Conch Café for the first night's official welcome dinner. Tristan immediately noticed the latest young recruits sitting up front at the Seasquirt tables. They looked just as clueless as he did last summer. *Just wait,* he thought.

Director Davis tried out a few new jokes, which went over about as well as his old ones. He then introduced Coach Fred. The campers ate from the not-from-the-ocean buffet and drank lots of pink Sea Camp water. After dinner, the Snappers and Squids were directed to go to the Wave Pool for practice.

Before Director Davis left, he stopped at their table. "Looks like the twins, Julie and Jillian, won't be joining us this summer. They're on a trip to Africa with their parents. Digging fossils, I believe. So it'll just be you five."

The teens nodded.

Sam nudged Tristan.

"Oh, yeah," Tristan said. "Uh, Director Davis."

"Yes?"

"We ran into Snaggle-Tooth in the lagoon. He was showing us his teeth."

"Yes, they are quite nice."

"He also asked if we'd heard about some fish dying. Somewhere around an island, Virgin something."

"Virgin Gorda," Hugh added. "Where is that?"

The director paused noticeably before he spoke. "Virgin Gorda is in the British Virgin Islands in the northeastern Caribbean."

"Snaggle-Tooth asked if we were going to investigate," Tristan said.

"Starting with the questions already, are you? Well, there has been a report of a fish kill in the area. A colleague of ours is investigating. It's nothing for all of you to worry about. Besides, if I were you, I'd be much more concerned about getting to the Wave Pool before Coach Fred shows up."

Tristan and the other Snappers turned to the Squid tables. They were empty. The older teens had already left for the Wave Pool. Not only were the Snappers behind, they also forgot that on the first night they got to dive in right after dinner. The group had to go back to the bungalow to change into their swimsuits. With barely a nod to the director, the teens sprinted for the door, forgetting all about the dying fish and the island named Virgin Gorda.

By the time the Snappers got to the Wave Pool, the Squids were already diving through and riding two-foot waves. Thankfully, Coach Fred wasn't there yet. He was still at the show for new campers. Tristan watched as one boy did an impressive 360, spinning completely around on his stomach as he rode a wave in.

"Look, we kept the waves nice and small for you kiddies," shouted the Squid who just did the 360. He was a stocky, dark-haired teen with thin lips and a flat, crooked nose that looked like it had been on the wrong end of a fist a time or two.

"Cute, dude," Ryder shouted back. "Like, let's get some real waves in here and we'll see who surfs 'em better."

"No," Sam said firmly. "These are just fine." She turned to Ryder and punched him in the arm. "Give us a break. We're not all, *like*, California surfing dudes."

The Snappers joined the older Squids in the pool. Tristan, Hugh, Sam, and Rosina practiced how to swim through and ride the waves—nothing fancy. Ryder, on the other hand, took every opportunity to show off his jumping and surfing abilities. He leapt out of the waves and somersaulted. He glided atop the crests, swerving back and forth like a dolphin riding the wake at a ship's bow.

After a particularly long ride in, Ryder turned to the flat-nosed Squid. "Yo, like, let's see ya do *that*, Squid-boy."

"Lame and tame," the teen responded. "Check this out." The boy dove into the pool, swam out, and came up on a wave about to break. He did another 360 on the cresting wave, this time twisting as he whirled around. He then streaked underwater to where Ryder was standing. "Now that's how it's done, pea brain."

"Is that the best you've got?" Ryder asked.

"It is in *these* waves. We have to keep 'em small for you baby campers."

Tristan was sick of the two boys' smack talk. He turned to Brianna. "Make the waves bigger so they can show off for awhile. Maybe that'll shut them up."

"Yeah, do it," another teen said.

Coach Fred had entrusted his bedazzled wave controller to the mocha-skinned girl who made Tristan go all googly-eyed. He tried not to stare at Brianna while she contemplated the buttons on the sparkly controller. With a smirk, she pressed one. The waves grew larger. Soon four-foot-high walls of water rolled through the pool. About halfway across, the waves steepened, curled over, and broke into a churning mass of whitewater.

Ryder and the Squid boy glared at each other and then dove into the pool. Tristan rapidly lost sight of them in the swirling whitewater. Minutes later, two heads popped up out by where the waves were breaking. The boys saw one another and ducked under.

They swam farther out until they were just beyond the breakers. They stopped, treaded water, and bobbed up and down. The two boys glared again at each other and then turned to watch as a wave approached. The Squid boy tried to shove Ryder out of the way to get the best position. But Ryder grabbed his ankle and pulled him briefly underwater.

Tristan and the others moved right to the water's edge to get a better view. As the next wave approached, the water began to rise under the boys. Side by side, they started kicking.

"What is going on here?"

Coach Fred strutted to where the startled teens stood on the beach. He was still in his camouflage pants and sparkly red sequin vest. "You are all supposed to be practicing, getting used to your webbed feet again." He glared at Brianna. Avoiding eye contact, she handed over the controller.

Ryder and the Squid boy surfed in, but nobody was watching. Coach Fred had their full attention. When the boys' heads popped up in the shallow water next to the beach, Coach Fred waded in and grabbed each by the arm. "That'll be enough for tonight, boys."

The Snappers made their way back to the bungalow. On the way, Sam leaned over to Hugh and Tristan to whisper, "One day, Ryder's big head is going to get him into trouble."

7

SQUIDS VS. SNAPPERS

THE NEXT WEEK AT CAMP WAS SPENT TRAINING hard. So hard, the teens had little time to think about potential spies; revenge-seeking, yacht-owning shark killers; or fish dying near some far-off island. Especially long hours were spent at Coach Fred's ocean boot camp. He set up buoys in the lagoon for the Snappers to swim around. He rigged floating lines they had to jump over or dive under. He placed weighted sticks on the bottom to see how fast the campers could find and recover them. And just to make it harder, he added some large, powerful, and very sneaky distractions—dolphins Toosha and Scarface. They sprinted by unexpectedly, cut off the campers, or playfully nipped at their toes. Rosina tried to fend off the dolphins by shooting slimy strands of mucus at them. After that, they harassed her the most. The least disrupted was Sam. It seemed marine mammals were a little biased when it came to her.

In the swimming exercises, Tristan was the fastest, while Ryder excelled in anything that involved jumping. Sam always found the weighted sticks first—after all, she had her own undersea quick-find tool—echolocation. Hugh and Rosina were just happy to complete each challenge, especially with the dolphins involved. Coach Fred's boot camp was not where they shined. They did far better in sessions with Ms. Sanchez, when they worked on their communication skills and other talents.

One afternoon, when they arrived at the lagoon for what they thought was going to be another grueling session of ocean boot camp, the teens were surprised to find the Squids already there. It was the same group of campers who had been at the Wave Pool the first night. Coach Fred was standing on the dock holding two sets of colored neoprene vests, one red and one blue.

"Gather round, my little campers," Coach announced. "Time for a friendly Sea Camp competition. It's an excellent means to strengthen your skills and show off your teamwork—*I hope*. I assume you've all had plenty of water today." He stared pointedly at the teens.

Tristan got the message and chugged down more than half of the bottle in his backpack. The other campers did likewise. He glanced around nervously. They'd never had a team competition before. Tristan's history in athletic competitions at home was nothing short of a series of humiliating disasters.

"Of course, the winners will get bragging rights," Coach said. "But for some added motivation—the bungalow that wins gets to go on a little excursion this evening for some homemade ice cream at Rita's place down the road. Now there's one delicious treat, and I'm not just talking about the ice cream, fellas."

The campers turned to one another with an expression like they just tasted the world's sourest sourball. Just the thought of Coach Fred romancing the ice cream lady made them all squeamish.

"To win this, you'll need to work together and use your skills strategically. Teamwork is very important here at Sea Camp," Coach announced. "Okay, here's how it's going to work. Somewhere out in the lagoon, I've placed two treasure chests on the seafloor. One has a red flag on it and one a blue. You must find your team's chest, bring it to the beach, and open it. Inside is a set of clues to where you will find the pieces to a puzzle. Once you've found the pieces, put the puzzle together. The first team to complete their puzzle and tell me what it says wins."

Coach handed the red vests to the Squids and gave the blue ones to the Snappers. "I want this to be a clean challenge. Use your skills well, and be smart about it. Oh, and one more thing—no help from Scarface, Toosha, or any other dolphins. That would be too easy. Other sea creatures? Well, that's up to you. You have ten minutes to come up with a plan. Starting . . . now!"

Tristan huddled up with the other Snappers, while the Squids did the same a short distance away. As they talked, each teen put on his or her vest. Hugh's vest got stuck half-way over his head with his arms sticking straight up. Sam had to help him by pulling it down.

Ryder watched, rolling his eyes. "We are in serious trouble."

Tristan was watching the Squids, sizing up the competition. He wondered what skills they would use. Brianna happened to glance his way and smiled shyly at him.

"Hey, like, no flirting with the enemy," Ryder derided Tristan.

Rosina scowled at him. Hugh and Sam looked shocked.

"I wasn't flirting!" Tristan blurted out, his face turning red. "I was just checking them out. I mean, I was trying to figure out what skills they would use."

"One minute left," Coach shouted.

Sam stared disapprovingly at Tristan and then turned back to the others. "Like I was saying. Once we find it, how are we going to get the chest to the beach?"

"Okay, campers. Five, four, three, two, one, that's it for strategy," Coach announced. "Everyone over to the beach."

Tristan couldn't believe they thought he was flirting. He just looked at the girl. She was the one who smiled. He jogged over to the dock with the others. He glanced again at the pretty Squid. For some reason he couldn't help himself. She caught him looking her way and again smiled. He turned away quickly, stumbling right into Hugh.

"Make me proud," Coach yelled. "Get ready . . . *go!*"

Anthony Price, the Squids' pint-sized fish-talker, ran for the water and dove in. He swam out into the lagoon. Sam ran into the water as well. She dove in, swam about twenty feet out, and ducked under. Rosina took off for the dock.

The rest of the red team spread out along the sand, forming a widely spaced line. The flat-nosed, dark-haired surfer Squid seemed to be their leader. He confidently shouted, "Forward." Together, they dove, swam out into the lagoon, and then popped up to reform their line.

"A search grid. Good strategy, Squids!" Coach yelled.

"Go, Sam. Hurry, Rosina," Tristan shouted.

Rosina ran to where Henry was perched on a dock piling. After a short teenager-pelican powwow, the bird took off and began gliding high up over the lagoon, looking down.

"Interesting, Snappers," Coach commented.

The Squids continued their coordinated swim in the lagoon.

Tristan pointed offshore. "Oh, no, check out the fish."

A school of small silver fish leapt repeatedly out of the water in front of the Squids. A head popped up amid the porpoising fish. It was Price. He looked toward the Snappers and waved with the smirkiest expression ever. He then dove back in among the leaping fish.

Rosina joined the other Snappers. Tristan could hardly contain himself. He wanted to get out there and start searching. He wondered if their great strategy was so great after all. He heard a sharp whistle. Fish boy was waving the red team over.

"Nice work, Price. Looks like the Squids have found their chest. Better get a move on, Snappers," Coach shouted.

"Where's Sam?" Ryder complained. "What's taking her so long?"

Moments later, Henry circled the group and then landed near Rosina. Sam ran out of the water. Both girls began talking at once. The boys looked from one girl to the other, their heads ping-ponging back and forth.

"Whoa," Tristan finally said. "One at a time."

Sam nodded to Rosina.

"Henry says the chest is near the big brain coral next to where Scarface likes to rub his back in the sand."

Tristan and the others looked at her like she just spoke in a language no one on Earth could possibly understand. "Where the heck is that?"

"Don't worry, follow me. I know," Sam said running into the lagoon.

"Hope your sonar works better than Henry's directions," Ryder said.

"Hey," Rosina growled.

They sprinted for the water. Tristan tripped in the soft sand, doing a perfect nosedive onto the beach. Typical, he thought. He jumped up, hoping nobody, especially Brianna, had noticed. Tristan dove into the lagoon and quickly caught up with the others. About 150 yards from shore, Sam dove down and pointed to a yellow coral covered with squiggly ridges. Some eight feet behind it and to the right was a three-foot-long brown chest with a blue flag strapped on top. The water was about twelve feet deep.

Back at the surface, Ryder swam to gain speed and jumped up to see the Squids. He came back to the group treading water over the chest. "They've found their chest, but it doesn't look like they're moving it yet."

Ryder and Tristan dove down and tried to pick up the wooden box. The other teens put their heads underwater to watch. The two boys strained, but the chest barely came off the sand.

"It's too heavy to carry," Tristan said back at the surface.

"What if we push it?" Sam suggested.

As a group, they dove down and tried to push the chest forward. It moved about an inch before getting solidly stuck in the sand. The teens headed up.

Ryder jumped again to see how the other team was doing. "They've started moving to the beach."

"Maybe one of us should go over there and see how they're doing it?" Hugh suggested.

"Uh, wait," Rosina said. "I have an idea. I think. Something Ms. Sanchez said last year. Remember, she told us that some snails use their mucus to travel over the sand to go faster."

The others shook their heads.

"What if I put some slime down in front of the chest and then you guys pull it over the slime?"

"Worth a try," Tristan said.

Ryder looked doubtful, but the others agreed to give it a go.

"Give me a minute," Rosina said before diving down and shaking her hands in front of the chest.

Tristan was watching from the surface when something big bumped his legs. His heart leapt and he flinched, instinctively curling his feet in. He swiveled around. It was Snaggle-Tooth. *Hey, what's happening? What you guys doing?*

Seeing the sand tiger shark, Hugh casually swam behind the others.

Rosina came up for a breath and went back down.

Tristan told Snaggle-Tooth about their challenge against the Squids. The shark asked if he could play too. Tristan told the other teens about the shark's offer.

"He should help us move the chest. Push it for us," Ryder suggested.

Sam smiled mischievously. "I have a better idea."

After she explained and the others enthusiastically agreed, Tristan told Snaggle-Tooth what to do.

Rosina came back to the surface. "Okay, try it now. Every few feet, I'll try to add some more mucus. Just hope I don't run out or anything."

"Wait a minute," Tristan said. "You're going to want to see this." He rose up out of the water, straining to see the red team. The other Snappers did the same. At first, they couldn't see any of the Squids. They were all underwater moving the chest. Seconds later, there was a flurry of arms and legs at the surface. A Squid girl screamed. The red team scattered, swimming away in all directions. In the center of the ruckus, a large dark gray fin broke the surface and began circling. The Snappers fist-pumped the air, laughing. The other team had just been punked by a shark.

"C'mon, let's go," Tristan said. "Once they realize it's just Snaggle-Tooth playing, they'll get back to moving their chest."

The group submerged. Tristan and Ryder grabbed the handles on each side of the chest and pulled. Hugh, Sam, and Rosina pushed from behind. At first the chest barely moved, catching again in the sand. Then the slime kicked in. The chest shot forward, sliding smoothly over the bottom. The teens popped up for a breath and went back down. Rosina gave up pushing to focus on releasing globs of mucus in front of the chest. They made good progress and soon were about halfway to shore. The teens gathered on the surface to rest.

"It's a tie. You're neck and neck!" Coach Fred shouted from the dock.

The teens dove back down. They pulled and pushed. But they were getting tired, and the chest was moving more slowly. Hugh and Sam suddenly dove to the side. A large, gray snout nudged the chest from behind. Snaggle-Tooth had returned to help. The chest barreled toward the beach. Soon it was too shallow for the shark. Tristan thanked him for his help and the teens dragged the chest out of the water onto the sand.

Hugh collapsed. "I've been slimed!"

The mucus Rosina had shaken off her hands was on the sand, the chest, and all over the teens.

"Uh, sorry about that," Rosina said with a slight smile. "But at least it worked."

"Just think of that nice cool ice cream, sweet and delicious," Coach Fred yelled. "Better get hopping, Squids. Snappers have taken the lead!"

Tristan looked down the beach. The other team was just nearing the beach. "C'mon, you guys. We're ahead. Let's open this thing up."

A blue rope was wrapped about the chest and tied with a stack of tight, round knots. The teens tried to untie the rope, but the mucus on their hands made it impossible. They wiped the gooey slime off on their swimsuits, then on each other. They rinsed their hands off in the water, scrubbed them with sand, but it hardly helped. Tristan glanced down the beach. The other team was now on the beach and beginning to work on the rope around their chest.

"Hold on," Hugh said. "Let me try something."

The others looked at him doubtfully, but backed away. Hugh ran for the water, dunked under quickly, and returned to the chest. He closed his eyes, concentrating, fingering the knots.

"What's he doing? We're going to lose just standing here," Ryder barked.

Hugh's fingers seemed to somehow lengthen and

narrow, working their way into spaces impossibly small. The knots started to loosen. Hugh opened his eyes and began untying them. The others jumped in to help. The rope fell away from the chest.

"Cool, how'd you do that?" Tristan asked.

"Something Old Jack taught me last summer," Hugh said, smiling. "Wasn't sure I could still do it."

"Nice job, everyone. It's neck and neck again," Coach shouted.

They opened the chest. Inside was a rectangular lead weight attached to an iPad encased in sturdy plastic.

Ryder grabbed the iPad. "Now what?"

"Here, let me," Hugh said, taking it from the teen. He turned it on. A satellite image of the beach and lagoon came up. A text box then popped up that read: *Follow the three clues to your puzzle pieces.* Hugh pressed the number one icon. It was positioned over the lagoon dock. *Here's where we started, here's where we finish. Carry me below, then off you go.*

Rosina threw up her hands. "What the heck does that mean?"

"Do you think it's waterproof?" Tristan asked.

"Yeah, I bet it is," Hugh answered. "And I bet it also has a GPS unit in it. C'mon." He ran for the dock. The others followed. The red team was sprinting just ahead of them. "I think we have to bring it under the dock."

They dove in and swam beneath the dock's wooden planks. Treading water, Hugh held up the iPad. A loud ding rang out like the chime of a clock. A number two icon popped up on the screen.

Tristan looked over at the red team. They were also getting their second clue.

From overhead, they heard Coach's voice. "Nice work, red and blue teams. Time to dig in, so to speak!"

Hugh read from the screen, "Like buried treasure, this one will take some real hands-on attention. Fifty paces south from the dock, next to the tree for number three."

They swam back to shore to where the dock began.

"How big is a pace?" Hugh asked. "I mean, look at Sam's feet; they're small compared to yours, Ryder."

"Even better question, which direction is south?" Tristan asked, looking around.

Hugh stared at the iPad screen. There was a compass rose in one corner. As he turned the iPad, the compass spun. He stood next to the dock, facing the lagoon, and lined up the image on the screen with what he saw. Pointing to his right he said, "That way."

Ryder pushed Hugh aside. He put one foot in front of the other, pacing off in the direction Hugh had pointed. "One. Two. Three . . ."

"Look, the Squids are going the other way," Sam said. The other team was also pacing off, but headed in the opposite direction. "Go faster."

Ryder stopped to look at the other team. He then turned back. "Uh, guys, where was I?"

"You were on twenty-four," Hugh said calmly.

"Twenty-five. Twenty-six . . ."

At fifty paces, they came to a pair of palm trees. One stretched out over the water.

"Guess we should start digging," Sam said.

"Where exactly?" Rosina asked.

"Beside the trees," Tristan answered.

They dropped to their knees and started frantically digging anywhere and everywhere next to the two trees. Tristan turned to see where the other team was. The Squids had also started digging. Sand was flying everywhere.

"Hey, watch it," Rosina snapped, brushing sand from her hair.

"Sorry 'bout that," Tristan said, shrugging good-naturedly and thinking, *Now she knows how it feels*. At least the sand wasn't gooey like her slime.

"I've got something," Sam shouted.

The others converged on where she was digging. The tip of a blue ribbon stuck out of her hole. They helped scoop the sand away, uncovering a rolled-up piece of paper like an ancient scroll. Sam swiftly untied the blue ribbon around the scroll. On it were just two words—LOOK UP.

The teens' heads snapped skyward.

"There! Out by the coconuts, hanging over the water!" Tristan yelled.

Hidden between the fronds of the palm tree that stretched out over the lagoon was a hanging blue bag.

"How are we going to get *that*?" Rosina questioned.

Ryder walked over to the palm tree and jumped up. He wrapped his arms and legs around the trunk and started to shimmy his way up. About five feet up, he started to slip. At first it was just an inch or two. Then he slid all the way to the ground, landing hard on his butt.

"Not as easy as it looks!" Coach Fred shouted to them.

Ryder glared at him. "No problem. I've got a better idea, anyways." He ran for the water.

"Wait," Sam shouted. "I know what to do."

But Ryder was already swimming away from them.

"Look, what if we build a human pyramid," Sam suggested. "I'm pretty light. I could be at the top. I did it once in gym class."

"That might work, but we'll need Ryder to do it," Tristan said.

Tristan shouted to him. The teen was swimming fast toward where the tree hung out over the water. Ryder leapt up and reached for the hanging blue bag. But he wasn't high enough and fell empty handed into the water. And the landing wasn't pretty. Ryder did a stomach-searing belly flop like when he first discovered his talent for jumping.

The others shouted to Ryder to come back to the beach so they could try Sam's teen tower idea. But he waved them off, swimming around for another try.

"Way to go, Squids!" Coach shouted. "Excellent skill use, Winters."

Tristan looked over. "Oh, no."

One of the girls on the other team was climbing another palm tree that hung out over the water. She was scrambling up monkey-like, amazingly fast.

"How's she doing that?" Sam asked.

They were quiet, contemplating the girl's spidey skills.

"I know," Hugh said. "She must have sticky hands and feet. Heard about that last year. Like a sea star's tube feet. They have sticky-suction cup tips."

"Cool," Tristan said. "I mean, as a skill and all."

"Ryder, come back," Sam shouted louder.

But Ryder either didn't hear or was ignoring her. He tried again to jump for the bag, but again came up short. He finally gave up and headed for the beach, where the others were still shouting and waving at him.

"The water is, like, too shallow to get good height," he complained.

"Didn't you hear us?" Rosina snarled. "They've just about got their puzzle pieces."

"What?" Ryder scowled. His frown deepened when he saw the Squid girl out on the tree. She had just grabbed the bag with their puzzle pieces.

Sam explained her idea again. The teens sprinted for the water. It was only a few feet deep directly below the bag. Tristan, Ryder, and Rosina stood facing one another with their arms outstretched and braced. Hugh helped Sam climb onto their shoulders. She stood up and reached for the bag.

"I'm too low," Sam yelled down.

"Good *try* there, Snappers," Coach shouted.

"We'll have to lift her up with our hands," Tristan said.

The others looked at him like he needed a straight-jacket. He sort of thought the same thing. But they had to try something.

"We can do this. I'll take this foot. Ryder, you take

the other one. And Rosina and Hugh, you guys help keep us steady."

"Stand on our hands!" Tristan yelled up to Sam.

Sam looked down at them. "Okay, but hurry. I don't think I can stay up here much longer." Her legs were starting to shake, and their teen tower had begun to lean.

They put their hands under Sam's feet.

"One. Two. Three!" Tristan shouted. They raised Sam up over their heads. She reached for the bag, but still she was just a little too low. As their teen tower began to topple, Sam sprang up in a last-ditch effort. The others tumbled into the water, and Sam stretched, reaching up as far as she could. Then, she too fell hard into the water. Sam came up spitting out seawater and coughing. That was it, Tristan thought. They just lost the challenge. Then Sam raised one hand. She had the blue bag! Tristan and the other Snappers whooped and hollered, racing back to the beach. Sam quickly untied the bag and dumped the puzzle pieces onto the sand.

"You've got some time to make up," Coach Fred shouted to them. "The Squids are already working on their puzzle!"

The others backed off and let Hugh look at the pieces. They had already decided he'd be the best at it. He stared at the interlocking wooden pieces. Each had lettering on it.

"The Squids just about have it," Coach yelled.

"You've got this, Hugh," Tristan said.

"Yeah, no problem," Sam encouraged.

Hugh seemed to figure something out and began putting the pieces together.

"Sea Camp Rules!" shouted the Squids.

"Excellent job, red team," Coach said. "Well done. It was extremely close—up until the tree, that is."

Hugh finished the puzzle and shrugged. The other Snappers looked at Ryder, shaking their heads.

"Hey, I almost had it. We would have won."

"Okay, everyone over here," Coach Fred said. "Shake hands. Good job, campers! Nice use of your skills. After dinner, Squids meet me at the park entrance for our trip to Rita's. Better luck next time, Snappers."

Disappointment showed on their faces. Ryder left the beach quickly, saying something about how he needed a shower. The other Snappers followed more slowly. After a celebratory swim, the Squids ran by. As she passed, Brianna hit Tristan on the arm. "Good move with Snaggle-Tooth. Almost had us."

Hugh grinned at Tristan, while Rosina and Sam gave him looks like they wanted to shove a spear through his chest.

"What?" Tristan said, beaming.

8

A FISHY SITUATION

No one knew whether it was the ice cream, something else they ate, or a quick-acting, fast-spreading bug. But the morning after the Squids went for their tasty reward, they all felt horribly ill. They were now holed up in their bungalow, barely able to get out of bed, and regularly revisiting what they had consumed over the past day or so. It was not going to be a pretty or sweet-smelling day for the Squids.

"Kinda glad we didn't win that challenge after all," Hugh said to Tristan and Sam at breakfast.

"No joke," Tristan replied.

"Yeah, I saw Coach Fred on the way in. He didn't look so good either," Sam told them.

Just then, Director Davis strode into the Conch Café followed by Doc Jordan and Ms. Sanchez. They looked concerned and in a rush.

"Campers, listen up," Director Davis announced. "There's been a mass stranding of dolphins in the southern Bahamas. Doc Jordan and Ms. Sanchez will be leading a team there to help. Campers in the Dolphin and Shark bungalows may go. Pack your bags and meet outside the Poseidon Theater in thirty minutes."

A large group sprinted for the door while others shouted that they wanted to go too.

"I'm sorry; only the senior campers may go. The rest of you will remain here to continue your training."

"What's going to happen to the dolphins?"

"How come they got stuck on the beach?"

"Wish we knew," Doc Jordan answered. "Sometimes dolphins or whales beach themselves like this when they are sick or injured, and they are very social animals. If one member of the pod goes aground, then the others may follow it. Or sometimes there's been activity nearby that uses sound on a frequency that injures the dolphins or disrupts their navigation system."

"Will . . . will they *die*?" Sam asked, choking up.

"Hopefully not. We are going to try our very best to save as many as possible. There's already a response team on site from the Marine Mammal Stranding Network. We'll be working with them."

"Okay, back to breakfast, everyone," Director Davis ordered. "There'll be a change in your schedules while Ms. Sanchez and the Doc are gone. Squids have the day off for obvious reasons. Seasquirts, to the lagoon for the morning, and Snappers, meet in the chemistry lab."

The camp leaders quickly jogged out the door.

After breakfast, Tristan, Sam, and Hugh went through the side entrance of the Rehab Center on their way to the chemistry lab.

"Hang on a sec," Hugh said. "I want to check on Old Jack and tell him what I did with my fingers yesterday."

They searched for the octopus in his retiree condo complex in the aquarium room. There was no sign of the six-armed cephalopod. Tristan checked the old guy's favorite pickle jar. Hugh looked under a pile of rocks and in a cylindrical plexiglass climbing tube.

Sam was staring curiously at a pink plastic teacup sitting on the sand in one of the tanks. "Hey, come look at this."

There was something curled up inside the dainty little cup, and three small white sticks hung over the side.

"What the heck is that?" Tristan asked.

Hugh leaned closer. "I think it's the baby octopus we rescued from the birds." He rinsed his hand with seawater from a nearby squeeze bottle and stuck it into the tank. Hugh reached in cautiously until his fingertips were nearly touching the plastic teacup. A small knob of a head rose up. Two tiny eye-slits opened. The baby octopus stared at Hugh's fingers and then blanched white. Hugh's fingers flashed pale in response.

"Yup," Hugh told them. "A couple of badly sprained arms and a concussion."

Seemingly out of nowhere, two large, suckered arms then wrapped around Hugh's arm. Startled, he jumped back. "Very funny, Jack."

"Yeah, good one," Tristan laughed.

A rainbow of color washed over the larger octopus's body. A similarly colored wave traveled up Hugh's arm.

Hugh smiled. "Old Jack's not too happy. He says the baby octopus has invaded his space and is getting all the attention."

The large octopus unwrapped his arms from Hugh. Sitting beside the teacup, Jack then used three of his arms to gently stroke the small, recuperating creature.

"Looks to me like he likes his new roommate," Sam noted.

"C'mon," Tristan said. "We'd better get going or we'll be late."

Hugh told Old Jack about how he used his fingers in the challenge, and then said good-bye to the octopus retiree and his new, but supposedly bothersome, friend. The campers hurried through the connecting door into the chemistry lab. Rosina and Ryder were already there, along with Director Davis and Flash, the camp's tech wizard. The older teen spent most of his time on the computer and monitoring system in the Situation Room.

The director stood at the front of the room. "Nice of you three to join us."

They sat down on high stools behind a long bench. Tristan checked out the newly renovated lab. It was divided into two sections. One part was a wet lab with running seawater and rows of tubs and tanks. The other section was dry with several long benches running across the room. Computers, a few microscopes, and some other instruments he didn't recognize sat on the benches.

"Last summer we went over the major ocean currents," Director Davis announced. "This year you're going to learn how to use a computer model to investigate them further. We use this software to track pollutants and debris—all the plastic, oil, and other chemicals we humans are sadly dumping into the ocean. The computer model is also very helpful in search and rescue operations. Flash here is the real expert."

"Hey. How's it goin'?" Flash said. "Okay, grab a computer and then click on the spinning globe icon on your screen."

Each of the teens moved in front of a computer. When Tristan clicked on the spinning globe, it opened to a world map of flowing ocean currents.

"These are the world's major ocean currents and their general direction of flow," Director Davis explained.

"Right," Flash added. "If you click on any of the currents, a new screen will pop up. It will show details about that current and allow you to do some pretty wicked stuff."

"Go ahead and start exploring the software," Director Davis suggested. "We'll come around and see how you're doing."

"Check out the track-and-trace feature," Flash

urged. "That's the really cool part. Especially since I've modified it. You can release a person, a drop of oil, or an object anywhere in the ocean and track where it might go."

Tristan scanned the ocean currents, clicked on a few, and was just about to try the track-and-trace feature when Hugh nudged him. "Hey, check it out. Here's that island Snaggle-Tooth was talking about—Virgin Gorda. It's in this cluster of islands up here." He pointed to the top right corner of the Caribbean Sea. To the southwest were Puerto Rico and the US Virgin Islands.

Sam leaned over to see as well. "Those must be the British Virgin Islands, like the director said."

Hugh clicked on the tracer sidebar and chose an object from the options list. He then clicked on a spot in a wide channel between Virgin Gorda and an island to the west, Tortola. A yellow rubber ducky popped up on the screen. It started moving southwest with the currents in the channel between the two islands. The rubber ducky was then swept into a swirl of water and began going around and around, stuck between two smaller islands labeled Peter and Norman. It suddenly shot out of the swirling eddy, went south, and got caught up in a stronger westerly flow to the south of Puerto Rico. It was in the Caribbean Sea. The teens stared at the screen, fascinated by the winding path of the toy. It soon took a sharp right turn, got sucked into a flow between Puerto Rico and the Dominican Republic/Haiti, and headed north.

"Look where it's going," Tristan said, pointing to the islands of the Bahamas.

Just then the director walked over. "What are you three so interested in?"

Before they could answer, Coach Fred pushed through the lab door. He still looked alarmingly pale and a bit rough around the edges. He hurried over to the director and spoke quietly to him.

Director Davis turned to the Snappers and looked them over as if deciding something. He pursed his lips. "I don't know about this."

"They did well in the challenge for the most part. And their skills are progressing," Coach Fred said.

Tristan glanced questioningly toward Sam and Hugh, wondering what was going on.

"It seems we have a little situation on our hands," Director Davis said.

The lights in the lab flickered. Tristan wondered if the "situation" had something to do with the power. There had been two power outages since camp began. Was it Rickerton? Tristan's heart beat a little harder just thinking about the man.

The director hesitated. He glanced with concern at the lights and then turned to Coach Fred, his eyebrows raised. The lights stopped flickering and he continued, "There've been a series of mortality events in the British Virgin Islands."

Tristan, Sam, and Hugh exchanged knowing looks.

"The cause is unclear, and a colleague in the area has requested our help. However, all of the senior campers are still helping with the stranded dolphins, and the Squids are clearly in no shape to go."

"We'll go!" Tristan blurted out excitedly.

The director ignored him. "Unfortunately, we just can't wait any longer. This could have a serious impact on the region and more if it spreads. I've already contacted your parents." He paused. "After some discussion, they've agreed to let you go—some more readily than others."

Tristan knew what that meant: his mother.

"Coach Fred will also be going. I expect you all to do exactly as he says."

They nodded, though Hugh and Rosina did so with slightly less enthusiasm than the others.

"Remember, you will be representing Sea Camp. Your actions can affect us all deeply."

Tristan was sure that last comment was also meant for him.

"Your job will be to work with Coach Fred and our colleague down there to investigate what is going on and try to find the cause. Now go pack your backpacks, and meet outside the Situation Room in an hour. Oh, and if any of you would prefer to stay here, that's fine as well. Just let me know."

Tristan could hardly believe it. They were going on an official mission, even though they were only second-summer Snappers. Cool. And he couldn't imagine what the director had said to his mother that convinced her to let him go.

As he was leaving the lab, Tristan paused, looking back. Coach Fred was standing next to a tall, thin man he didn't recognize. He had wild, steel-gray hair that resembled a badly built bird's nest, with matching scruffy eyebrows, and his clothes were rumpled as if he just fought his way through a powerful windstorm. The man was whispering to Coach Fred and looking around as if to ensure he wasn't being overheard. He furtively handed something to Coach Fred. Tristan couldn't see what it was.

9

SPY GADGETS 'R' US

JUST OVER AN HOUR LATER, COACH FRED AND Director Davis led the teens to Sea Camp's hidden runway. Tristan was distracted, thinking about the fact that they were going on an actual mission and about just how many ways he could screw up. If he did something stupid, this could be his first and his very last official mission. He nearly tripped over a rock on the path and then stubbed his toe on the edge of the airstrip's asphalt, bumping into Hugh.

"Sorry 'bout that."

Hugh just nodded. Tristan then realized that since they'd been told about the mission, Hugh had hardly said anything. Maybe he didn't want to go. Should he say something? It wouldn't be the same if Hugh didn't go. Besides, they needed him. Who knew when morphing your skin like an octopus would come in handy, and his communication skills were really good. Tristan decided not to say anything, hoping that Hugh was just nervous like he was.

Parked about halfway down the runway was a small jet airplane. It was noticeably larger than the one they'd flown in last year.

Ryder was the first to board after Coach lowered the stairs. "Now this is the way to travel."

The director winked to Tristan as he entered the plane. "Confiscated from some drug runners. Got it cheap with shipwreck funds."

Tristan gawked at the inside of the plane. It was light, airy, and luxurious. The seats were made of soft, cream-colored leather; some faced forward, others backward, with small tables between them. There was even a couch on one side.

"Okay, everyone grab a seat and buckle up," the director told them. "I'll be up front with Coach till we level off."

Ryder and Rosina took seats facing forward up front. Tristan and Hugh sat facing the back across from Sam with a small table between them.

Director Davis cracked a bad joke over the intercom, something to do with sea stars and lighting up at night. He then told them to ensure their seatbelts were secure, explained where the emergency exits and inflatable lifejackets were, and told them how to use the oxygen masks that would drop from the ceiling should the cabin become depressurized.

"Don't remind me." Hugh cinched his seatbelt tighter.

Tristan smiled, trying to look relaxed to reassure both himself and his friend.

"Okay, this is your captain speaking," Coach Fred announced over the intercom. "We'll be flying southeast to Beef Island—ETA about four hours. Haven't flown one of these small jets for a while. Shouldn't be too much of a problem. We can probably do a roll or maybe a loop if you'd like."

"No!" Hugh and Rosina shouted. They were both already trying to squeeze the life out of their armrests.

The plane powered up, taxied down the runway, and soon they were speeding through the air, climbing steeply. Once they leveled off, Director Davis left the cockpit. He grabbed a small bag and a heavy plastic case from a compartment at the front of the plane and went to the couch across the aisle from Tristan. A loud click sounded as he opened the plastic case.

"Okay, campers, a few items to distribute. Then I suggest you all take a nap as the next few days are going to be busy and undoubtedly physically demanding."

The director handed each of the Snappers a stretchy, black GPS tracking bracelet. He then passed out something that resembled a large, blue, plastic egg. "Put the tracking bracelets on, please. No fiddling with them or the software this time." He winked at Hugh.

"We are quite proud of this next item. It's a new Sea Camp design."

Tristan turned the plastic egg over in his hands, trying to figure out exactly what it was. The other Snappers did the same.

"Like, dude, what the heck is it?" Ryder asked.

"At the same time, squeeze the top and bottom of the container," the director instructed.

Tristan squeezed the egg. He heard a distinct pop, and the thing opened. It was hinged on one side. There was something inside, but he wasn't sure what that was either. It was made of a transparent, rubbery material and looked a lot like a jellyfish.

"Say hello to robo-jelly—the latest in robotic undersea sensors. Once released into the ocean, robo-jelly will become neutrally buoyant at the depth released and then drift in the direction of the current. While tracking water flow, it also measures pressure, temperature, salinity, and pH, and will also detect an array of chemicals."

"Awesome," Hugh said, turning the silicone-encased robot in his fingers. "This is one jellyfish I might actually like. How do you get the data from it?"

"Good question, Hugh. The robo-jelly will periodically go to the surface and send its data back to Sea Camp via a satellite link. Then it will sink back to the depth it is tracking. Keep the robo-jellies in their eggs until you're ready to use them. The container is watertight. When robo-jelly is released and gets wet, it automatically turns on."

"How will we know when to use it?" Sam asked curiously.

"The colleague we'll be working with in the islands should be able to help with that. And here is a map of the area you'll be working in. Get familiar with it, and then, as I said, try to get some sleep. Oops, almost forgot one more very important item."

The teens looked up expectantly. Tristan wondered what other cool gadget they might get. He felt like James Bond. Maybe they'd get to use an underwater car that fires torpedoes and releases an ink smoke-screen or has an ejector seat.

"Lunch!" the director said as he passed out boxed meals. "There are drinks in the small refrigerator in the back. Help yourselves."

Lunch was good, but Tristan was disappointed that it wasn't another undersea gadget.

"Hey, how about some food up here for the one flying the plane," Coach Fred said over the intercom.

Director Davis chuckled and carried two of the box lunches into the cockpit.

Tristan offered to get Hugh a drink. He didn't think his friend was going to undo his seatbelt anytime soon. While they munched on sandwiches, Tristan, Hugh, and Sam examined their maps.

"There's Beef Island, where we're headed," Hugh pointed out. "It's right beside that island, Tortola, and pretty close to guess what?"

"Virgin Gorda," Sam and Tristan answered together.

Along with Tortola and Virgin Gorda, there were smaller islands to both the south and north, including Norman, Peter, Mosquito, Great Thatch, and Little Thatch. Some specific locations were also marked on the map—The Baths, Deadman's Cove, Invisible Bay, Rogue Rocks, and Treasure Caves.

The director came back through the plane to get drinks and noticed the teens staring at their maps. "Bet you're wondering where those names come from." He sat on the couch across from them.

"It's quite a story actually. The British Virgin Islands were discovered by Columbus in 1493 and soon became a favorite hideout for pirates. Some of the most dubious and infamous characters of the high seas sailed the waters of the BVIs. The sheltered coves and uncharted reefs of its some forty small islands were great places for the pirates to stage raids from and stash their loot—at least that's what people say. Notice Great and Little Thatch Islands. Those were named after Edward Teach, also known as Blackbeard."

Rosina and Ryder had turned around and were now listening as well.

"And Beef Island, where we'll be landing, was—as the story goes—home to a widow who poisoned a band of thieves during a dinner party. The conversation during that dinner must have truly been *toxic*."

When the campers failed to laugh at his joke, the director continued, "Pirates are said to have buried treasure on Norman Island, and supposedly it inspired Robert Louis Stevenson's book *Treasure Island*. Who knows what you'll come across during your investigation!"

Tristan found Norman Island on the map. It was the island the yellow rubber ducky had circled near in the computer model. Treasure Caves was on the southwest side of the island.

"Are there, like, pirates there now?" Ryder asked.

"Not that I know of," the director replied. "But you never know where unsavory characters will pop up." He raised his eyebrows at them and then headed back to the cockpit.

"Not very reassuring, is he?" Hugh said to Sam and Tristan.

Unsavory characters? Surely the man was just joking, as usual. Tristan thought again of Rickerton. At least that was something they wouldn't have to worry about. He looked over at Hugh, who was examining the robo-jelly again. Sam was drumming her fingers on her seat's armrest. Her eyes moved nervously from Tristan to Hugh to the map and then out the window.

"Okay, everyone settle down and get some rest," Director Davis said from up front. "We'll be touching down in a few hours."

Tristan, Hugh, and Sam sat quietly talking, but together the drone of the plane and the soft leather seats were like sedatives. Soon their eyelids got droopy, and their heads began to bob. Just before Tristan nodded off, he glanced out the window. *Were there still any pirates in the British Virgin Islands?*

10

THE *R/V REEF RUNNER*

TRISTAN DREAMT HE WAS FALLING. HE WAS SUR-
rounded by water in his dream, yet it felt like he was
spiraling down through air. He snapped awake and
instantly realized it wasn't a dream, at least the falling
part. The plane had just dropped sharply along with
Tristan's stomach. Nobody aboard was asleep now.

"Nothing to worry about," Director Davis said over
the intercom. "Just a little turbulence. Please remain
seated with those seatbelts fastened."

Ghostly pale and verging on green, Hugh clutched
his seat's armrests with a rigor mortis grip. "Yeah, like
I'm going to get up and start twerking right now."

Tristan stared out the window. It was not a comforting sight. A towering, dark cloud billowed upward,
growing taller and blacker by the minute. Lightning

flashed within. "Looks like we're flying around a storm."

"Ya think?" Rosina muttered.

The plane angled sharply to the left and then banked right.

"Stay calm, campers. A little storm's no problem for this expert pilot," Coach Fred boasted. "We'll be down shortly."

Looking down, Tristan could see the ocean through breaks in the clouds.

"Down? Did he say down?" Hugh groaned. "There's nothing but water down there."

The plane dropped again, and a gust of wind shoved it sideways. The teens gasped, each of them turning varying shades of green.

"I'm sure there's land down there, somewhere," Sam said. "I mean, I'm sure it's close. We just can't see it. But it's down there, probably right in front of the plane. I'm sure of it . . . sort of."

The plane shuddered again, slowed, and angled down.

"Water, I just see water," Hugh moaned.

Tristan heard the landing gear lower. They were definitely descending. He stared anxiously out the window. Hugh was right: there was no land or runway in sight. Rain streamed across the windows and lightning flashed. The sharp crack of thunder reverberated through the airplane. Tristan and the others jumped at the sound. He gripped the armrest and looked out the window again. The windswept ocean flashed by below.

Tristan shut his eyes and then opened them, deciding it would be better to watch when they crashed into the sea. He'd probably have a better chance of surviving that way.

A flash of green passed by, and then the edge of a runway came into view. They were about to land. Tristan let out the breath he didn't even realize he'd been holding. Another strong gust of wind shoved the airplane's back end sideways, and thunder boomed. Tristan crossed his fingers as sweat began to trickle down his neck. Suddenly, the plane's engines revved, powering up loudly. They angled skyward, climbing fast and steep. Tristan's heart hammered in his chest.

"Nothing to worry about," Director Davis assured them over the intercom. "We're just going to wait a bit for the squall to pass before landing."

The teens sat still and uncommonly quiet. Hugh barely seemed to be breathing. He looked like he wished he could teleport himself somewhere, *anywhere*, else.

They headed east and began to circle within a thick, gray shroud of clouds. More turbulence. Tristan's stomach did another flip-flop. He was beginning to wish he were someplace else as well. If he survived the crash, his parents would definitely pull him out of Sea Camp. The plane banked once more and continued to circle.

A very long ten minutes later, the clouds around them began to break up.

"Look down, everyone," Director Davis suggested over the intercom.

Sunlight broke through the parting clouds, spot-lighting a green hilltop on a small island. The ride smoothed out, and a loud sigh of relief echoed through the airplane. A larger, longer island came into view. It was skinny and low at the ends, but hilly in the middle.

"That's Virgin Gorda down there," the director announced. "Columbus thought the island resembled an attractive, pleasantly plump woman lying down, so he named it the fat virgin. Ha, that's a good one."

They passed over a stretch of dark water, a clus-ter of rocky islets, and then a small, crescent-shaped island. It, too, was hilly and green at the middle, with rocky cliffs along one side and a long, white beach on the other. Tristan thought he saw some small huts behind the beach and what appeared to be a sprawl-ing mansion atop the cliffs. He pointed it out to Sam and Hugh.

"All clear. Taking her down," Coach announced.

They headed west past a few more small islands and then began to descend. Tristan felt the plane slow. He knowingly held his breath this time as the ocean flashed by below. Just as the runway came into view, the airplane dropped steeply. It bounced once and then settled onto the asphalt. Coach hit the brakes. As he was thrown forward, Tristan exhaled and prayed they wouldn't slide off the rain-slickened pavement.

"A snap, Snappers," Director Davis said, chuckling. "We're making a tight turnaround here. Our contact should be waiting. I'll be picking up a pilot and head-ing back to Sea Camp . . . things to take care of. But I'll be monitoring your progress and staying in close communication with Coach Fred. Good luck and, above all else, stay safe."

The plane taxied down the runway, passing what looked to be the regular airport terminal where passengers were just getting off a commercial flight. As soon as they stopped, Director Davis opened the door, lowered the stairs, and ushered the teens off. Coach Fred led them toward a low, white, concrete building. Walking briskly toward them and waving was an athletic-looking woman wearing a tan baseball hat and a fire-engine red foul weather jacket that fell nearly to her knees.

"Wasn't sure you'd make it in," the woman announced. "That was one nasty squall that just went through." She shook Coach Fred's hand, smiling. "I'm Dr. Margaret Gladfell, but please just call me Meg. Guess I don't need these anymore." She took off her hat and the foul weather jacket. Underneath, she had on flowered shorts and a T-shirt that said *Virgin Islands Institute* over two circling fish in silhouette. Her dark blonde hair came to her chin in a perky bob. And when she smiled, small lines crinkled around her bright hazel eyes.

"Uh, just a little rough coming in. Not too bad," Coach Fred said, running his hand over his dark, slicked-back hair.

Tristan was expecting some bluster about how the storm hardly tested his amazing piloting skills, but instead, Coach seemed to almost stumble over his words. And Tristan could swear the man blushed when he shook the woman's hand. That was a first.

Before Coach could introduce them, Meg said, "Well, I'm just glad you made it in. No time to waste. We can save the rest of the introductions for the ship. It's all set to go. I've taken care of the necessary paperwork and stocked up. It's just a short way to the dock from the private terminal here."

The scientist turned and strode toward the low, white building. They had to jog just to keep up with her. A taxi van was waiting for them outside. They piled in. Coach then loaded their bags along with some bottles and several large jugs of Sea Camp water. The van left the airport, made two quick turns, passed through a parking lot full of beat-up, dusty cars, and pulled up alongside a wooden dock.

Tristan stared at the boat tied up at the dock, thinking maybe they made a wrong turn.

"We're going on that?" Rosina asked.

"Like, this must be some sort of joke," Ryder added.

"I know she's not much to look at," Meg said. "However, our newer vessel is down with engine problems. Anyway, this one's plenty seaworthy and a good work boat."

Tristan and the others got out of the van. They gazed at the vessel with obvious doubt regarding her seaworthiness. The ship was some sixty feet long. Its steel hull was spotted with rust and the remains of what once may have been a coating of forest-green paint. The faded white superstructure was two stories high. And the chipped, warped deck appeared in need of some serious TLC or a complete overhaul. On the side of the bow was written "R/V Re Run".

"What kind of name is Re Run?" Rosina asked.

"No, no. It's the *Reef Runner*, just missing a few letters is all," Meg said. "Been meaning to get that fixed."

A narrow gangplank stretched from the dock to the ship.

Meg led the way aboard. "C'mon, captain's below and anxious to get going."

The teens hesitated until Sam slung her backpack over her shoulder and jumped onto the gangplank. "C'mon, you guys, she looks fine. This'll be great."

The others followed her aboard, clearly less enthusiastic about their next mode of transportation. Tristan crossed the gangplank especially uncertain. Once aboard, he promptly stubbed his toe, stumbled into Hugh, and nearly stepped on the tail of a large orange cat curled up on the deck. The cat eyed him like he would be the first to "walk the plank." *Great start,* Tristan thought.

They gathered on the open stern deck. Meg pointed out a rusty A-frame used to deploy nets and other instruments off the ship. She then showed them a small, gray, inflatable boat sitting on a cradle to the side, and led them into the ship through an open garage-like area. As they passed through, Tristan recognized a small, remotely operated vehicle with a camera on it attached to a huge spool of cable. Some scuba gear sat off to the side, stored in a wire cage.

The teens weaved their way around more equipment before going through a door-sized hatchway. Tristan hit his shin on the raised ledge at the base, nearly tumbling in face-first. He decided the ship's tight spaces and littered deck were going to be seriously bad for his health. *So much for a more bruise-free summer.*

They entered the ship's science lab. A computer, two microscopes, a box-like instrument, and a stack of petri dishes sat on a long bench on one side of the small room. Above a sink hung beakers, small nets, and some sieves. Beneath the bench were two stools and a small freezer. On the other side of the room were some bookshelves, a cramped, square, open workspace, and a printer. All of the equipment was strapped to the wall with bungee cords. Tristan stared at the bungee cords, thinking, *That can't be good.*

"This is the ship's small but very practical lab," Meg explained. "We can process most types of samples here. We don't have a flow-through seawater system like on our new ship, but we can still take water samples and analyze them for many parameters. We can also preserve samples and ship them to the institute for further, more detailed analysis."

The scientist moved to another door going toward the bow. "Up forward is the main salon and galley. There's one head on this deck, and above is the bridge and captain's cabin. Your cabins are on the deck below, along with another head, and some storage. The engine room is aft. Now, let's go see the captain."

Hugh whispered to Tristan, "Head?"

Sam chuckled. "That's the bathroom."

They went through a narrow corridor and another hatchway into a larger, more open room—the main salon. Rectangular tables with bench seats sat along the back and sides facing a window-like opening into the galley. The galley's cramped cooking area was no bigger than the inside of a minivan. Up front, steep stairs went to the deck above, as well as the one below. On either side of the room were doors that led outside. A stubble-faced older man sat at one of the tables. Beside him was a fidgety twenty-something woman with her hair under a bandana. She wore a spotted apron that seemed to scream: *Please wash me!* A chart was laid out on the table in front of them.

"'Bout time," the man said, scowling. "What were you doing out there, playing hopscotch or something? Can't believe I've got to ferry a bunch of kids around to study some dead fish. Fish die all the time. It's especially good when they end up in my stomach."

"Coach Fred, campers, I'd like you to meet Captain Hank," Meg said. "Don't worry, his bark is worse than his bite."

"Don't bet on it," the captain muttered. His short, dark hair was peppered with gray like the stubble covering the lower half of his lean face. His skin resembled well-worn and creased leather, a testament to years spent at sea in the tropics.

Impervious to the captain's gruff manner, Coach Fred sat down next to the man. "Nice to meet you, Captain. Let me introduce the team. This here is Ryder

Jones, Tristan Hunt, Samantha Marten, Rosina Gonzales, and Hugh Haverford."

Captain Hank barely acknowledged their presence, but Meg nodded to each of them in turn and said, "And this is Sarah. She's a critical part of the operation—the steward. She's the ship's cook."

Sarah said hello and then jumped up and scurried into the galley. The captain waived a mug at her. She returned to fill it with a thick, dark liquid that Tristan guessed was some gruesome form of coffee.

"Go below and find a cabin—two beds in each," Meg told them. "Store your gear and then meet on the stern. As soon as the first mate, Charlie, is back, we'll be leaving the dock."

The captain scowled. "Better be soon."

Ryder and Rosina dashed below, clearly wanting first pick of the cabins. Hugh, Tristan, and Sam waited to descend to the lower deck.

"I didn't realize we'd be living on a . . . a boat," Hugh groaned.

Sam grinned. "Don't worry. I go out with my dad all the time. It's great."

Hugh looked at her like she'd just told him how much he likes swimming with sharks. Tristan didn't think he was going to be so in love with the boating life either.

They went below. Sam and Rosina were in one cabin. Hugh and Tristan were in another. That meant Ryder would end up bunking with Coach Fred. Tristan was sure that was not what Ryder had hoped for when he rushed below.

11

SEASICK

On the ship's stern deck, a young man, perhaps in his early twenties, scampered about readying for departure. He had brown hair twisted in dreadlocks tied back in a thick ponytail. His holey gray T-shirt hung loosely over a pair of baggy, frayed shorts, which were held up with a piece of twine. The young man's scruffy clothes and wild hair were in stark contrast to his movie star good looks. He had a chiseled chin, a straight, narrow nose, and eyelashes that were so dark and long they looked fake.

"Hey, y'all watch your step now," the dreadlocks guy told the teens as they gathered at the stern. "And don't go tripping over Abbott—that furball's always in the way. Safety briefing once we get underway."

It took a moment for Tristan to connect the dots.

The guy was Charlie, the first mate, and Abbott was the cat he nearly tripped over. The cat now sat nearby watching as if supervising Charlie's work. Its thick fur was orange-and-white striped, and there were tufts at the tips of its large, pointed ears. Given its size, Tristan thought Abbott the cat was more like Abbott the not-so-small dog.

The teens stood on the deck awkwardly, not sure where to go or what to do. Tristan was mostly just trying to stay out of the way and not stub his toe or trip over anything else. With a belch of black smoke from the stern, the ship's engine rumbled to life and the deck began to vibrate. This seemed to rouse the cat, as it lazily stretched its limbs and strutted off toward the bow.

"Is that, uh, normal?" Hugh asked worriedly. "I mean the smoke and all the shaking?"

The first mate shrugged. "More or less."

Although the smoke soon cleared, the deck continued to rattle disturbingly. The smell of diesel permeated the air. Charlie untied the dock lines, and as the *Reef Runner* pulled slowly away, he hauled in several giant, orange rubber balls that had been hanging between the ship and the dock.

Tristan glanced at Hugh. Hugh's gaze was fixed on the dock like he wanted to leap for it before it was too late. Ryder was at the side of the ship watching the water rush by. Tristan figured he was probably wondering if anyone had ever surfed in the ship's wake. When he looked to Sam, Tristan was surprised to see that both she and Rosina were staring kind of dopily at the first mate.

Coach Fred and Meg then joined them on the stern. Charlie explained where the lifejackets and life rafts were, and what signals the captain would sound if there was an emergency, like a fire, if someone fell overboard, or, in the worst case, if they had to abandon ship.

"Watch y'all's toes onboard," he went on. "Lots of cleats and other toe-stubbers around. When we get outside the harbor, keep one hand on the ship at all times. She can be a little pitchy. Yep, think that covers it. Okay, see y'all later." And with that, the first mate hurried toward the bow and out of sight.

Tristan couldn't help but notice how Sam and Rosina watched him go, thinking: *What's up with that?*

"We're off," Meg announced. "We'll head south and then work our way back north to Virgin Gorda. Tonight we'll be anchoring in Deadman's Cove off Peter Island. Trip there's not too long. Let's go inside so I can catch you up on things." She lowered her voice. "Besides, I'm looking forward to hearing what you all can do."

Tristan glanced around before going inside. It was beginning to get dark, and he watched as small clusters of lights flickered on along the shore and on the low brown hills of the island they were passing. He then followed the others into the main salon. They sat down around the chart still laid out on one of the tables.

Meg showed them their location off Beef Island just to the east of Tortola. "We'll be entering Sir Francis

Drake Channel here and heading south to Peter Island. Deadman's Cove is pretty protected, so it should be a calm anchorage for the night."

"Dr. Gladfell," Coach Fred said brusquely, as if beginning an official interrogation. "What are the positions of the mortality events so far?"

"Well, Mr. Coach," the scientist replied, very businesslike. "They are the starred locations on the chart." She smiled at the teens, raising her eyebrows good-naturedly at Coach's so-serious tone. Tristan decided he was going to like the scientist. She pointed to several stars on the west coast of Virgin Gorda and on the small islands to the south. "There's no clear pattern in time or space in the die-offs. In addition to fish, we've seen some other animals affected and sponges that just seem to disappear. There's been some coral bleaching, but we think that may be due to climate change and unrelated to the fish kills. It's all very puzzling. We've never seen anything like it here."

Tristan felt the motion of the ship change.

"Must be turning into the channel," Meg told them. "Might get a little bumpy till we reach the islands to the south." She then began to describe in more detail each of the sites and what had been reported or found.

Tristan tried to pay attention to what the scientist was saying, but when the ship began to roll he seemed to lose all ability to think. The deck had become one giant seesaw. It rose steeply on one side and dropped on the other. Then the other side rose while the opposite side fell. Coach Fred grabbed the chart as it skated toward the edge of the table. Sam slid across the bench. Tristan and the others grabbed onto whatever they could. Obviously enjoying the ride, Sam giggled. Hugh and Rosina, however, turned a color that reminded Tristan of several-months-old, moldy Cream of Wheat. He once left of bowl of it under his bed by mistake, so he knew what he was talking about. Even Ryder had gone a little pale. Tristan felt okay, though he didn't dare move as the ship rolled from side to side.

"Time to get your sea legs, campers," Coach Fred announced way too merrily.

"We can finish this in the morning," Meg said, noting the color and expression on Hugh's and Rosina's faces. "Maybe some fresh air for you two." She helped the two teens up and ushered them to a side door leading outside. Sam followed. Tristan got up and immediately fell back down. He then lunged from one handhold to the next, making his way unsteadily after the others. Ryder said something about needing to unpack before heading below to his cabin.

"Take a seat here," the scientist suggested, helping Rosina and Hugh onto a deck box along the outside of the ship. "Let me get something that might help."

"Just kill me now," Hugh groaned.

"No, me first," Rosina added right before she ran to the side and fed her lunch to the fish.

Hugh joined her at the rail, tossing his cookies too.

"Don't worry, you'll get used to it," Sam told them a little too perkily.

They both shot her looks like daggers.

Tristan hadn't felt bad before, but once he saw the other two lose their lunch, he began to feel queasy. "Uh, gotta go, sorry guys." He staggered back inside.

Meg was on her way out carrying bottles of water and two of the biggest pink pills he'd ever seen. Tristan heard her say, "Here, try these. If you can keep them down, it should help."

Tristan fell onto a bench in the main salon. Meg came in, and Sam soon joined them.

"Two survivors out of five isn't bad," Coach Fred noted.

For now, Tristan thought. He tried to think of something other than the rolling, heaving deck or what he just witnessed outside. For some reason, the camp's computer model came to mind along with a question he'd been thinking about. "Do you think what's going on here has anything to do with, you know, the stranded dolphins in the Bahamas?"

The scientist paused thoughtfully. "Hard to say, really. It's possible, given the regional currents, but that's quite a distance for something to spread. I would also expect there to be a more regular track or pattern in the impacts if whatever this is was spreading with the currents. We've had fish kills here before due to an algae bloom and an oil spill in a marina. But this is different. The one thing I can tell you—word is getting out, and people are worried. Overfishing has significantly reduced the fish population here, and this could prevent any sort of recovery and destroy the region's reefs and tourism industry. We need to find out what is causing these strange die-offs before it's too late. That's why I contacted Director Davis."

She leaned in closer, whispering, "So, what *can* you do?"

Coach glanced around and then spoke quietly. "The captain, first mate, and steward don't know about your *skills*. And we'd like to keep it that way." He then nodded to Sam and Tristan.

"I can echolocate and communicate with whales and dolphins," Sam whispered eagerly. "After last summer at camp, I worked on it at home in Maine. Of course, I couldn't tell anyone, except Mom and Dad. But I went out with Dad on his lobster boat to look for whales. We even saved a whale that was caught in some derelict fishing line. Dad cut the line off with his knife while I told the whale to stay calm and that we were there to help. Since then, my dad's really warmed up to the whole Sea Camp thing."

"I didn't know you saved a whale," Tristan said to Sam. "Very cool."

Sam beamed.

"And what about you?" Meg asked Tristan.

"I can communicate with sharks and rays, and I'm a pretty fast swimmer. Unfortunately, I didn't get to practice much like Sam. My folks are scared someone will find out about me, and, well, I did have a little *incident* with a shark some fishermen were going to kill."

"Yeah, and you saved it," Sam said.

Tristan nodded, while Coach shook his head and gave him the what-were-you-thinking look.

"Well, how about that," Meg said. "What about the others?"

Coach jumped in. "Jones is an excellent jumper, and Gonzales has good bird communication skills and mucus deployment."

"Mucus? You don't say."

Just then, the steward strode into the salon. She took the chart off the table. "Sorry, we'll be anchoring soon. I need to get ready for dinner." She turned to Sam and Tristan. "You two can help."

"I'll go see how our friends outside are doing," Meg offered.

"I'll join you," Coach said.

As they left, Meg grabbed a packet of saltines sitting near the window looking into the galley.

As the ship rolled, the deck continued to seesaw. Tristan wasn't sure how much help he could offer given that he could barely stand up. He prayed there was nothing breakable involved. The steward brought in a stack of heavy plastic plates, looking to pass them to Tristan. She pointed to a plate-size space surrounded by inch-high walls on the ledge in front of the galley window. Tristan stood up to grab the plates, and the deck tipped especially steeply. He wavered drunkenly, bounced off the table, and then smashed into the ledge, smacking his elbow hard.

Sarah smiled kindly and looked to Sam. "How about you help, and—Tristan, is it? Why don't you just take a seat for now. Seems a little safer that way."

Tristan rubbed his aching funny bone and dropped

onto a bench. He wondered how long it took to get one's sea legs. On the bright side, he wasn't puking his guts out.

A little while later, the ship slowed and made another turn. Within minutes, the rolling eased. Tristan heard the captain calling to the first mate. The engine quieted, and the heavy rattling of the anchor chain echoed through the ship. Tristan got up and peeked out through one of the side doors; it was pitch black. There were no lights anywhere. He guessed they were in Deadman's Cove and that it was deserted.

The steward announced that dinner was ready. Coach Fred ate with Captain Hank, Meg, and Charlie. Ryder reappeared from below and joined Sam and Tristan at the other table. Hugh and Rosina stuck their heads in, seemed to get one whiff of food, and then disappeared back outside. The meal was served family style. Bowls filled with Caesar salad and string beans were passed around along with a platter of hamburgers and cheesy pasta. Tristan noticed that Sam kept glancing toward the other table.

They ate quietly. Tristan hoped his food would stay down, having no desire to join the hurling club outside. Plus he was still nervous, thinking about all the ways he could screw up on their first real mission, especially given his parents' warning regarding any more *incidents*. At least he hadn't broken or spilled anything, yet.

After dinner, Meg and Coach Fred sat drinking coffee and talking quietly. The teens decided to turn in early. A combination of excitement, nerves, travel, and, for some, seasickness had worn them out.

When Hugh stumbled into their cabin, Tristan told him what Meg had said about the die-offs. But Hugh hardly seemed to hear. Within minutes of lying down, he was asleep. Tristan had taken the top bunk. If Hugh got sick during the night, he definitely did not want to be lying below on the receiving end. With the now gentle sway of the ship, Tristan soon fell asleep as well.

12

TREASURE CAVES

THE OUTRAGEOUSLY LOUD CLANGING OF POTS AND pans in the galley one deck up was the worst wake-up call ever, like an enormous church bell rung right over Tristan's head. He woke up with such a start that, for a moment, he had no clue where he was. Nearly falling out of the top bunk quickly set him straight. Tristan leaned over and looked down at Hugh. "Hey, how ya feeling?"

Hugh licked his dry lips. "Wonder what's for breakfast?"

Tristan smiled. That was a good sign. After a decent night's sleep, Tristan felt better. He was still worried about messing up, but he was less anxious now and more excited to see what the day ahead would bring. He sat up and climbed down from the top bunk without falling. It was a good start.

The boys threw on T-shirts and shorts, and then took turns in the head, which was about the size of a broom closet with a toilet, sink, and shower all crammed inside. They climbed up the steep stairway to breakfast. Plastic tubs set out on the table held an assortment of cereals. Tristan decided to try a couple of baked eggs from a cupcake tin also on the table. He tipped the pan to scoop two eggs onto his plate. They slid out faster than a greased pig, skated straight across his plate, and slid to the deck.

Cereal sounds good, Tristan thought.

After breakfast, Coach Fred stood up to address the group. "Rise and shine, Snappers. First day of the mission. Swimsuits on, then go see Charlie on the stern for snorkeling gear." He nodded at Charlie and then winked at the teens. "We're heading out on the inflatable to reconnoiter several sites on Peter and Norman Islands. I'll bring the water."

Again, he winked overtly to the teens. Tristan thought the captain, steward, and first mate would have to be seriously dense not to have noticed. Also, he had no idea what *reconnoiter* meant.

The teens met Charlie on the back deck. It was a hot, sunny day in the British Virgin Islands. A few puffy, white clouds drifted by overhead, bringing short periods of shady relief in the already humid heat.

Sam nodded toward the snorkeling gear and whispered, "Guess it's for appearances."

Tristan stepped up to the first mate.

"What size fin?"

"Not sure."

"Really? Well, try these to see if they fit." Charlie handed him a pair of short, black fins. "And see if this mask fits."

The fins fit Tristan fine and he started pulling the mask's strap over his head.

"No, not like that. Just stick it on your face without the strap and suck in through your nose. If it stays on, it's a good fit. Man, I thought y'all were supposed to be some sort of teen wonders in the water."

Tristan just shrugged and tried the mask on the way Charlie suggested.

The first mate stared at him curiously. "You know how this works, don't you?" He was holding up a snorkel.

"*Yes.*" Tristan took it from him.

Meg pulled up alongside the ship in the small, gray, inflatable boat that had been stored on deck. She was at the back operating the outboard engine. She took the campers' snorkeling bags and piled them out of the way. Coach then handed her a backpack full of Sea Camp water bottles and helped each of the teens into the boat.

"Be back by noon," the scientist called out to the first mate. "We'll check the radio on the way out."

Sitting on the side of the rubber inflatable, Tristan got his first good look at Deadman's Cove and Peter Island. The small cove was horseshoe-shaped and surrounded by steep, rocky cliffs. The water was calm, clear, and dark bluish-green in color. The island seemed to be just a few uninhabited, plant-covered hills. He didn't think they were tall enough to be called mountains, but certainly higher than anything back home in Sarasota.

"We'll head to the site farthest south then work our way back," Meg told them. "We've had one confirmed fish kill in the area and a few anecdotal reports."

She sped the inflatable south toward the far end of Deadman's Cove, where a group of dark, pointed rocks sloped into the water like the humps down a dragon's back. As they passed, the flat water of the cove turned to small, choppy waves. The inflatable sped over the little waves. Tristan and the others bounced, not unpleasantly, on the boat's rubber sides.

Soon they came to another small embayment. Several boats were tied up to mooring balls within the inlet. A fancy yacht sat beside a dock in front of a few small wooden buildings. People waved from the dock.

Meg waved back. "That's Peter Island Yacht Club. They've passed on some of the reports from boaters in the area."

They continued south. Large catamarans and several big powerboats cruised by, going in the opposite direction.

"Along with its history of pirates . . . *arr*, matey," Coach said. "The BVIs are well known as one of the best places for bareboating."

The teens rolled their eyes at the man's attempt at pirate humor.

"What's bareboating?" Hugh asked.

Tristan thought maybe it meant that people here liked to go boating naked or something.

"That's when you rent or charter a boat to cruise on vacation," Meg explained. "Here it takes little time to sail or motor from one island to the next. And the islands are full of beautiful little bays and beach bars for boaters to enjoy. Along with a few luxury resorts and exclusive hangouts for the rich and famous, of course."

"Hey, doesn't some rich dude, like a mega-billionaire, have his own island around here somewhere?" Ryder asked.

Meg smiled. "Yes, Ryder. I believe you are talking about Necker Island to the north."

"Do other, like, famous people have homes here? Will we see them?"

"Doubt we'll see any really famous people. I believe there is someone associated with Google on one of the other privately owned islands, and a big-time venture capitalist on another—I hear he invests mainly in hotels, oil, and the pharmaceutical industry—and, once, the Queen of England visited on her yacht, the *Britannia*. It is a British territory after all."

They skirted a couple of jagged, dark rocks sticking out of the water. It was the westernmost tip of Peter Island.

"Hang on," Meg instructed. "Till we reach Norman Island up ahead, the ride's going to be a bit bumpy."

Minutes later, the inflatable hit the first more sizable wave. Both the boat and the teens went momentarily airborne. When the boat landed, they bounced. Tristan grabbed for the rope running along the side of the inflatable, thinking that getting tossed out would not be good and could constitute an *incident*. Then he heard giggling. Seated across from him, Sam was enjoying the boat bounce-house. Tristan decided her oh-so-happy, boat-loving attitude was going to get annoying very soon. They hit another wave.

"Look, no hands!" Ryder shouted as he raised both arms over his head.

When the boat landed, they again bounced, and Ryder grabbed for the rope—that made Tristan feel better. Hugh and Rosina were both grimacing and had a white-knuckle death grip on the side ropes.

Something silvery then jumped out of the water right in front of the inflatable. The fish spread its fins out like wings and glided effortlessly over the water.

"Look, flying fish," Meg shouted over the whine of the outboard engine.

Several more silver missiles leapt from the water, skimmed over the sea surface, and then disappeared. Tristan smiled, thinking of the flying fish that were part of the attack squad last summer. He'd since read somewhere that they leap out of the water to avoid predators and can cruise up to 40 miles per hour over the sea surface. And, as he saw in the Bahamas, they can also knock a man right off a jet ski.

Tristan gazed farther ahead. He could see Norman Island. It was smaller than Peter, hilly, and from what he could tell, also mostly uninhabited. The side of the island looked as if giant bites had been taken out of it, creating several semicircular coves. In the distance, something large and dark leapt out of the water. It twirled, flashed white, and landed with a terrific splash. "Did you see that? Something big just jumped."

"Probably an eagle ray or manta ray," Meg told them. "They jump out of the water all the time around here."

Just past the northern tip of Norman Island, the ride smoothed out. The teens relaxed their grips on the ropes. They came to another large embayment. It was lined by sparkling white sand, and the water was an astonishing shade of turquoise. Two sailboats were anchored just offshore. They continued on. After rounding another rocky outcrop, Meg slowed the boat.

"Here we are, and just as I hoped, no one else is here yet. It's a popular snorkeling site for tourists."

In front of them lay another semicircular cove. A sheer wall of tan rock lined the cove and dropped steeply into the sea as if it had been carved with a giant knife. Behind it was a high, brown hill topped by scrubby, low-lying trees and bushes. And, like an enormous pair of eyes, two high-arching caves sat side by side at the water's edge. The water in front of the caves was invitingly clear and light emerald green. Tristan had never seen anything like it.

Meg cut the engine. "This is Treasure Caves. The story is that a pirate once buried his loot here. People have searched and searched, but no one's ever found anything even remotely valuable."

They coasted up to a floating white ball about the

size of a big beach ball. Coach Fred went to the front of the inflatable, leaned over on his belly, and pulled up a looped line attached to the ball. He tied it to a line from the bow of their boat. He then came back and gave each camper a bottle of Sea Camp water, encouraging them to drink.

As Tristan swigged the pink-tinted water, a small wave hit them from the wake of a passing boat. He choked and spilled half the water down his shirt. The other teens snickered. Coach gave him a questioning look. Tristan shrugged and tried to look confident.

"Okay, Snappers," Coach instructed. "Here's the plan. You'll swim over to the caves with Dr. Gladfell, who will then lead you in."

The scientist added, "We've had reports of some die-offs in the area. There's almost always a school of copper sweepers inside the caves and sometimes an octopus or two. It'll be good place to start our investigation."

"Uh, Dr. Gladfell, what are copper sweepers?" Hugh asked.

"Please, Hugh, call me Meg. They're relatively small schooling fish that like to hang out in caves or crevices in reefs."

Coach looked at Hugh. "Haverford, use your communication skills to question the fish about any marine life fatalities in the area or if they've noticed anything out of the ordinary in the water."

"And everyone keep your eyes out for anything that doesn't look healthy," the scientist said. "I'll be with you if you have any questions." She pulled on her fins and readied a mask and snorkel. "Of course, I need these."

Just then, a small yellow head popped up next to the boat. They heard the faint intake of air.

"Turtle!" Sam exclaimed.

The others turned to see, but the sea turtle quickly tucked its head under the water and disappeared.

Coach Fred spun around, surveying the surrounding area, and then said, "Snappers, deploy!" The teens sat staring at Coach with a perplexed expression, so he added, "Jump in."

Tristan, Sam, and Ryder slid into the water almost immediately. Hugh and Rosina remained aboard, staring uneasily into the sea. Meg encouraged them in as she, too, slipped in.

Once in the cool ocean, Tristan felt calmer yet energized. He dove. It was only about ten feet deep, and giant, blocky, tan rocks lay at various angles on the seafloor. He swam through a wide V-shaped crack between two big rocks, and then circled one the size of a porta-potty. His leg brushed against something soft. Tristan twisted around. It was a dark brown sea whip growing up from a rock. It had long, soft branches coming off a central stalk, like a short, furry underwater tree. He glanced around; there were more sea whips scattered about on the rocks and bottom. Tristan headed to the surface for a breath. Along the way, he noticed some orangey antler-shaped corals.

Tristan dove back down. He saw something odd on

top of a large, flat rock and swam over to investigate.
It looked like a collection of tall, tan pillar candles.
Tristan swam closer. Make that *fuzzy*, tall, tan pillar
candles, only they were corals. He waved his hand
gently by one. Thousands of thin, brown tentacles
with tiny, white tips fluttered like a wheat field in gusty
winds. Awesome. Tristan waved his hand again, and
a fish swam up to watch. At least, he thought it was
a fish. The creature bore a striking resemblance to an
ornate serving platter. Its body was flat, dark brown,
and oval shaped, with bright yellow, ribbony fins lining
its narrow top and bottom. The fish also had a small,
straight fan for a tail, and its head narrowed to a little
puckered-up yellow snout. It was definitely the weird-
est-looking fish Tristan had ever seen. It peered back
at him, maybe thinking the same thing. The serving
platter fish began paddling slowly, backing up. Tristan
wanted to follow it, but he needed to go up for air.

At the surface, Tristan scanned the area for the
others. They were nearing the caves. He swam to
catch up. Meg was treading water with the others at
the entrance to one of the caves. "Everyone okay?"

They all nodded and held up their webbed hands to
show the scientist.

"Now *that* is cool."

Meg led the group into the cave. The light quickly
dimmed to a dull gray. Tristan again dove down. He
stared at the walls. They angled in and were covered
with what looked remarkably like splatters of bril-
liantly colored paint. There were splotches of vivid

pink, lavender, and rich reds intermingled with vibrant spots of yellow. Lumps of orange also dotted the rock canvas. Tristan popped up to the surface and heard Meg explain that much of it was sponge or something called coralline algae.

"What's the bright orange?" he asked.

"Oh, that's *Tubastraea*, also known as orange cup coral. Look closely. Some have their tentacles out to feed on zooplankton. The coral polyps look like small flowers."

Sure enough, when Tristan dove down and looked closer, he saw rings of orange tentacles poking out from small, orange cups. He peered farther back into the cave. A brief flash caught his attention. It was like sunlight reflecting off a mirror. Tristan swam toward it curiously.

The cave got darker except for one spot, where sunlight piercing through a hole in the rocky ceiling lit up a column of water. A school of coppery-silver fish swirled in and out of the sunlight. Each was flat and the size of a large serving spoon. And when the light hit a fish just right, there was a fleeting glint off its shiny body. In a spiraling dance, the school of fish began to move toward Tristan. They swam past him to Hugh, surrounding the teen like a living tornado. Hugh spun around within the circling fish.

Treading water at the surface, Sam smiled at Hugh. "Looks like you've made some friends. Ask them if they've felt bad or seen any sick fish."

Hugh submerged.

"Hey, you guys. Look over here," Rosina shouted to them from farther back in the cave. She was holding onto a shelf-like ledge and pointing to something.

Tristan had to move closer to see what she was pointing at—*bodies*; dead bodies, to be exact. There were dozens of fish, a couple of moray eels, and an octopus piled up on the ledge.

Tristan recognized some silver-and-pink striped fish. "Hey, those are squirrelfish."

"That's right," Meg confirmed after swimming over. She turned to Hugh, who joined them. "Find out anything?"

"A few nights ago, the water outside the cave started smelling bad, so the sweepers hunkered way back inside. A wave washed in that bunch of dead fish and things." He pointed to the ledge.

"Do they know what caused it?" the scientist asked.

"Nope, no idea."

"Could they tell you anything else?"

Hugh shook his head. "They said they pretty much keep to themselves here in the cave."

"Okay, lets head out and see what else we can find out."

"Are we just going to leave them here?" Sam asked, staring at the dead creatures.

"I'll take a few samples to see if we can figure out what killed them," Meg answered. She put several dead fish in a plastic bag, sealed it, and placed it in a yellow mesh bag she'd brought along. "Let's see if you can find any other organisms to question."

The teens swam out of the cave the same way they came in. Before he reached the entrance, Tristan stopped and stared ahead. Just outside the dim and shadowy cave, sunlight turned the water a radiant aqua blue. The contrast was mesmerizing. So much so that when Tristan exited the cave, he nearly missed the four-foot long nurse shark cruising by. But the shark must have sensed or seen him. It stopped abruptly, cocked its head, and settled on the bottom. It then laid perfectly still. Tristan took a breath and dove to it. The shark was motionless, as if wanting to blend into the seafloor and go unseen.

Tristan listened but didn't hear the shark saying anything. *Hey, hi. I'm Tristan.*

The shark remained as still as an undersea statue and just as silent.

Strange, thought Tristan. Sharks had always responded to him. Was there something wrong with the shark? Or him? He tried again. *Hi. I'm Tristan. Nice cave.*

The shark shook its head, and Tristan saw one eye briefly turn his way.

Hey, I can see you. Why won't you talk to me?

The shark glanced at him. *Go away!* It then swam off the bottom and under a rock. But the space was barely big enough for just the shark's head. Its whole body and tail stuck out. Tristan went to the surface for a breath. The other teens saw him. He waved. "Shark." Tristan then dove back to where the shark was trying, rather unsuccessfully, to hide.

Your whole body is sticking out. That's not a very good hiding place. What's wrong?

The shark backed its way slowly out of the hole and then glanced nervously around before staring directly at Tristan. *Bugger. You're gonna bloody get me in trouble. If they see me talking to you, mate, I'm dead or worse.*

Who? What are you talking about? We're just here to figure out why the fish and stuff are dying.

Clear off. Save yourself while you still can.

Just then, out of the corner of his eye, Tristan thought he saw something moving in the distance. It was an indistinct form at the edge of his eyesight's range. But it looked big.

Bloody hell! Now I'm sunk. The shark flicked its tail and shot off.

Tristan stared into the blue water around him. Whatever he saw was gone. Tristan went after the nurse shark, but it was too late. The shark had also vanished. He swam back to the boat. The others were hanging onto the side of the inflatable.

"Hey, did you guys see something swim by out here?"

They shook their heads, swiveling around.

"What did you see, Hunt?" Coach asked from the boat.

"Not really sure, but it looked kinda big."

Hugh's eyes got wide.

"What about the shark?" Sam asked. "What did it say?"

"It wouldn't talk to me. It was strange. Said something about getting into trouble if it talked. Told me to clear off, then swam away."

"How big was the thing you saw?" Hugh asked, spinning around nervously.

Tristan just shook his head.

As they discussed the shark's odd behavior, a sea turtle popped up next to Ryder. Raising its cute, yellowy head for air, the turtle swam smack into his chest.

Ryder pushed it away. "Whoa, like, dude, watch out."

Sam and Tristan swam over. The sea turtle's domed shell was brownish-green and about two feet across. It flapped its long, speckled front flippers and swam straight into Sam. Its gaze seemed unfocused, and its head bobbed unsteadily.

"Hugh, can you talk to it?" Sam asked.

"Nope, can't speak sea turtle."

"Tristan?"

"Nope, me neither."

"Birds for me," Rosina offered.

They turned to Ryder. "Hey, why are you looking at me? I can't talk to the dumb turtle."

As Meg climbed into the boat, she said, "We've seen sick sea turtles like this before. In an algae bloom a few years ago, the sea turtles seemed to be affected by a toxin released by the algae. They appeared to be confused, weak, and had trouble breathing. Let's get it into the boat. I'll radio the institute to arrange a rescue."

Sam and Tristan held onto the sea turtle while the

other teens climbed into the inflatable. The sea turtle made no attempt to swim away. Its head lolled from side to side.

Meg wet a towel she'd brought along and laid it on the boat's deck. She and Coach Fred lifted the sea turtle from Sam and Tristan and placed it on the towel. They put another wet towel on top of the turtle. While they untied the boat from the mooring ball, Meg radioed the Virgin Islands Institute, telling them they rescued a sick sea turtle and asking for transport to the wildlife center in St. John. Coach Fred sat at the back and cranked up the outboard engine. They began motoring slowly away from Treasure Caves.

A loud thumping sound soon drew their attention skyward. It was a familiar noise to the teens after last summer. Flying toward them from the north was a helicopter.

"That was fast," Hugh said.

Meg looked up. "We don't have a helicopter. Probably just some rich guy going to his island."

The helicopter was painted yellow, and as it neared, Tristan thought he could see someone leaning out, possibly with binoculars or a camera with a giant zoom lens.

Ignoring the helicopter, Meg told Coach to head northwest toward a small island just visible in the distance. A speedboat from the wildlife center would meet them there.

The helicopter circled once and then flew back in the direction it came from. The thumping from its rotating blades faded quickly.

"Those are Rogue Rocks," Meg said, looking toward their destination. "Supposedly, pirates would lure ships there to wreck and then steal the valuables."

It was slow going as they tried to avoid any big bounces or bumps that might further stress the sick sea turtle. From a distance, Rogue Rocks looked like a small island. Once they got closer, Tristan realized it was just a bunch of big, dark rock piles. Meg pointed to a narrow passage between two of the towering piles of dark stone. Coach steered the boat through into a hidden circular cove where the water was exceptionally calm. The loud drone of a powerful engine again drew everyone's attention. Tristan glanced up, thinking it was the helicopter again.

Meg pointed to a boat speeding their way. "There they are."

A huge white rooster tail of water shot up behind the fast-moving powerboat. It slowed to thread the narrow entrance to Rogue Rocks and was soon pulling up beside the inflatable. Meg said hello to the three people aboard, and the group carefully passed them the sea turtle. She then explained what happened and thanked them for the quick response. The animal rescue team waved good-bye as their boat cruised slowly away. Once outside of Rogue Rocks, the driver powered up and they blasted off. The boat was quickly gone from sight.

"Let's head back to the ship to get these dead fish on ice and figure out where to go next," Meg said.

Coach steered the inflatable back toward Deadman's Cove. On the way, he asked if anyone wanted to try his or her hand at driving. Sam was quick to volunteer. She swerved a little at first, but then steered straight, grinning from ear to ear.

Tristan glanced back at Norman Island with a million questions swirling through his mind. *Was there really treasure there? What was up with the shark, and why was it acting so weird? And what killed the creatures they found in the cave and made the sea turtle sick?*

13

GIANT BOWLING BALLS

"Saw some sponge; it looked okay. Anyone see anything that looked sick? Anything blotchy, blackened, or bleached white?" Meg asked.

Back at the *Reef Runner*, the campers had just finished lunch in the main salon. They all shook their heads.

"Dr. Gladfell, what do you think killed the things in the cave?" Hugh questioned.

"Meg. Call me Meg."

Hugh nodded sheepishly.

"Don't know yet. Analysis of the samples we took should tell us more."

"Was there anything unusual about what you found?" Coach asked.

The scientist paused for a moment. "As Tristan

pointed out, there were some squirrelfish, along with other fish, a few moray eels, and an octopus."

Tristan thought back to what Ms. Sanchez told him at the Rehab Center. "Squirrelfish are nocturnal."

"Yes, that's right," Meg responded. "Come to think of it, all of the dead organisms we found in the cave tend to be more active at night."

"What does that mean?" Hugh asked.

"Not sure. It could be that whatever killed them was somehow linked to their nighttime activity."

"How about the shark? It was acting kinda cuckoo," Tristan added.

"Have sharks ever responded to you like that before?"

"No."

"Hunt, tell us again what it said." Coach Fred instructed.

"Said it would get in trouble, that we should clear off, save ourselves."

"Save ourselves from what?" Sam asked.

"Don't know."

Meg cleared a space on the table and unrolled the chart. With a pencil, she added a new star next to Treasure Caves on Norman Island. "Looking at the other mortality events, this one is the farthest south. Most have been closer to Virgin Gorda. I think we should head up that way and visit a few of these other locations. Besides, then I can arrange to ship the dead fish to the institute on the evening ferry from the Bitter End Yacht Club. I'll ask the captain to reposition the ship here." She pointed to a small landmass just north of Virgin Gorda—Mosquito Island.

"If it's okay with you, Coach, on the way we could make a quick stop here, at The Baths." She pointed to the southwestern edge of Virgin Gorda. "It's the most popular spot on the islands and not something to miss, even for all of you."

Coach grudgingly agreed to a short stop. He urged the campers to make it quick and warned them, as usual, not to do anything stupid. He also reminded them not to put any of their *unusual* in-water skills on display in what could be a crowded public place.

About an hour later, the *Reef Runner* slowed and turned toward shore. Tristan, Sam, and Ryder were sitting outside atop the deck box on the port side. They'd been there since lunch and had seen five rays catapult themselves high out of the water, along with the fins of several dolphins at the surface. At least, they assumed they were dolphins.

Tristan stared ahead. "Check out all the boats. This must be the place."

"Yeah, and most of 'em are, like, way nicer than this old tub," Ryder griped.

Tristan ignored Ryder. He'd been doing that a lot lately. Ever since the challenge at Sea Camp, Ryder had been getting on Tristan's nerves even more than usual. He was right about one thing, though—there were some pretty nice boats moored where they were headed. A sleek, blue-hulled sailboat with glistening teak woodwork caught his eye. Nearby, sat a wide catamaran and next to that a shiny, white yacht. The other moorings held smaller sailboats or powerboats outfitted for deep-sea fishing. One boat, however, was definitely worse off than the old research vessel they were on. Compared to it, even the *Reef Runner* was large and luxurious. It was a beat-up wooden dinghy barely bigger than a bathtub. Tristan hoped that whoever owned that boat hadn't had far to travel.

He examined the shoreline, wondering what attracted so many people. Nestled between two rocky hills was a short, white-sand beach with a small, thatch-roofed hut behind it. It looked like a nice little beach and bar, but no big whoop. The ship motored closer to shore. Tristan soon realized the rocky hills weren't exactly hills. They were piles, several stories high, of the biggest, roundest gray boulders he'd ever seen, like stacks of giant rock bowling balls.

The captain cut the engine as they approached an empty mooring ball. Charlie leapt onto the bow, carrying a long pole with a hook at the end. The *Reef Runner* glided to a stop, and the first mate expertly reached down to snag a looped line attached to the floating white ball. He put the loop around a cleat at the ship's bow and gave the captain the thumbs-up.

Tristan was enviously watching the first mate's balance and agility when Hugh and Rosina appeared from inside, followed by Meg and Coach Fred.

Meg smiled. "Never get sick of this place."

"What's so special about it? Looks like just a bunch of rocks on the beach to me," Rosina scoffed.

"I can answer that," Hugh offered. "I was just inside reading about it. The rocks at The Baths are made of granite and formed millions of years ago. Wind and waves wore them down over time into these giant round boulders. Underneath the boulders, there are trails and hidden pools."

"Well done, Hugh," the scientist said. "Exactly right."

"Can we swim in the pools?" Sam asked excitedly.

"They're more like wading pools," Meg told them. "They get a little deeper at high tide, but you'll want to stay in the shallow areas by the trail. Charlie will bring you to shore in the inflatable. He'll drop you off and then return in about an hour. That should be plenty of time to explore the boulder trail. It's well marked."

After slathering themselves with sunscreen, the campers piled into the inflatable. They were barefoot and in their swimsuits. The teens waved to Coach and Meg as Charlie ferried them to shore. The captain stood at the bow, scowling at the departing group. Sam waved at him as well, but the man simply turned on his heel and headed inside the boat. "Not the most friendly sort, is he?" Sam said to the first mate. Charlie just shrugged in response.

Charlie drove slowly, steering around the boats as well as swimmers going in seemingly random directions. He beached the inflatable on the sand. Tristan was just climbing out when the whine of powerful engines echoed across the water. He twisted around to see the incoming boat and tumbled right out of the inflatable onto the sand. Charlie snickered while the other teens just smiled, like Tristan tripping was an everyday occurrence—which it pretty much was. Tristan swore under his breath, brushing off the sand. He eyed the boat that was just cruising slowly by the *Reef Runner*. One of the men aboard waved to their ship's captain who was back at the bow. The powerboat pulled up to an adjacent mooring. Tristan thought maybe they were friends of the captain—that is, assuming he had friends, given his not-so-sparkling personality.

"I'll be back to get y'all in about an hour," Charlie told them. "Just follow the signs. And don't go off the trail. Never know when one of these big rocks may fall."

"*What?*" Hugh snapped.

"Just kidding," Charlie laughed. "These rocks haven't moved for thousands of years. It's perfectly safe. Trail starts that way." He pointed down the beach to a sign with an arrow that said "To Devil's Bay."

"That was a good one," Rosina said in a syrupy sweet voice, smiling weirdly at the good-looking first mate.

"Yeah, a good one," Sam added. "Thanks, Charlie. See you later."

The boys exchanged questioning looks, obviously wondering why the girls were acting so nice, especially Rosina.

The group walked around some oiled-up sunbathers and then passed the small beach bar, where people were drinking beer and laughing. Nobody paid much attention to the teens as they approached the trail entrance. It was a dark, narrow, triangular passageway that led beneath two of the huge granite boulders.

They had to go through one behind the other. Ryder ran ahead on the hard, packed sand. Tristan followed, ducking down and taking care not to smack his head on the rocks overhead. Sam went next. She ran her hand over the smooth, gray, granite walls. Rosina followed, with Hugh bringing up the rear.

Tristan heard muffled voices—people talking somewhere in and among the boulders. He followed Ryder through the tunnel into a dimly lit cavern with a high boulder ceiling and a shallow pool in the floor. A single ray of sunlight pierced through a crack between the rocks overhead and flickered across the crystal clear water at their feet. Tristan stood in the water in sheer wonderment. It was the coolest nature-made kiddie pool ever.

"Not bad," Ryder said as he waded farther into the cavern.

Sam entered. "Wicked!"

Hugh and Rosina joined the others as they stared in awe at the natural beauty and flickering rays of golden light in the boulder-built cavern.

"Dead end that way," Ryder told them, coming back.

Tristan pointed to a frayed rope nailed to the side of a rock sloping up to their left. "I think the trail goes that way."

Using the makeshift handrail, Tristan took the lead.

He climbed up and across the smooth, sloped boulder. The others followed. Tristan gazed at the giant boulders all around them, feeling very small. The place was both mesmerizing and intimidating. About twenty feet later, he came to a short set of irregular rock steps. Tristan jumped down onto the sand. The colossal round rocks surrounding them sat one on top of another. Tristan looked up and could see blue sky. They were in a clearing in the boulder pile. He peered more closely at the rocks. Where sunlight hit the granite, small black and clear crystals sparkled like diamonds.

"It's beautiful," Sam said.

"Beautiful until one of those boulders rolls on top of us," Hugh noted sarcastically.

Tristan thought Hugh might be right. Some of the boulders around them sat solidly atop the sand or other rocks. Other boulders seemed precariously balanced at odd angles. Tristan stared at a boulder the size of a backyard shed that sat leaning steeply on a rounded edge.

"I really hope Charlie was kidding about the boulders falling," Hugh added.

"I'm sure he was," Tristan said swiftly, hoping it was true, and thinking if the boulder did roll, they'd be squashed like bugs.

Sam and Ryder jostled to be the first one up the next granite block stairway. Nearly sliding off on some loose sand, Tristan steadied himself and followed more slowly. The trail led to another tunnel. It was even smaller than the first one, and they all had to crouch down to go through. On the other side, the group ran into a couple going in the opposite direction. The man had a bulging round belly. Tristan said hello and watched as the guy attempted to crawl through the tunnel. Tristan paused, thinking they'd better be ready to push from behind—literally. After a succession of curse words that definitely would have gotten Tristan grounded, the big-bellied man somehow squeezed through.

The campers scrambled over a few more boulders and then came to another opening in the rocks. A sign said "Devil's Bay" and had an arrow pointing to the left into another tunnel beneath the boulders. Footprints in the sand also led in a different direction. It looked like an unmarked trail that went up a narrow rock chute between two boulders. Ryder took the unmarked trail.

"Hey, wait," Hugh shouted. "They said don't go off the trail."

"C'mon, don't be such a baby," Ryder yelled back.

Sam went up after him. Rosina shrugged and followed.

Tristan looked sympathetically at Hugh. "We can always backtrack."

Hugh nodded uncertainly and followed. They walked up through the rock chute, crossed a granite ledge, and then scrambled down into another cavern with little more than a puddle on the floor. At the far end of the cavern, they climbed up a series of steep rock steps to a natural lookout over the top of the boulder field. The teens clustered together and peered out over the maze of passages and pools below. In the distance, they could just make out the deep blue water of Devil's Bay.

"Hey, check out that rock. Kinda looks like a shark," Tristan said, pointing to a big boulder sticking up. It was thick and round in the middle, but gradually narrowed to a snout-shaped peak. A wide crack positioned just below the top looked like a mouth.

"You've got sharks on the brain," Rosina said.

"Besides, I think it looks more like a whale," Sam noted with a laugh.

"Maybe we should head back to the trail now," Hugh suggested.

But instead of going back, Ryder went the other way. He stepped down onto a small ledge and then disappeared.

"Woohoo!" They heard a splash.

The other campers followed and found a deep but skinny oval-shaped pool.

Ryder popped up, startling them. "C'mon, there's a cool tunnel you can swim through. Looks like it goes back to the main trail."

"I don't know about this," Hugh warned as the others jumped, splashing, into the pool.

Hugh sighed, shook his head, and then slid down the rock into the pool. He and Tristan swam through the tunnel, breaststroking one behind the other. Tristan gazed up at the boulder ceiling. He felt like an explorer on an adventure in some faraway land. This was definitely one of the coolest places he'd ever been. They climbed up and over another boulder and then slid down into a narrow cavern. The walls were about six feet apart, and the water on the sandy floor was less than a foot deep.

Sam turned to Ryder. "Where does the trail go?"

He was coming from the far end of the cavern. "Uh, well, it's kinda a dead end."

The others rolled their eyes at Ryder and turned to backtrack. Suddenly, a deep, muffled thud resounded within the cavern, and the surrounding boulders seemed to shiver for just an instant. The campers froze.

"Do they have earthquakes here?" Hugh asked nervously.

Tristan shrugged and then noticed a slight change in the light overhead. He glanced up. "Look out!"

Tristan shoved Hugh out of the way just as a small boulder crashed down from above. The others dove to the side. The round rock was about the size of an over-inflated basketball. It landed with a splash right where Hugh had been standing.

"Thanks," Hugh said as he stood up unsteadily.

"That was close," Sam said, also getting to her feet.

All Tristan could do was nod in agreement. It had been way too close. Hugh could have been killed. Tristan's heart was pounding. Their adventure in the boulder pile just went from exhilarating and awesome to I-want-my-mommy scary.

"Let's go back," Rosina urged.

No one disagreed.

Rosina went first, climbing over the rock to the tunnel that led into the other pool.

"Oh crap! Super crap! Crappity crap!"

When they caught up with her, Rosina was still mumbling something about crap. She was staring at another displaced boulder. This one was much bigger. And it had created a new rock roof over the oval pool, which meant—the way back was blocked.

Rosina scowled. "Who said we should go off the trail?"

"Or that the rocks here haven't moved for thousands of years?" Hugh added. "Anyone see another way out?" There was a hint of panic in his voice.

Tristan spun around, looking. Sam tried calling for help, but they were too far off the main trail and the boulders muted the sound. They swam back through the tunnel and climbed into the adjacent cavern.

"Okay, let's look around. There must be a way out," Tristan said, trying to stay calm. He looked up to where the boulder had fallen from, thinking maybe they could climb out. But there didn't seem to be a big enough opening or any way to climb up the smooth-sided round boulders.

"No way over here," Sam said from the left.

"Here either," Hugh added from the cavern's far end.

"We're, like, screwed," Ryder groaned.

"Yeah, that's real helpful," Tristan said. "Look, when we don't show up, they're gonna start looking for us. We just have to hang out and wait for someone to come and help us climb out or something." He hoped.

Hugh stared at his feet. "Uh, that may be a problem."

"Why's that?"

"The water. I think it's rising."

"Now is not the time to joke around," Rosina snarled.

"No, I'm serious. It was at my shins when we first came in. Now it's almost at my knees."

They all stared down.

"The tide," Sam said worriedly. "It must be coming in."

They scrambled around more, frantically looking for a way out. Soon the water was above their knees.

"Hey, wait. If the tide is coming in, there must be a connection to the ocean," Hugh suggested.

"Yeah, and it could be the size of a pea," Ryder countered.

The water crept higher.

The teens searched the shadowy cavern again, hoping to find something they missed before, some way to climb or swim out. But again, their search came up empty. They were trapped, and the water continued to rise. Hugh looked panicky. Rosina had gone pale. Tristan tried to think of something, anything, that might help.

"Hang on," Sam said. "Did you guys hear something?" She cocked her head to the side, listening. Then, without another word, she scrambled over the rock into the connecting tunnel to the deep pool.

"Did she, like, hear someone?" Ryder asked. "I didn't hear anything."

Hugh jumped, clearly startled. "What the . . ." He

stared down into the water where he'd just been standing.

Sam scrambled back into the cavern, grinning.

"What are you so happy about?" Rosina asked, staring at the water that was now nearly at her thighs.

"Help's here."

Hugh leapt up again. "Something's definitely down there. It just grabbed me. I swear."

Sam laughed, and the others looked at her like she was several cards short of a full deck.

"I thought I heard something. So I went back. There are a couple of dolphins nearby out in the ocean. They said there's an opening through the pool to where they are. It's too tight for them, but they sent help to lead us out." She pointed to Hugh's feet.

A suckered arm poked out of the water. Sitting underwater on the sand next to Hugh was a tan octopus. The octopus flashed purple and slithered onto his foot.

"Oh, yeah, okay, we should follow him."

"Ah, one problem," Rosina said. "We didn't drink any Sea Camp water. You know, no webbed feet in public and all."

"It's okay," Sam told them. "The dolphins say it's a short swim and there's an air pocket partway through."

Tristan breathed a sigh of relief. They'd found a way out.

"How short?" Hugh and Rosina asked in chorus.

"C'mon," Tristan said, trying to act cool and collected. "We can do this, even without the webbing."

"Not like we've got much choice," Ryder moaned, voicing Tristan's own thoughts.

"Whose fault is that?" Rosina snarled.

"Hey, how could I know the dang rocks would move?"

"C'mon, let's just go," Sam said before leading the group back through the tunnel.

In the pool on the other side, Hugh treaded water and looked up at the low boulder ceiling over their heads. He gulped. "Uh, is the water rising in here too?"

"That would be a yes," Tristan answered, knowing exactly what Hugh was getting at. As the water rose, their breathing space was shrinking. Tristan's pulse again quickened.

"The dolphins say the airspace is just after a ledge," Sam explained. "You can get a breath there if you need it."

"Maybe we should just wait for help," Rosina suggested nervously.

Treading water, Tristan stared at the getting-closer rock ceiling. "Who knows how long that could take? Besides, I don't think we have much time left in here— if you want to breathe air, that is. Hugh, you should go first with the octopus."

"Me? Go first?"

"Him? Dude, you've got to be kidding," Ryder jabbed.

"Yeah Hugh, you go first with the octopus," Sam agreed, ignoring Ryder. "Then send it back to lead each of us out."

Hugh shook his head, but then glanced up at the nearing ceiling.

"No time to argue," Tristan urged. "You can do this, Hugh."

The octopus pulled on Hugh's feet. "Okay, okay, I'll go."

Hugh took a couple of deep breaths, obviously trying to relax. After one last big gulp of air, he dove down, following the octopus as it shot out through a wide hole at the far end of the pool. The last thing Tristan saw were Hugh's feet as he made a sharp right turn underwater.

The other teens paddled silently in the pool, nervously waiting as the water continued to rise. The ceiling was getting uncomfortably close. Tristan was trying hard to stay calm. He started to think that one of them should go after Hugh. He was just about to suggest it when two suckered arms poked out of the water and waved at them.

Ryder went next. A few minutes later, the octopus was back.

"Rosina, you go," Tristan suggested.

"Uh, that's okay. You go, Sam."

Sam didn't hesitate. She dove into the underwater tunnel, following their eight-armed guide.

Now it was just the two of them. Tristan looked at Rosina. She was super pale and shaking. "You can do this."

Then their heads hit the boulder overhead. Tristan's heart began to hammer so hard he was sure Rosina could hear it. He started to breathe rapidly, feeling as if he couldn't get enough air. *Where's a paper bag when you need one?* Tristan took a deep breath, trying to slow his breathing and calm down. He could do this. They still had time. Besides, it wouldn't do them any good if he totally lost it. The octopus returned. Rosina looked at Tristan, then at the octopus, then back to Tristan. She shook her head. "I . . . I can't do it."

"Yes you can," Tristan said. "Go for it."

But Rosina didn't move. Her eyes were wide with fear. Tristan didn't know what to do. He couldn't just leave her there. His head scraped against the rock overhead. Soon he'd have to twist his head just to keep his mouth above the water.

"C'mon, it's just a short swim. The others made it. You can do this, but ya gotta go now," Tristan urged, willing himself not to panic.

She shook her head. Purely on instinct, Tristan grabbed Rosina by the shoulders and looked into her eyes. "We'll go together. I'll go right behind you. Now relax and take a deep breath. You can do this. *We* can do this."

"You'll stay right behind me?"

"Yes!"

That seemed to snap Rosina out of panic's tight grip. She nodded, took a couple of deep breaths, and then dove after the octopus's trailing arms. Tristan swam right behind her, knowing that if she hesitated or got stuck, he would probably drown—it might have been the bravest but dumbest thing he'd ever done.

The underwater passage was tight. Tristan pulled with his arms and kicked as best he could. He felt slow and awkward without webbing. He scraped his arm and then a foot on the rock walls, and then bumped into Rosina's feet. She flinched forward, hitting her knees. He knew that wasn't going to go over well. Tristan hesitated to give her a moment to get ahead. The scrapes stung. Rosina rose up slightly, and Tristan nearly ran headfirst into a ledge. His legs hit painfully as he pulled himself past. Rosina swam upwards. He followed. She was breathing in a small pocket of air. Tristan joined her. It was a tight fit, and as he squeezed in, Rosina smacked her head on the rocky roof.

"Ouch! Watch it."

"Sorry," Tristan said, smiling nervously. "Ladies first."

Rosina grimaced, took a big breath, and again dove after the octopus.

A few seconds later, Tristan followed. The underwater tunnel got wider and angled down. Up ahead, Rosina swam under a rock arch adorned with colorful splotches of algae and sponge. Tristan twisted onto his back as he went under, looking up. Air bubbles trapped underneath shimmered silver amid the rock's bright splatters. Then there was just open blue water and a bunch of legs hanging down. Tristan headed for the group at the surface. About midway up, he paused, thinking he saw something in the distance—a large, shadowy form swimming through the water. It was just like that morning. He stared harder, but couldn't make it out. Something was definitely out there. But *what*?

Tristan hit the surface, and Rosina punched him in the arm. "That's for running into me. Look at my arms and legs. I'm all cut up." She also nodded to him in a silent but obvious thank you.

Tristan nodded back, knowing she didn't want the others to hear how she'd panicked in the pool. At the same time, he realized that by helping her, he'd forgotten all about his own fear and pounding heart. Tristan looked at his legs. Blood was seeping out of the small nicks and scrapes from where he'd hit the walls of the tunnel while swimming out. He turned to the others. They were also all scraped up.

"Lucky we've got this healing skin thing," Tristan said, referring to their special genes that also gave them amazing healing powers in the sea. He then looked to Sam and the two dolphins that were playfully poking her with their beaks. "Thank your friends there. They saved us for sure."

"Yeah, yeah. Can we just go back now," Ryder said.

The dolphins next to Sam began squeaking nervously and pushing her toward shore.

"Uh, guys. They want us to get going. Something's out here they don't like. They said to go that way." She pointed to their left along the rocks.

The dolphins didn't wait to see what the group would do. They sped away in the opposite direction. Sam yelled thanks and quickly swam the way they had told her to go. The others followed. The octopus jetted along beneath Hugh. Tristan kept looking back, wondering what was out there and not sure he really wanted to know.

They swam into a small sandy cove and got out. A narrow path led back to the main trail.

As they walked, Tristan turned to Sam. "What was out there?"

"Don't know," Sam answered. "The dolphins didn't say."

Tristan thought about what it could be and just one thing came to mind. There'd been blood in the water. Not a lot, but still—blood had been seeping from their cuts into the water around them. *Shark. Was that what he'd seen in the distance?* Tristan couldn't be sure. Besides, he didn't want to believe that a shark could be a threat to him or the others. It must have been something else—but what?

Back at the trail entrance, Charlie was waiting. He was *not* happy. "Where've you been?"

"Remember that joke about the boulders falling?" Tristan said.

14

DINNER AT THE
YACHT CLUB

THE *Reef Runner* NEARED MOSQUITO ISLAND
around late afternoon. The last few hours aboard had
been busy for the teens. After their near-disaster of a
pleasure stop at The Baths, they were questioned non-
stop by the captain, Coach Fred, Meg, the first mate,
and the steward. Even Abbott the cat seemed curious about what had happened, trailing at the campers' heels wherever they went. They also learned that,
strangely, no other visitors at The Baths had seen any
boulders move, though a few people reported hearing a deep thudding noise and feeling some shaking.
Rumor was that there had been a far-off explosion or a
weak earthquake in the area.

With everyone listening, the campers were careful about how they recounted their escape from the

boulder pool. Certain details were purposely left out. The captain seemed especially curious about what had happened. Charlie thought the teens were exaggerating, while Sarah urged them to report the incident to the local authorities. Coach Fred and Meg convinced her and the others that it would be best to keep quiet about the whole thing, saying it was just a freak accident and that, fortunately, no one had been hurt.

For his part, Tristan was surprisingly happy. Sure, they were almost crushed to death by a boulder and then nearly drowned, but he stayed pretty calm—at least on the outside. And although only he and Rosina knew it, he probably saved her life. Tristan felt confident and proud, just like after last summer. If only his parents could see this side of him. He vowed not to worry so much about messing up or getting pulled from camp by his parents.

While the captain and first mate prepared to anchor off Mosquito Island, Coach Fred and Meg took the opportunity to have a more private discussion with the campers. They huddled on the stern deck out of the others' earshot.

"I'll be speaking with Director Davis in a bit," Coach Fred told them. "So whose brilliant idea was it to go off the marked trail to begin with?"

Silence. Though if Coach had been watching closely, he might have seen Rosina glance accusingly at Ryder.

"Check, got it, no snitching," Coach continued. "Well, nice job getting out of there without panicking."

Tristan stole a glance at Rosina, who seemed to be purposely looking away.

"Before I talk to the director, given this afternoon's little adventure, do any of you want to return to Sea Camp? After all, you are only Snappers, young and inexperienced for a mission like this."

Tristan didn't hesitate. "No way."

"Yeah, like, no way is right," Ryder agreed.

"We don't want to *leave*," Sam added. "We still don't know what's killing the fish and stuff."

Hugh and Rosina nodded in agreement, once again with slightly less enthusiasm.

Coach smiled and struck Tristan on the back so hard he nearly did a face-plant on the deck. "That's just what I wanted to hear. No quitters at Sea Camp! Had to ask though, camp policy and all."

"Was it an earthquake?" Hugh asked.

Coach Fred hesitated before answering. "Probably a small quake or maybe some construction on the island. But as I always say, it's better to be suspicious than get caught off guard. You should all remember that, one of my better mottos. We've discussed it, and our best guess is that it was indeed just a freak accident and nothing to worry about."

Tristan didn't think Coach Fred looked so sure.

Meg pulled out the chart they'd been using and unrolled it across the deck. "While you were at The Baths, we had a report of another fish kill." She pointed to Mosquito Island. "We're up here, just pulling into Invisible Bay. We'll anchor, and then, first thing in the morning, go check out the site." She pointed to a cluster of small islands to their south. "Here at Cockroach Island."

Hugh raised his hand. "Cockroach Island, really? And you want us to go there?"

Meg laughed. "That's just another old pirate name. There were so many cockroaches on the ships back then that they were regular guests at mealtime. The hardtack biscuits crawled right off the table."

"Yuck!" Sam said, cringing.

Rosina looked ill, while Ryder pretended to barf.

"I've also contacted the institute and arranged for transport of the samples we collected this morning. They'll go out on this evening's ferry from the Bitter End Yacht Club. I've spoken to the owner, an old friend, and she's arranging things on their end. She also invited us for dinner. It's a short ride across Gorda Sound, and given what you've all been through today, it might be a nice treat. Assuming you're staying and it's okay with you, Coach?"

"Looks like we're all staying," Coach Fred said proudly. "As for this evening, I'm not sure they have the table manners for the Bitter End. But if you all agree to be on your best behavior?"

The campers rolled their eyes at the man and then nodded in agreement.

Meg leaned in closer to the group. "By the way, how did you really escape from that pool and come away without even any cuts or scrapes?"

They recounted the whole story, this time filling in the missing details.

The inflatable cruised across Gorda Sound, the long bay that separated Virgin Gorda from the smaller islands to the north. The winds were light, the seas calm, and a speckling of high clouds streamed across the early evening sky. The captain, first mate, and steward stayed aboard the research vessel.

Coach Fred was at the back, operating the outboard engine. He wore khaki shorts with a bright white, logo-free polo shirt. He didn't look thrilled about their dinner date at the yacht cub. The campers were dressed in their finest attire, or about as good as it could get: a pair of clean shorts and a Virgin Islands Institute T-shirt provided by Meg. The scientist was also in a T-shirt paired with a blue sarong skirt decorated with white silhouettes of fish. She pointed out the nearby islands.

"That's Virgin Gorda to our right, of course. To your left is Prickly Pear. The next island to the north is Eustatia, and behind that, Necker Island."

"Dr. Gladfell, does anyone live on Prickly Pear?" Hugh asked as they cruised by the small tan one-hill island. It had little vegetation, steep-sided rocky cliffs, and just a few pockets of sand along the shore.

"It's Meg, Hugh, and no, no one lives there. It's a national park."

"What's that island past Necker?" Tristan asked. He could just make it out in the distance.

"That's Scar Island."

"Eagle ray!" shouted Sam. She pointed to a large ray swimming gracefully beside the boat. It had a long, whip-like tail and a purple back with white spots.

"Turtle!" Tristan yelled from the other side of the inflatable.

The campers leaned over to his side. A sea turtle's small yellow head had just broken the surface. As soon as it noticed the boat, the creature took a gulp of air and dove.

"Glad to see that one looks healthy," Meg noted.

Continuing across Gorda Sound, they saw another eagle ray, two more sea turtles, and an enormous gray stingray lying motionless on the sand. As they neared the Bitter End Yacht Club, Coach maneuvered the inflatable around a maze of moorings and boats, along with people paddling kayaks or trying to windsurf. He aimed for a dock running alongshore. Behind it was a two-story wooden building painted chocolate brown with blue-and-pink latticed trim. It reminded Tristan of a giant gingerbread house. Meg scrambled forward to the bow to fend off the dock. She then held the boat steady so Tristan and the others could climb out. Tristan did it without so much as a stumble. Things were looking up. Coach passed them a small cooler containing their dead fish samples and got out as well. Meg secured the line from the bow to a cleat.

"Hello, there! Welcome to the Bitter End Yacht Club."

A light-haired, elderly, and notably fit woman scurried out of the building to give Meg a long, tight hug. She wore a flowery sundress with matching flip-flops. Her skin was wrinkled but not in a loose or flabby way, just enough to highlight how spry she was for her age. She also had intelligent blue eyes and round rosy cheeks that scrunched up when she smiled. For some reason, Tristan immediately liked the woman.

"We're so glad you could make it. I'm Mary. My husband and I own the Bitter End. I've arranged for Alvin to give you a tour before dinner. That will give Meg and me a chance to catch up."

A heavyset man pulled up beside the dock in an extra-long golf cart. "Y'alls a-ready fors a ride?"

"We'll meet you at the restaurant after the tour," Meg told them.

"Hops on in," Alvin said, smiling. He was missing several lower teeth so that when he spoke, his words were slurred.

Coach gave them another of his classic don't-do-anything-stupid looks before following the two women into the office building.

"I'll shows you the northern sides first. Me, this is wheres I'd stay in if I's was a guest."

The campers piled into the cart. Alvin drove down a narrow, packed-sand road that curved around the office building and behind a similarly decorated restaurant. They came to a beach with people lying on lounge chairs under palm trees. Buoys off the beach marked a large, rectangular swimming area. In the middle floated a giant, round, blow-up trampoline. A couple of kids were bouncing on it, laughing, and trying to push each other off into the water. Tristan eyed the trampoline, thinking it looked like fun.

They continued down the winding shoreline road.

It was lined with palm trees and tall bushes bursting with pink and white flowers.

"Uh, Mr. Alvin, what's that place out there?" Sam asked, pointing to a tiny island between where they were on Virgin Gorda and Prickly Pear Island.

"Oh, that's Saba Rock. Justs a bar and hotel out theres. Famous fors the tarpon feeding. Every nights for happy hour, theys feed the tarpons. Puts on a real show."

The road curved to the right. Tristan gazed out over the lagoon stretching out behind Saba Rock. "How far away is that island?" He pointed to the far side of the lagoon.

"Eustatia? She's abouts a mile off, give or take. Now, sees the cottages ups the hill. Get greats wind, no needs for ACs or anything."

The guest cottages sat in three long rows like wooden blocks stacked up the steep hillside. A network of wooden stairs and boardwalks provided access to the rooms. Tristan decided the view must be great, but he wasn't so sure about climbing up all those stairs every day.

They drove north along the shore beside the lowermost row of cottages. Alvin turned onto a steep, paved road that went up behind the last set of rooms.

"Here's where we drops 'em off if they don't want to take the stairs."

Tristan looked out over the water to Eustatia Island. The view of the lagoon was breathtaking. Enhanced by the sun now low on the horizon, the contrasting colors seemed almost too vivid to be real. It looked like an abstract oil painting with wide swaths of royal blue, streaks of bright turquoise, and patches of deep green.

"What's the long tan area?" Tristan asked, looking at a wide stripe about three-quarters of the way across the lagoon.

"And what are all the really dark spots?" Hugh questioned.

"That tan's a coral reefs, kid," Alvin answered. "Can't get across that one, too shallow. Thems there dark spots, they is piles of them black spiny urchins. Watch out for thems, they'll stick ya bads. Okay, nows hang on while I turn around and go down. We'll go a littles faster ways back."

Alvin swung the cart around swiftly. The teens slid across the seats, reaching for something to hold on to. If Tristan hadn't grabbed hold of Sam, she would have gone flying out. They raced down the steep incline, careened around the road's wide turn, passed the beachfront, and arrived back at the buildings. Rosina and Hugh looked ready to jump for it as Alvin slowed, but he just kept driving.

"Now, we'll go to the souths side of thes property."

Alvin kept up a running narrative as he drove slowly along the now cobblestone, slightly wider shoreline road. "Overs here, that's the watersport shack. Ya can rents just about anything that floats there."

Tristan checked it out. The adjacent beach was packed with small Hobie Cat catamarans, windsurfers, paddleboards, and kayaks.

"Over heres," Alvin said, pointing to the other side of the road. "That's the Sailing Club. There's the shops for clothes and stuffs. Next one's the stores for foods and that's a bar. Got good pizza theres."

A few minutes later they stopped beside a wide tree with big, flat, green leaves that resembled lily pads, and long, narrow clusters of green, grape-like balls. Tristan recognized the Sea Grape tree from Florida. He used to chuck the green grape things at his sister.

Alvin pointed to several more rows of cottages stacked on the hillside toward the other side of the property. "Here's the rest of them rooms. There's a pool and another beach downs that ways. Across here, that's the dive shop and these two docks are for them big boats."

Two long finger piers extended out into Gorda Sound. Several people with suitcases were boarding a green-hulled workboat tied up to one. Stacks of boxes sat nearby, waiting to be loaded, including the cooler containing the dead fish. Tristan figured it was the ferry Meg had mentioned. He then noticed the boat at the end of the other long dock. The sparkling white yacht was long and sleek with dark-tinted windows. People in fancy clothes were milling around on an upper deck at the stern.

"Hey, like, who owns that boat?" Ryder asked.

"That's Mr. Marsh's," Alvin told them.

"Who's Mr. Marsh?" Hugh asked.

"Hugo Marsh. Owns Scars Island, very private. C'mon, dinners time."

Alvin swung the cart around, nearly dumping Sam out again. The teens hung on as he sped back toward the restaurant. When they got out, Hugh and Rosina looked a little wobbly.

Dinner was served on an outside patio. Mary joined them and explained how lucky they were to be there for the weekly seafood buffet, a real treat for the guests. There was fish chowder, seafood salad, and numerous serving dishes all filled to the brim with cuisine from the sea. Two chefs manned a barbeque, grilling fillets of mahi mahi, salmon, and giant shrimp. Coach Fred, Ryder, and Rosina dug heartily into the from-the-ocean fare. Sam, Hugh, and Tristan stuck to the strictly non-seafood options like hamburgers, fried plantains, and beans and rice.

"You don't care for seafood?" Mary asked. "It's all sustainably caught or farmed in an environmentally friendly way, if that's the problem. We're even serving lionfish—nice and flaky, once you cut off the poisonous spines. They're invasive, you know. Don't belong here, but we've been seeing more and more of them. Lionfish gobble up the small fish and crustaceans on the reefs. And they have no natural predators here. My dive guides kill 'em every time they see one. Plus they're pretty tasty."

"Seafood allergy," Hugh said quickly.

"Yeah, me too," Tristan added.

Sam stuffed a big forkful of rice and beans into her mouth and just nodded.

"Oh, well that is a shame. Let me know if you're still hungry. I can always have our chefs prepare something else for you."

The teens chewed and shook their heads to indicate they had plenty to eat.

Mary wanted to hear all about how they liked the islands and what they'd been doing. Coach watched the teens like a hawk, attentive to their every word. It led to an especially awkward conversation. Mary also asked if they'd learned anything new about the mysterious fish kills and disappearance of sponges. Meg was just explaining that there was little to tell when a new party of diners arrived at the restaurant. The Bitter End's owner waved, excused herself, and went to say hello.

Heads turned as the group made its way to a reserved waterside table. Two of the men wore well-pressed navy suit jackets, khaki slacks, and polo shirts. The women accompanying them had on short, body-hugging dresses and shoes with skinny stiletto heels at least four inches high. Tristan stared at the shoes. He couldn't imagine how anybody could walk in them, especially in the sand or on the dock. His attention was then drawn to a tall man at the back of the group. He was lean, strangely tan bordering on orange, and wore flowing, white drawstring pants with a matching gauze shirt. He strode toward Mary with a confident, charismatic flair, running a hand through his silky, shoulder-length, streaked hair.

"Is that guy wearing pajamas?" Tristan whispered to Hugh.

"I think that's Hugo Marsh, the big-time investment guy I mentioned before," Meg told them in a hushed voice. "He owns Scar Island." She paused. "Do you know the story behind the island's name?"

Mouths full, the teens just shook their heads.

"Supposedly, there was a brutal pirate captain who was served a stew he didn't care for. Upon tasting one spoonful of the stuff, the captain whipped out a dagger and sliced the man's cheek to show his displeasure. And that man was just the waiter. The chef was promptly tossed off the ship. Anyway, the captain named the island 'Scar' because its shape resembled that of the wound he gave the waiter. It was supposed to remind his crew and others not to cross him or provide bad food service." Meg chuckled before adding, "Hope you all left room for dessert."

The teens' attention quickly turned to a table stacked high with an incredible assortment of sweets, including cupcakes mounded with frosting, small custard-filled tarts, and giant peanut butter cookies. Tristan already felt like he was about to explode. Still, he had to make at least one trip to the dessert table. Hugh and Ryder somehow made repeat visits.

After dinner, the group waddled back to the dock in a collective food coma. With all the added weight, Tristan was sure their small boat would sink.

The inflatable was now being rocked by choppy waves, and the wind came in gusts.

Meg glanced skyward. "Looks like a squall coming through. We could wait for it to pass or head back and try to outrun it?"

15

ADRIFT

"A LITTLE RAIN'S NOT GOING TO HURT ANYONE," Coach announced. "Let's head back. Besides, don't want to keep the kids out too late and all."

After some serious head shaking, the campers struggled, bellies full, into the inflatable. Meg started the engine while Coach stood at the bow to release them from the dock. Cables on the nearby sailboats rattled in the strengthening wind, and it started to drizzle.

"Hang on," Meg told them. "After we get past the boats, I'm going to give her some gas to try to beat the squall. And you all might want to scoot back. It's going to be a little wet up front."

The campers shimmied back on the boat's rubber sides, squeezing together. Meg turned the inflatable away from the well-lit yacht club and navigated slowly around the rocking boats and empty mooring balls. She then swiveled the throttle to increase their speed. The boat rose higher out of the water, and soon they were speeding through the night toward Mosquito Island. Just a sprinkling of lights dotted the barren islands around them. The inflatable bounced roughly over the wind-driven chop, and spray blew in over the front. The rain fell harder. The campers scrunched farther back, trying to stay warm and dry.

They were in the middle of Gorda Sound, about halfway back, when trouble struck. A stuttering cough interrupted the steady whine of the engine. Meg gave it more gas and the outboard engine returned to an even drone. Minutes later, there was another sputter and then . . . silence. The inflatable jerked and slowed, just as the skies let loose a punishing deluge. Shielding his eyes from the pelting rain, Tristan looked back. The lights of the Bitter End had disappeared. They were enveloped in a dark cocoon of falling water, and the only sounds were the whistling wind and the drumming of rain against the boat's rubber hull.

Meg tried to restart the engine. Coach scrambled back to help. But the motor remained eerily quiet. They were now adrift in the dark in Gorda Sound—more specifically, in the boat channel.

From her backpack, Meg pulled out a small dive light and radio. "*Reef Runner, Reef Runner*, come in?"

No answer. Even if there had been a response, it would have been hard to hear in the wind and rain. She tried again as Coach continued to work on the engine.

The campers were dripping wet, and rainwater began collecting at their feet.

"We could, like, swim back," Ryder shouted.

"'Fraid not," Meg yelled back. "Not safe out here in the boat lane, plus there are dangerous reefs and rocks to go around. You could get sliced up pretty badly."

"I might be able to lead us with my echolocation," Sam offered.

"Not this time," the scientist said. "But you can wave this around in case any boats are headed this way." She passed Sam the dive light. "*Reef Runner, Reef Runner*, come in?"

Still no response. Tristan and the others sat nervously quiet as the boat continued to drift. Thankfully, the wind soon began to let up, and the rain was tapering off. The squall was passing.

Tristan pushed his wet hair back from his face and looked out over the water. There wasn't much around. As he stared at the ocean's dark surface, a burst of blue-green twinkling grabbed his attention. He leaned over to get a better view. A dark form passed by. He sat up. "Did you see that?"

"See what?" Sam asked.

"Something just swam under the boat."

The other campers leaned over and stared nervously into the water. Rainwater dripped from their hair and noses. Hugh shivered. Something dark and about four feet across swam by. In its wake was a sparkling trail of blue-green light. Another form passed by, its whole body outlined in glowing, glimmering light.

Tristan breathed a sigh of relief. "Rays."

Now that he knew what to look for, Tristan's eyes adjusted, and he could make out the wide, diamond-shaped forms swimming beside the boat. "Three of them."

"Maybe they want to help," Sam suggested.

"Maybe."

"Well, we're not going anywhere anytime soon, Hunt," Coach interjected. "Hop on in and find out."

Tristan glanced at the others and then at the dark, choppy water.

Hugh seemed to know what he was thinking. "Uh, we don't know what else is out there."

"C'mon, the rays wouldn't be here if there was, like, something bad down there," Ryder scoffed.

"Then you go in," Hugh countered.

"Remember, dude, I can't speak ray."

Tristan took a deep breath and reminded himself of his vow to be more confident. "No, no, I'll do it." He swung his legs around to the outside of the boat and turned to Coach Fred. "You don't happen to have any Sea Camp water with you, do you?"

"No, but I have something else that might work just as well."

The campers all turned to him.

"Our new chemist at camp has been working on this for months. Granted, it's still in the experimental stage, but worth a try."

Sam turned the dive light toward Coach. He pulled a small plastic bag out of his pocket. Inside were some red, rubbery-looking pills. "It's Sea Camp water in a concentrated pill form—we think."

He handed a pill to Tristan, who said, "You *think*? Is it safe?"

"Yeah, yeah, Hunt, nothing to worry about."

"Go on, try it," Ryder urged. "I would."

Tristan rolled his eyes and then looked to Sam and Hugh. They just sort of shrugged. "Okay, I guess."

He swallowed the pill and waited, hoping he wouldn't choke or go into some kind of tongue-chewing convulsions.

"How long before it starts working?" Hugh asked.

"No idea," Coach answered.

The sound of a powerful boat engine somewhere in the distance interrupted the conversation.

"Quiet!" Coach urged, cocking his head and listening intently.

For several minutes, nobody said or did anything. Tristan sat on the side of the boat and waited. The engine noise got noticeably louder.

"It's headed this way," Coach told them.

"Should be some emergency paddles in here," Meg said urgently. "Anyone see them?" She looked to Sam. "Keep waving that light to let them know we're here."

It was a quick search. No paddles. And from the sound of it, the oncoming boat was big and bearing down on them fast.

"Use your hands, start paddling," Coach ordered. "We need to get into shallower water and out of the boat channel."

The teens leaned over the sides of the boat and began paddling. Simultaneously, Coach shoved Tristan into the water. "We could use that help right about now."

Tristan popped up and floated beside the barely moving boat, letting his vision adjust to the darkness. He looked for the rays. They were circling nearby. Two had white spots on their backs, which made them easier to see. The other ray was larger, solid black on top and white underneath. It had two weird, flat projections in front of its mouth. Tristan recognized it—a manta ray. He glanced around, wondering if anything else was out there. *Don't think about it*, he said to himself. Tristan then silently said hello to the rays.

The manta ray swam directly at Tristan. It turned abruptly, flashing its white underside.

In his head, Tristan heard the ray. *Who are you, and what are you doing here?*

Man, Tristan thought, *the animals around here sure aren't very friendly.*

The manta made another pass. *Who do you work for?*

I don't work for anybody. We're just here to help figure out why things are dying.

The manta circled in close. *Yeah, that's a bit dodgy. But you don't look like those other wonky chaps and I can't talk to them. Why are you skulking about out here at night?*

Skulking? We're not skulking.

Either way, you blokes better bloody start moving. There's a big ol' boat headed this way.

Tristan rolled his eyes. *I know that. That's why I got in. Our engine's dead, and we could use some help getting out of the way.*

The sound of the approaching boat was now disturbingly loud, and Tristan could feel the thrum of its propellers in the water. On the inflatable, Sam was frantically waving the dive light back and forth. The others paddled harder, but the boat was heavy and they were fighting against the remaining breeze.

"Hey, uh, Tristan?" Hugh shouted. "Hurry it up, buddy."

The manta ray made another pass by Tristan. He knew it was trying to decide if they were trustworthy. After an excruciatingly long few seconds, the ray told him what to do. Tristan popped up and told the others.

Coach speedily tied a wide loop in the line from the bow and tossed it to Tristan. "We need to move *NOW.*"

On the inflatable, they could see the hull of a large white powerboat headed straight for them. Sam aimed the light directly at the boat, swinging it from side to side.

Tristan grabbed the rope from Coach and kicked to the front of the inflatable. With his webbed feet, he shot forward—the pill had worked. He held the loop out so the wide manta could swim through. He let go, and the rope lay hooked under its two weird front flap-like projections and around its outstretched, wing-like fins. The two eagle rays picked up the back of the loop in their mouths. The rays waved their broad, powerful fins and swam forward. The inflatable resisted. Then, slowly, it began to move. Tristan grabbed the line to help pull, kicking hard.

The powerboat was nearly on top of them. Someone else leapt into the water from the boat. Ryder grabbed the line. He nodded to Tristan and began pulling as well.

Tristan felt a powerful rumble in the water. He kicked even harder, not wanting to be crushed under the boat or ripped to shreds by the propeller. He couldn't understand why the boat hadn't turned away; they must have seen the light Sam was waving. Tristan glanced behind him. A huge, glowing wave of white water at the boat's bow was almost on top of them. He turned back, kicked, and prayed.

Either the powerboat turned at the very last minute or its bow wave pushed the inflatable just enough, because somehow they escaped being run over or sliced in half. But it had been dangerously close. Seconds after the boat passed, its giant wake hit them like a tsunami. The inflatable rocked violently and nearly flipped. Sam was tossed out, and the others were thrown to the deck in a twisted pile of limbs and bodies. The team up front stopped pulling.

Coach Fred jumped up quickly to check for injuries: a few bumps and a cascade of bruises. Luckily, no one was seriously hurt. But they'd lost the handheld radio overboard.

"I'd like to know who was driving that boat," Coach Fred said angrily. He called to the teens up front, "Nice work, boys. Do you think you could get us back to the ship?"

While Tristan asked the rays, Sam looked up from the water. "Hey, Coach, I'm in the water already. Can I pull too?"

Coach handed her a red pill, and she passed him the dive light.

With the team pulling up front, the inflatable now moved slowly but steadily. They glided out of the Gorda Sound boat lane and toward Mosquito Island. For the most part, Tristan was too busy pulling to talk to the rays. But once, when the water got scarily shallow, he asked the manta not to run them aground. The manta ray responded by saying something about a reef, a shortcut, and not to worry. The rays then swung them into a narrow channel lined with thickets of branching coral. Tristan popped his head up and watched uneasily as they passed frighteningly close to the sharp coral. Rounding the tip of Mosquito Island, the *Reef Runner* came into view, lit up by its bright stern deck lights.

Tristan let out a long, tired sigh. Just before they reached the ship, he thanked the rays for their help. Tristan also asked why the animals in the area were acting so funny and if the rays knew anything about the die-offs. The manta ushered the eagle rays off and then paused. It told him it would come back in the morning when it was alone. Tristan climbed into the inflatable with the others.

Now alongside the *Reef Runner,* Coach Fred threw the line from the bow to the first mate.

Captain Hank strode up to the rail and angrily pushed Charlie aside. "Where've you all been?"

"Engine problems," Coach answered.

"How'd you make it back?"

"We tried the radio, repeatedly, before it went overboard," Meg replied. "Lucky these kids are strong swimmers. They pulled some, and we walked the boat through the shallow areas."

The captain eyed them suspiciously. It was not the reaction Tristan had expected.

The first mate bowed his head and shrugged apologetically. "Sorry, found these tucked away under some lifejackets. Thought they were in the boat." He was holding up two narrow plastic paddles. "I'll check out the engine."

"You do that," the captain huffed. "Hard to get good help around here. At least you made it back without damaging my boat, but I'll want a replacement for that radio."

What about us, like, not getting run over and chopped up or anything? thought Tristan.

"Yes, thanks," the scientist said sarcastically. "*We* all made it back safely."

Wet, freezing, and totally exhausted, Tristan could think only of jumping into a warm, dry, non-hazardous-to-your-health bed. The rush of adrenaline during the near collision had faded, and the food he'd consumed at the Bitter End weighed heavily in his stomach. He and the others made a beeline for their bunks. Sam was the only one who even took a shower before climbing under the covers.

Tristan lay in his bed, wrapped snugly in the sheets and blanket. His eyelids felt so heavy he could hardly keep them open. But he wasn't quite ready to go to sleep. He looked down at Hugh in the bunk below.

"Hugh," Tristan said softly. "Hugh?"

No response except a gentle snore. Tristan lay back and let his eyes close, thinking. The animals were acting awfully strange, and the campers had had two near-death accidents in just one day. Was that normal for a mission? Did campers nearly get killed on a regular basis, and it was just something the director neglected to mention? Or were they just having a really, really bad day? Right before he fell asleep, Tristan decided it must be his serious bad luck. Though somewhere back in the recesses of his mind, he wasn't so sure.

16

HERDED BY SHARKS

Short but powerful squalls swept through the British Virgin Islands throughout the night. They'd spun off a low-pressure system building in the Atlantic Ocean. No one in the islands paid much attention to the storms, as it was early in hurricane season.

As morning broke over Mosquito Island, the rising sun turned the fish-scale clouds overhead a fiery orange-red. The air was already thick with humidity. The teens sat eating quietly in the main salon. Tristan was sure Coach Fred had asked the steward to bang the pots and pans even louder that morning. Still, the campers were more asleep than awake at the table, tired from the previous night's adventure. He'd seen Rosina doze off and nearly drown in her cereal bowl. After breakfast, Coach Fred ushered the group to the stern deck.

"Snappers, muster up," Coach barked. "Earlier this morning, a boat towed Charlie in the inflatable to the Bitter End to flush out the engine and lines. Looks like our problems last night were caused by water in the gas. Once Charlie comes back, Meg and I will be heading out to Cockroach Island to recon the site of that last fish kill. Probably won't be till sometime this afternoon. In the meantime, I've got a call with the director this morning to discuss yesterday's events and what our options are."

Through his early-morning fog, Tristan picked up on the fact that Coach had said that just he and Meg would be going out in the afternoon. "Aren't we all going to Cockroach Island? Not that I really want to go to an island named after cockroaches."

"The senior campers have returned from the dolphin stranding, so we thought they could—"

Tristan was suddenly wide awake. "What?"

"But wait, you're going to bring them here?" Sam questioned. "And send us home?"

No way, Tristan thought. After all they'd already been through and done . . . now they were going to be replaced with senior campers? Just the thought made Tristan want to either scream or puke; he wasn't sure which. They'd never live it down. They'd be the laughingstock of Sea Camp. He'd been nervous before, at times scared, but now he was mad.

"Coach, you can't send us home *now*. It's not like anything that happened was our fault. We don't know what's causing the fish kills. And the manta from last night said it would come back today to tell me what's going on."

"Hold on, hold on." Coach held up his hands. "Nothing's been decided yet. But this is a lot for you all to handle. You're only Snappers. We're lucky no one was hurt yesterday."

Hugh raised his hand.

"Yes, what is it, Haverford?"

"How did water get in the gas?"

"We believe it was from the squall last night. Look, outboard engines are notoriously temperamental. Having one break down is not all that surprising. I've already spoken to our *wonderful* first mate about the absence of paddles in the boat and the radio issue. I don't think anything like that will happen again."

"Then why, like, make us leave?" Ryder asked. "We kicked it yesterday, dude."

"Yeah," said Sam.

"*Yeah*," added Tristan.

Even Hugh and Rosina nodded their heads.

"Uh, Coach?" Sam said.

"Yes, Marten, now what?"

"The red pills. Just so you know, they kinda worked too well. My, I mean, our webbing didn't go away right after we got out of the water. I still had some when I climbed into bed."

"Interesting," Coach mused. He then handed each of the campers a bottle of Sea Camp water. "We'll stick with these for now."

"I thought we had to leave?" Tristan questioned.

"As I *already* said, nothing's been decided." Coach rolled his eyes and turned to Meg, who was standing nearby. "It's just that the situation here seems to be a little more complicated than we expected."

Tristan wondered what *that* meant.

Meg smiled at them. "The captain mentioned a reef nearby and suggested we take a swim this morning while we wait for the inflatable. I thought we could check out the shoreline and then head to the reef. The water here is very calm, so it'll be an easy swim, especially for all of you. We could also release a couple of those drifters you brought along." She lowered her voice conspiratorially. "Might be a good opportunity to prove you should stay. We might even find that manta, Tristan."

The teens agreed enthusiastically. Clearly, no one wanted to leave and face the disgrace and humiliation of quitting or getting kicked off their first official mission before it was complete.

"Do you have your robo-jellies with you?" Coach asked.

The teens shook their heads. Tristan, Hugh, and Sam offered to go below to get theirs.

When they were in the passageway outside their cabins, Tristan paused. He turned angrily to Sam and Hugh. "Can you believe it? They're thinking of sending us home and bringing in some senior campers. That would totally stink. I don't know about you guys, but I want to stay and find out what's really going on."

"Yeah," Sam said. "Totally. We have to stay. Something's not right here. It's strange how all the animals are acting and everything that happened yesterday."

Tristan nodded. "I bet Coach thinks something weird is going on too, and that's why he wants us to leave."

Hugh just stared at them worriedly and turned a shade whiter.

Coach called down from the deck above, "C'mon, Snappers, get a move on!"

The teens grabbed their robo-jellies. On the way back, they ran into Coach Fred heading to the bridge. "I'm going to distract the captain so he won't notice that Dr. Gladfell is the only one actually using snorkeling gear." Then, surprisingly, he looked almost warmly at the campers and spoke softly. "Look, I know you want to stay and that nothing that happened yesterday was your fault. In fact, you all did quite well. Just be careful out there this morning. If you can come up with some new information without any more trouble, maybe I can convince Director Davis to let you stay."

Tristan, Sam, and Hugh were so shocked they just stood there with their mouths hanging open. The angry pit in Tristan's stomach lessened. Now he *had* to find that manta ray.

"Well? Don't just stand there."

The three teens sprinted for the stern. When they arrived, Ryder was just jumping in. Rosina was already in the water. A rope ladder hung from an opening in the side of the ship. Meg put the robo-jellies in her yellow mesh bag. The teens each drank about half a bottle of pink water before also jumping in. The scientist then donned her fins, mask, and snorkel and joined them. She led the group on the surface toward shore.

Tristan swam beside Sam and Hugh, behind the others. The water was calm, warm, and well lit by the morning sun as it passed between clouds. Tristan glanced at the sandy bottom, but he wasn't really paying attention. He was thinking about the manta ray and hoping it would show up soon.

Sam let out a muffled cry. Tristan reacted instantly, turning to see what was wrong. With her hair streaming behind her like wheat-colored seaweed, Sam raised her eyebrows in surprise and smiled to him underwater. Bubbles of air escaping from her mouth rose toward the surface. She pointed to a small cove ahead that was surrounded by big, tan rocks. Between the rocks, the sand was bright white and the water was amazingly clear. It was also teeming with fish, tens of thousands of fish, maybe even millions. An enormous, shimmering cloud of two-inch-long silver fish literally filled the water. Tristan kicked gently toward the astonishing abundance. He floated through a narrow crevice between two rocks and into a shallow pool. It was a rock hot tub filled with fish. The fish parted gracefully as he floated in. He watched as sunlight glinted off their silvery sides. So captivated by the fish-filled rock hot tub, Tristan quickly forgot about everything else. He felt relaxed and at peace. Tristan floated for a little while longer and then swam to a small beach where the others were standing waist-deep in fish-filled water.

"This is so cool," Sam said, swirling happily around in the fish. "I've never seen so many fish. Never swam with so many fish. Did you see how they moved? Hugh, what are they saying? What have they seen? Did I say this is *soooo* cool?"

Hugh shook his head, exasperated. "Cool for you, maybe. Half of them are trying to talk to me, all at the same time. It's like crazy fish voices in my head. Seriously, you could go nuts here."

Meg took off her mask and snorkel. "They all look healthy; that's good. Hugh, take a breath and try again. Ask if they've seen or felt anything odd in the water."

"Okay, I'll try, but don't expect much." Hugh took a deep breath and floated amid the fish.

"Any sign of the manta, Tristan?" Sam asked hopefully.

He shook his head.

Hugh stood up. "Dr. Gladfell, I mean, Meg, they can't agree on anything. One fish says sometimes at night they start feeling bad and it comes from the north. Another fish says it's in the mornings and comes from the west. A lot of them say the others are crazy, that there's nothing wrong."

"Dude, like, that's no help at all," Ryder groaned. He looked bored, as did Rosina, who was dribbling mucus into the water. She watched as it spread from her hands out over the surface.

A bunch of fish suddenly leapt out of the water in front of the group. Like a wave of porpoising silver bullets, more fish jumped. Tristan wondered if something was chasing them. *Maybe it's the manta? Some-*

thing else? He tentatively put his face underwater and looked around. Something silver, narrow, and about a foot long raced by. Barracuda.

Just as Tristan popped up to tell the others, seemingly out of nowhere, two huge black birds swooped down and nearly knocked him over. Each had long, narrow wings, a white chest, and a forked tail. Reaching down with sharp talons, the giant birds grabbed at the jumping fish. One bird flew off empty-handed, but the other came away with a wiggling, silver catch.

Two more black birds swooped down, but instead of going after the leaping fish, they chased after the bird with a meal dangling from its talons. The bird carrying the fish swerved, ducked, and then shot skyward, trying to lose its pursuers.

Rosina studied the birds. "What are they?"

"They're frigatebirds," Meg answered.

"How come they don't just dive in for the fish?"

"They can't swim or even get wet. Frigates are opportunistic feeders. They feed on fish however and whenever they can get them. As you can see, they often steal fish from each other or other birds. That's why they're also known as pirate birds."

As if to demonstrate the fact, several more frigatebirds joined the dogfight, swooping, diving, and hovering in an all-out attempt to steal the one bird's catch. It was an astonishing aerial display—*Top Gun*, bird style.

"Hey, maybe you can talk to them," Tristan suggested to Rosina.

"They look kinda busy right now."

"Okay, looks like we're not going to find out any-thing here," Meg told them. "Let's head out to the reef the captain mentioned to see what's there and then release the robo-jellies. Follow me."

The group paddled out through the shimmering cloud of fish. Hugh swiveled around manically as he passed through. Tristan grinned. He was glad he didn't have hundreds of fish voices in his head. Soon the swarms of fish thinned out, giving way to empty sand and smooth, blocky, tan rocks. As Tristan swam, he looked around, again hoping to spot the manta.

The group swam along the shore and then headed seaward. Tristan watched below him as the bottom changed. Wisps of sea grass now sprouted from the sand, and there were scattered green sticks with bushy tops sticking up like short paintbrushes. Last summer, Ms. Sanchez told him what they were, but he'd forgotten. He was pretty sure they were some type of algae. Tristan then noticed another algae; this one was easy to remember. It was named *Halimeda* and resembled clumps of green cornflakes strung together in chains. When they first saw it in Florida, a heated cereal debate arose among the campers. Tristan voted for cornflakes, while Rosina argued that it looked more like strings of green granola. Sam was convinced it resembled moldy oatmeal.

Tristan then saw some white fish with yellow stripes along their midsections. They were poking around in the sand, looking for food. Two whiskers hung from each fish's chin. He'd seen similar fish in the lagoon at Sea Camp—they were goatfish. The bottom continued to change as they swam farther offshore. The water deepened, and there were scattered corals, sea whips, and a few more fish swimming along the seafloor. Tristan noticed a small brown damselfish darting in and out of a pile of coral and rubble. He figured it was probably tending to its algae farm and would attack him if he got too close. Last year in the Bahamas, Hugh swore one had nearly bitten off his finger. Another of those weird serving-platter fish swam by; this one was purple with iridescent blue lines on its body and translucent fins running along its top and bottom.

Tristan dove. A yellow brain coral about the size of a grapefruit sat atop a pile of old reef rubble. Small purple and red spirally things stuck out of its surface. They resembled miniature Christmas trees and looked soft. He tried to touch one, and it instantly withdrew into a tube. The reaction was so fast it reminded him of someone flinching after touching a hot pan. Tristan had no idea what they were and made a mental note to ask Meg. He then noticed a cluster of long black spines sticking out of a nearby hole. Assuming it was a black spiny sea urchin, like the ones Alvin had warned them about, he kept his distance. He returned to the surface and looked around for the others.

The rest of the group was following Hugh. He was chasing something on the bottom. Tristan swam over and tapped Sam on the leg.

"Octopus," Sam said. "Won't talk to him."

Hugh stopped swimming and pointed to another small stack of coral rubble. He shrugged his shoulders and came to the surface. "Won't come out. No matter what I say."

Just then, Tristan noticed something on the sand in front of the reef. It was square and seemed to be wiggling on the inside. He swam closer for a better view. The others followed. It was a fish trap, about three feet in length and two feet wide. The wiggling came from all the fish crammed inside and mashed up against the trap's wire mesh. Many of the fish had cuts from the metal. A big, droopy-eyed grouper stared sadly at Tristan. It was squished between two squirming black-and-yellow French angelfish.

The teens gathered overhead on the surface.

Sam looked horrified. "They've even caught really small fish. They can't even be big enough to eat."

Meg nodded. "They're trying to outlaw this type of trap fishing. It does terrible damage to the fish population and reefs here."

"Let's let them out," Tristan suggested.

"Yeah, like a prison break," Sam said.

Meg glanced around nervously. "Okay, but do it quickly. Messing with someone's trap is dangerous business."

Tristan and the other campers swiftly dove down to the trap and looked for a way to release the fish. Sam found a hinged door with a latch on it and tried to open it, but it was stuck. Ryder tried to muscle the door open, but it still wouldn't budge. Rosina pushed the teen aside and coated the latch and hinge with a blanket of slippery, slimy mucus. Sam tried again, and the door swung open.

Fish came pouring out. Some shot out like small rockets; others cruised slowly away, a little wobbly. The big grouper exited and stopped in front of the teens. Tristan couldn't tell what it was saying or thinking, but he could swear the fish was smiling. Soon the trap was empty.

Meg pointed to a small boat cruising along the reef to their south.

"I think we'd better move on, just in case. Let's go north and then release a couple of those robo-jellies."

After a short swim, Meg stopped and turned to the teens. "This looks like as good a spot as any. Sam, if you would, reach into the bag and get a robo-jelly. Rosina, how about you release another?"

The girls each took a plastic blue egg from the yellow mesh bag.

"Like, squeeze the ends," Ryder told them.

"Yeah, *like*, I know," Rosina replied sarcastically.

They squeezed, and the eggs popped open. Each girl removed the rubbery, robotic jellyfish from its case, giving the case back to the scientist.

"Where should we let them go?" Sam asked.

Meg pointed into deeper water. "Swim a little way out and then, Rosina, why don't you release yours on the surface. Sam, you dive down a few feet and release yours there."

The girls nodded before swimming out into the open, blue water. Tristan floated on his stomach, watching them go. Something bumped his feet. He thought it was Hugh, but then realized his friend was floating right in front of him. He hesitated before turning around. A large black manta ray was just swimming past. Its bright white underside flashed as it flapped its wide fins.

There you are, chap. Do you want some info or not?

Excited that the manta had finally shown up, Tristan turned to tell the others. But before he could get a single word out, Sam came racing back. Rosina was right behind her.

"Uh, I think there's something out there," Sam said shakily. "I was echolocating after I released the robojelly. I . . . I think it's big."

"What is it?" Hugh asked, going a little green.

"Shark, I think, maybe two."

Tristan turned to the manta ray. It flicked its fins. *Gotta go!*

"Hey, wait," Tristan yelled out, but it was too late; the manta ray was gone.

Tristan had a weird feeling, and not the one he usually got when sharks or rays were around—it was as if the hair all over his body was standing straight up. *These sharks might not be the kind to chitchat with.*

Meg and the others turned to Tristan. He was about to say, "Let's get the heck out of here," when two huge, dark gray dorsal fins broke the surface about forty feet away. One began heading to their right, the other to their left. The group moved closer together.

"Okay, stay calm," Meg told them. "We've never had a shark attack in the British Virgin Islands."

"There's always a first time," Hugh moaned.

Tristan ducked nervously underwater to look at the sharks. They were enormous, fat, and gray on top, white underneath. *And* they were circling. Then Tristan noticed something strange—an unusual hump just in front of their dorsal fins.

Curiosity won out over fear or even common sense. Tristan floated away from the group and closer to the sharks. They were bull sharks, like the one he saved on the beach. That could be good, he thought. Then one of the sharks turned toward him. *Or maybe not so good.* The shark swam directly at him. Tristan tried to simultaneously backpedal and communicate with it. *We're friends, good humans, not very tasty.* The shark was silent, and its eyes looked weird—sort of cloudy and unfocused, like it was looking at him but not actually seeing him. When the shark was just two feet from Tristan, it stopped. Then it hung perfectly still and just sat there. Tristan stared at the shark, barely moving, or breathing, for that matter. He knew he should probably be scared, if not terrified. But Tristan was intrigued and confused by the shark's odd behavior. Why was it acting so strangely? The big bull shark then simply turned and rejoined the other shark still circling the group.

Tristan had seen what the bump in front of its dorsal fin was. Now he was really confused. He swam back to the others. "They're not saying anything, and they've got something on their backs. I . . . I think it's a camera."

"A camera?" Sam asked.

Tristan nodded.

"Okay, let's worry about that later," Meg told them. "For now, let's try moving slowly back to the ship. Keep together."

The teens began sculling gently, moving toward the ship in the distance. The sharks made a closer pass and then began swimming back and forth, blocking their path. The group stopped moving.

"Uh, how 'bout we just go to shore?" Hugh suggested, clearly trying hard to stay calm.

"Yes, Hugh. Let's try that," Meg agreed.

When they tried moving toward shore, the sharks again got in their way. Tristan attempted once more to communicate with the sharks. Nothing. Their pointy-finned friends then began making passes closer to the campers, opening and closing their mouths threateningly and showing off hundreds of razor-sharp teeth. Backing away, the group headed offshore. The sharks again blocked the way. Tristan realized what they were doing.

"They want us to go that way." He pointed to the one direction they had not tried. "And I don't think they're going to give us much choice."

"Like, let's go that way," Ryder said.

The others nodded enthusiastically.

They swam northeast away from Mosquito Island and the research vessel. The sharks stayed close behind, making sure no one went even the slightest bit off course. They were being driven, herded like cattle.

Tristan saw an island not too far away. He recognized it—Prickly Pear. He and the others swam for the shore. The sharks quickly cut them off, forcing them to bypass Prickly Pear and continue swimming.

After what seemed like forever, another island came into view. Again, the group headed for it. This time, the sharks didn't block their path but instead stayed close behind, snapping their toothy jaws, egging them on. When they reached the tip of Eustatia Island, all Tristan wanted was to get out of the water and *away* from the sharks. That, however, presented another problem— the rocks on this part of Eustatia were covered with sharp, hard little spikes. The teens stared at the rocks and then back at the two giant fins circling nearby.

Rosina cursed as she climbed out of the water. Sam tried to swim along the shore, but the sharks drove her back. She joined the others as they scrambled painfully over the sharp rocks toward the beach on the island's eastern side. "Ouch! Ouch! Crap! Double crap!" Their feet got cut up and bloody.

Trying to avoid a particularly wicked-looking rock, Meg stepped into an adjacent water-filled crack.

"Damn it!" the scientist exclaimed as she leapt out of the water with one foot raised. Tristan and the others gathered around. He didn't have to ask what was wrong. Her foot was swelling up like a balloon. It was also heavily polka-dotted with tiny black spots.

The teens helped her over the last set of spiky rocks and onto the sand. She sat down, holding her foot up. "Stepped on one of those bloody sea urchins."

"Uh, Meg," Hugh said shyly. "I read that you're supposed to, well, you know, pee on it."

"No, no," Meg replied quickly. "Nobody's going to urinate on my foot."

"Thank god," Hugh sighed.

"Just help me down the beach," she said. "Oh, no, look at *your* feet."

Tristan stared at his feet. Like the others, blood was seeping out of numerous small but deep cuts. He shook his head. "Don't worry; these will go away once we get back in the water."

They helped Meg hobble a short way farther down the beach. Her foot had become even bigger and redder than before. Blood ran in rivulets from cuts. It looked horribly painful. They helped her sit down and looked around for help. The beach was deserted.

"Can you see the *Reef Runner* or any other boats to wave down?" Meg asked.

They shook their heads. Invisible Bay was now truly invisible behind the tip of Eustatia Island and Prickly Pear. And Saba Rock, off in the distance, blocked the view to the busy waterfront at the Bitter End Yacht Club.

"But, like, I don't see the sharks anymore," Ryder said, peering into the water.

"I . . . I think they're gone," Rosina added nervously.

The campers walked cautiously into the water up to their knees to let their cuts heal. Sam then lay down and made some clicking noises.

"Hard to tell what's past that coral reef," she told

them, pointing to a narrow channel of water and a long stretch of reef. It ran nearly the entire length of Eustatia Island. At the reef's top, rubble, a few corals, and the tips of more black spiny sea urchins stuck out of the water. Tristan realized it was the reef they'd seen from the cottages at the Bitter End.

"Maybe I could jump over the reef and swim to the Bitter End," Ryder offered.

"Or I could swim around it," Tristan added.

"No, if you misjudge it, you'll be worse off than me," Meg said, wincing with pain. "Besides, I think we should all stay together, and Coach is expecting us back anytime now. Once he realizes we're missing, they'll start looking for us."

Sam played with her black rubber tracking bracelet. "Yeah, glad we still have these on."

Tristan noticed a trail through the scrub. It went up the hill behind the beach. "What about going up there? Maybe there's a house or something." After he spoke, he thought: *Could that be why the sharks drove us to the island?*

"Worth a try," Meg said. "Why don't you and Ryder hike up the trail a little way and see what's up there."

Tristan looked at her horribly swollen, black-dotted foot and decided not to say anything about wondering why the sharks had driven them to the island. Right now they just needed to find help.

Just as the two boys started up the path, the drone of powerful outboard engines drew their attention back to the water. A speedboat was rounding the northern tip of Eustatia heading into the deep water on the opposite side of the reef. It seemed to be going to Saba Rock or the Bitter End.

Rosina jumped up and down, waving at the boat and screaming for help. The others joined in. The boat slowed, did a U-turn, and sped back the way it had come.

"Hey, where are they going?" Rosina groaned.

The boat turned, swinging in toward the island.

"Had to go around the reef," Meg sighed.

The boat's deep, V-shaped hull and big twin outboard engines prevented the driver from pulling up to the beach. Instead, the man stopped the boat just offshore. Another man hopped out and waded over to the group. He was middle aged and wore khaki shorts, a buttercup-yellow polo shirt, and a matching baseball hat. He was also unusually large, overly muscled, and had a weird look on his face. He was smiling, but Tristan thought it looked kinda fake. He decided the guy resembled an ex-pro-wrestler gone preppy who wasn't very happy about it.

"You folks need some help?"

"Yes," Meg answered. "Stepped on a sea urchin in the rocks. We could use a lift back to our ship in Invisible Bay."

The man leaned over to examine Meg's injured foot. "We've got a doctor back at the island. I suggest we go there instead and get that treated. It'll be much worse if it gets infected."

Tristan wondered what island he was referring to.

"That's fine—in fact, sounds like a great idea," Meg replied. "But could you radio our ship, the *Reef Runner*, and let them know what happened and where we're going?"

"Ma'am that's not a problem. We'll be happy to."

The man lifted Meg up as if she weighed nothing and carried her to the waiting boat. The teens followed. He helped them in as well. Tristan gazed worriedly at his feet as he climbed aboard. The cuts were healed, but he still had webbing. He hoped the strangers were too busy to notice. Meg sat on the deck with her foot raised. The man who helped them into the boat wrapped her foot in a towel and told the huge, similarly dressed driver to radio their ship.

"*Reef Runner, Reef Runner*, come in?"

The driver started the boat's twin engines. Tristan sat on a padded bench at the boat's stern. The roar of the big outboards was ear blasting. He saw the driver talking on the radio, but could only assume the man was speaking with someone on their ship.

17

THE PSYCHO SPA

The speedboat raced across the water, rounding the northern tip of Eustatia Island. Necker Island came into view. They turned right toward another more distant landmass. With the twin engines at full throttle, it took little time to reach the island. The driver slowed as they approached a long but empty dock. To the right were several small finger piers with more speedboats tied up alongside.

As they came to a stop, Tristan noticed a change in the weather. He'd been so preoccupied by the I'd-love-to-eat-you sharks, the foot-slicing rocks, and the exhilarating boat ride that he hadn't noticed the thick gray clouds rolling in or the wind picking up.

"Welcome to Scar Island," said the muscleman who helped them into the boat. "I called on our way in to inform the doctor of the injury."

The dock rattled as two ultra-fancy golf carts rolled toward them. Each cart had a sleek yellow frame that curved over three rows of white, cushioned seats. A little yellow flag at the front made the vehicles look weirdly official. A woman hopped out of the first cart to arrive. She was wearing a buttercup-yellow lab coat. Tristan decided whoever was in charge had a serious obsession with the color.

"I'm Maria, one of Mr. Marsh's doctors. Where's the injury?"

While the doctor examined Meg's foot, the teens disembarked onto the dock.

"I'm Dr. Meg Gladfell, from the Virgin Islands Institute. We're grateful your boat showed up when it did." She looked to the driver. "Were you able to reach our ship?"

"Yes, ma'am. Told them what happened and that we were bringing you here."

"Thank you. These are my, uh . . . students from a summer class at the institute." She gave the teens a look like she hoped they'd go along with her. "They're here studying coral reefs."

"That's nice," the doctor said. "Let's go get this foot cleaned up."

The men lifted Meg out of the boat and gently put her into one of the carts, keeping her foot raised. Ryder and Rosina went with her, while Tristan, Sam, and Hugh rode in the other vehicle. The carts' drivers were dressed just like the men in the boat; neither said a word.

As the yellow carts rolled down the dock, Tristan whispered, "What about the cameras on the sharks? Did you guys see them?"

"No, I was too busy looking at their *teeth*," Hugh answered.

"Why would there be cameras on the sharks?" Sam asked. "Do you think that's why they're acting so weird?"

"Maybe someone's studying them," Tristan suggested. "I've seen television shows where they glue cameras onto animals to learn about them. You know—a shark-cam. But they're not supposed to affect the shark's behavior."

Hugh whispered, "Well, lucky the boat showed up when it did."

"Yeah, *lucky*," Sam said suspiciously.

Hugh and Tristan looked at her questioningly.

Sam shrugged. "I'm just sayin', given everything that's happened, I'm not sure what to think. Remember what Coach said: better to be suspicious rather than surprised. Or something like that."

Then it started to rain. Tristan wanted to talk more with Sam and Hugh about what they'd seen and everything that had happened. But the loud patter of raindrops striking the cart's roof made further discussion impossible. He tapped his foot nervously and stared out into the rain, thinking. Tristan felt a confusing mix of emotions. He was relieved to have escaped the strangely behaving sharks, and wanted to know why they were acting so weirdly—along with all the other animals in the BVIs. He was also angry that they still might be thrown off the mission and replaced with senior campers. Unexpected and dangerous things kept happening to them, and they still had no idea what was causing the die-offs. *Something* was going on in the British Virgin Islands, and now, more than ever, Tristan wanted to know what it was.

The fancy, yellow cart struck a bump and the rain abruptly stopped. Tristan leaned out and glanced up—a rock ceiling. They'd entered a tunnel. Yellowy-gold lights lined its rough, dark, rock walls. The drivers slowed as they went around a wide right-hand turn. The carts then rolled to a stop. They were in an underground cavern. It had a high ceiling and was about the size of a big gymnasium. Tristan's attention was drawn to a nearby dock. Tied up alongside was a small submarine. Except for the big transparent bubble at its front, like a giant bug's eye, the sub was painted pitch black. A bunch of milk-crate-like baskets sat nearby, along with some transparent plastic tubes and a stack of metal drums.

The doctor climbed out of her vehicle and pointed to a set of stainless steel doors. "Here's my lab. I've got some medical supplies inside. Should be able to bring down the swelling and put something on there to prevent infection. Dr. Gladfell, if you'll come with me? Kids, the drivers will take you to a room where you can dry off and get cleaned up. We'll meet you up there shortly."

Before Meg or the teens could say anything, the carts began rolling away. Tristan looked back curiously as the injured scientist disappeared behind the steel doors. *What exactly was this place?*

The carts then sped up and went around several switchbacks before exiting the tunnel. Back outside, Tristan noted that the rain was now just a drizzle. They stopped beside a stone walkway lined with neatly trimmed and manicured plants. Overhead, a green-and-white striped awning flapped in the breeze. The walkway led to what looked like a large, elegant home built of dark wood and tinted glass. The drivers nodded to the teens, indicating they should get out. Tristan wondered if they could talk at all.

Ryder was the first up the path. Rosina followed. Sam, Hugh, and Tristan stayed a short distance behind, as usual.

Tristan looked at the house and then turned to Sam and Hugh. "I think this is the island we saw from the plane. Remember the big mansion on the cliffs?"

Just then, as Ryder was about to knock on the heavy wood door at the end of the walkway, it opened. Standing before them was a beautiful, dark-haired woman in a yellow sarong.

"There you are. Mr. Marsh is busy at the moment, but he asked me to show you to a room where you can get cleaned up. Mr. Marsh also thought you might like to have lunch. Please wipe your feet here." She pointed to a furry, buttercup-yellow mat. "And if you would, put on some slippers. Mr. Marsh doesn't allow bare feet inside." She motioned to a row of simple white terrycloth slippers.

The teens looked curiously at the slippers and then at one another. Tristan and the others shrugged, dried their feet, and put on a pair of slippers. He couldn't help but think it wasn't just the sea creatures in the British Virgin Islands that were strange.

"Please follow me," the woman said, as she led them down a narrow, yellow-walled hallway.

They came to a museum-like rotunda with several arched passageways leading off in different directions. A fountain surrounded by towering palm trees and tropical ferns sat at the center of the round room. Water trickled over a series of small, black stone waterfalls, creating a bubbling gurgle. The floor was made of a similar black stone polished to a high sheen. Tristan thought he heard music, and then realized it was chirping, like the sound of birds and frogs in a jungle forest or swamp at night. A cloyingly sweet smell hung in the air. Things were getting more bizarre by the minute. They followed the yellow-sarong woman through one of the arches into another hallway. Soft lighting created a golden glow inside. They passed several dark, wood doors, each with a carving of a fish or a bird on it. The woman stopped by a door adorned with a pelican, opened it, and motioned for them to go in.

"This is the pelican suite. There are some dry

clothes for you, and feel free to take a quick shower if you'd like. Lunch is in fifteen minutes. I'll come back for you then." As she left, she closed the door.

Tristan and the others just stood there staring. The spacious sitting room was luxuriously decorated. Overstuffed couches and chairs framed in rich, dark mahogany were covered in a soft, woven, buttercup-yellow fabric. To the sides were two bedrooms, and, in front, a cliff-top patio overlooked an endless sea of gray-blue. Littered throughout the room were yellow pillar candles of varying heights. Tristan noticed the same sweet smell as before, but this time recognized it—vanilla. Then he heard a familiar gurgling sound. A fountain with water bubbling over smooth, dark stones sat off to one side. Tristan wasn't sure what the point of it all was, especially the fountains—except that they made him want to pee. He went to find a bathroom. The same yellow-obsessed decorator had done that room as well.

Ryder fell onto the sofa, sinking in. "I don't know about you guys, but I could get used to this. Pretty cushy."

"Do you think this is Mr. Marsh's home or a hotel?" Sam asked.

"Or, like, some kind of wacko spa," Tristan suggested, walking back in. The overdose of yellow, candles, soft lighting, and pee-inducing fountains gave him the creeps.

Sam picked up a pair of white drawstring pants from a stack on a table. They were miniature versions of the ones they'd seen Mr. Marsh wearing the night before. Matching gauze shirts lay close by.

"No, thanks, I'm not into the pajama look," Tristan said.

"You guys gonna take a shower?" Rosina asked.

"Nah," Tristan said. "I'm pretty dry, and besides, something about this place is freaking me out. Let's just wait for Meg and then get outta here."

Ryder stood up and took some clothes from the pile. "Why rush, dude, this place is way nicer than that tub of a ship we're stuck on. The shirts aren't too bad. I'm gonna rinse off."

Rosina went for a quick shower as well and put a shirt on over her swimsuit. Tristan, Sam, and Hugh refused to do either. They got some dry towels and wrapped them around their shoulders.

There was a knock at the door.

18

GOLDEN-FRIED DELICIOUSNESS

THE SCRUMPTIOUS SMELL OF FRESHLY FRIED FOOD made their mouths water and their stomachs growl. The teens had been led to a room with a long, glass wall overlooking the ocean. At the room's center was a lengthy table made of gleaming, pale wood. None of the teens, however, were looking at the view or sitting at the table. They all stood staring at a magnificent buffet set out on a side table. The spread was incredible—stacks of cheeseburgers, platters of french fries, chicken fingers, mozzarella sticks, and jalapeño poppers. All were fried to crispy golden perfection. The smell was overpowering, trance inducing.

"Mr. Marsh will be in shortly. Help yourselves," said the soft-spoken woman wearing the sarong. She then left the room.

Ryder didn't hesitate. He grabbed a plate, stacked it high with fried goodness, and sat down in one of the chairs around the long table. "Now this is what I'm talkin' about."

The others stared at him and at the food uncertainly.

"What? I'm, like, starving."

Tristan's stomach rumbled loudly enough to make Sam giggle. He and the others hit the buffet, piling their own plates high with golden-fried deliciousness.

A few moments later, the woman returned, followed by Meg. The scientist's injured foot was wrapped in bandages, and she was on crutches. She hopped in on one white slipper. Right behind her was the tall, lean man with streaked hair they'd seen the night before at the Bitter End. He was again outfitted in flowing white gauze. The room's lighting made him appear even more strangely orange than before.

"Hello, students," Meg said. "Please say hello to Mr. Marsh."

Through mouthfuls of food, they muttered, "Hi."

"Hellooo."

His voice was deep and he stretched the word out as if trying to get it to flow like the water in his fountains. "Welcommme to my island. Before we go on, what would you like to drink? Water, iced tea, or some lemonaaade?"

The teens made their requests and the woman in the sarong left the room.

"Please, go ahead and eat," Marsh encouraged them. "Dr. Gladfell, may I get you a plate?"

"Yes, thank you, and please call me Meg."

"How's your foot?" Sam asked.

"Much better, thank you. Don't think I'll be doing a jig anytime soon, though. But the swelling's gone down, and I've taken a strong antibiotic to prevent infection. Mr. Marsh's doctor was quite helpful, and he was just telling me about the fascinating research they're doing here."

"Is it a spa or something?" Tristan blurted out, noticing the dark eyeliner the man wore to highlight his intense, light-blue eyes.

"Ho, ho," Marsh laughed.

Tristan thought he sounded like a fake Santa Claus who'd had a little too much Christmas cheer.

"Nooo, no. I just like to keep things relaxing for my fellow investors; a calm retreat in this busy, hectic world."

"What sort of investors?" Hugh asked curiously.

"We do mainly pharmaceutical research and development here, young man. Did you all see my submersible on the way in?"

They nodded.

"We search the ocean for chemicals that can be used to make new drugs. My scientists collect samples, extract compounds, and then test them in the laboratory to see what effect they might have on cells and diseases, such as cancer. But enough about that. How's the food?"

"Good."

Tristan's mouth was full and he wasn't sure what to make of Marsh, so he just muttered, "Fine."

"Have you discovered any new drugs?" Hugh asked.

Marsh answered in an exaggerated whisper. "Son, I'm not at liberty to say." He then nodded very obviously to Hugh. "So, I hear you're here to study coral reefs."

At first no one responded. After an awkward silence, Tristan said, "Yeah, over the summer." He looked sheepishly to the others and drank some of the lemonade the woman had returned with.

"Coral reefs are of special interest to my scientists. Many reef organisms use chemicals in defense against predators. Would you like a tour of the lab before going back to your ship?"

Tristan wanted to say yes, but his tongue had suddenly gone numb and he was starting to feel surprisingly sleepy. In fact, he could hardly keep his eyes open and his head up. He turned to Sam. Her head was already resting on her arms. She appeared to be sound asleep. *That's odd,* was the last thing Tristan thought before everything went dark.

19

AN AFTERNOON NAP

Tristan's head felt like a large bowling ball. Just holding it up was nearly too much for his neck, which seemed to have turned into a weak, rubbery noodle. He tried to open his eyes, but that was difficult as well. When Tristan finally managed to pry open his eyelids, he discovered that they were back in the pelican suite. Sam and Hugh were slouched next to him on the couch. He couldn't remember how he got there or even finishing lunch.

"Like, dude, my head feels like it's gonna explode," Ryder groaned from somewhere nearby.

"Mine too," Hugh muttered. "What happened?"

"I'll tell you what happened," Meg said angrily. "We were drugged."

"Drugged?"

"Drugged," Meg repeated. "The question is *why*?"

They heard voices outside the door. Seconds later, Mr. Marsh walked in. Another abnormally large ex-pro-wrestler guy in an equally big yellow shirt followed him in. The man held a strangely shaped silver gun, and it was pointed at them.

"Good afternoon. Hope you had a nice, relaxing nap. So good just after lunch to rejuvenate the mind and senses."

"Are you nuts?" Tristan blurted out. "You drugged us."

"Son, that's much too harsh. Just a little assistance for a midday siesta. Besides, you've got a big decision to make. First things first, though—those nice little black bracelets you're wearing. I'll take those, please."

The campers hesitated until the big guy with the gun stepped forward as encouragement. They handed their tracker bracelets to Mr. Marsh.

"Marsh, what is going on here?" Meg demanded. "We'd like to go back to our ship *now*."

"Meg, just *relax*, calm down."

"Make that Dr. Gladfell, and don't tell me to relax. This is outrageous."

Marsh walked over to her. His yellow-shirted ape guard stood by the door, watching attentively. Marsh took her hand. "I really tried to get you all to leave on your own. I thought for sure the little incident at The Baths and your escapade in Gorda Sound last night would do the trick. By the way, how did you get out of that pool in the boulders without help?"

No one said a word.

"Well, never mind that for now. We'll have plenty of time to discuss it."

He patted Meg's hand condescendingly, dropped it to her lap, and picked up a remote control. A wall-mounted flat screen flickered to life. At first the picture was just clear blue water rushing past. Then a group of legs treading water in front of a reef came into view. One person was wearing fins. The other five had no need. The image circled around the group and then honed in on one person. Tristan was staring straight at the camera.

"Seems there's something quite unusual about your students, Dr. Gladfell."

"I don't know what you're talking about."

Marsh smoothed the front of his pajama shirt. "Oh, but I think you do. I was just going to frighten you all off, maybe cause an injury or two so you'd have to leave the islands. Even had some men standing by to get you out of that boulder pool. And my boat turned just enough to miss hitting you last night. But after I saw this, well . . . I know a good business opportunity when I see one."

"*You're* causing the die-offs," Tristan said. "That's why you're trying to get rid of us."

After he said it, Tristan wished he'd kept his big mouth shut—again. Now his heart was pounding along with his head.

Marsh stared at him like a specimen to study. "Now, I checked your feet when you were *relaxing*. No Aquamen in the room. So, tell me, how does it work?"

Tristan looked away, and the others were silent.

Tristan instinctively hid his hands and feet, even though they weren't webbed anymore. He turned angrily back toward Marsh, seriously wishing he was a whole lot bigger and stronger.

"Look, I'm really not a violent or bad man. I'm an entrepreneur, an investor, always on the lookout for a lucrative deal." He waved his arms around. "And as you can see, I've been quite successful. I have partners all over the world and live quite comfortably. We could use young, bright minds like yours and your, shall we say, unusual physical abilities. Can you dive deep? How and when do the webs emerge?"

You could hear a pin drop in the room.

Marsh turned off the television and put the remote down. He headed for the door. "Look, I'll give you some time to think about it. I've got several of my investment partners coming in this afternoon. I know one of them is already very interested in the video feed from my sharks. You decide. Would you like the opportunity of a lifetime to work with us? Or are you going to turn down my very generous business proposition? And by the way, don't think your friends from that ship will be coming to help anytime soon. It really is an old, worn-out vessel. One never knows when the engine might fail or, god forbid, a crack develops in the hull."

The men turned abruptly and left. Tristan got up and tried the door—locked. He looked out the sliding glass doors. The sheer drop from the patio was at least 100 feet, maybe more.

"I'm so sorry, campers," Meg said. "I never imagined that someone might purposely be causing the fish kills."

"We don't even know how or why he's doing it," Hugh said.

"I believe I do," Meg told them. "In fact, I might have made our situation worse. I asked that doctor about the submersible and those large metal barrels we passed in the carts. Did you see them?"

"Yeah."

"She said they're empty fuel drums. But that didn't sound right to me, so I asked what they did with the chemicals they use and experiment with in the laboratory. She gave me some lame answer about how they are shipped to a disposal station nearby. But there's no such thing. We have a real problem with chemical disposal at the institute in St. John. She was lying, and she knew I knew it."

"You mean they're dumping chemicals into the ocean?" Sam asked.

"I get it," Hugh said. "They're using the submersible. It's not just for collecting samples. They're using it to dump their waste. And it's black so they can do it at night."

Meg nodded. "That's what I think too, Hugh. With the sub, they can go unseen and release their waste at different places, different depths, so there's no clear pattern in the impacts. And remember how the dead animals in the cave were more active at night?"

"We've got to stop him," Tristan urged.

"Yeah," Sam added.

"But first we need to get out of here," Meg told them.

Rosina stared out the patio doors. "What's he going to do to us if we don't agree to work with him?"

They shook their heads. Tristan definitely didn't want to think about the answer to that question—some sort of *permanent* relaxation?

"How'd he know about the tracking bracelets?" Sam asked. The others shook their heads in response. "Well, at least back at camp they'll know where we are."

Hugh turned to Meg. "So what do we do? Just sit and wait for them to figure it out and come get us?"

"That might take a while. They may not even realize we're in trouble, and it sounds like folks on the ship could have their own problems right now. Let's look for a way out."

"And figure out what we're going to tell this guy. I don't like his idea of taking it easy," Tristan added.

20

PAJAMA PANTS

There was no way out. They were trapped in Marsh's creepy psycho spa. Rosina stood by the patio doors staring out, while Ryder lay draped on the couch. Tristan and Sam paced like caged animals, and Meg sat nearby, tapping her fingers anxiously on a table.

Hugh picked up the television remote and began flicking through stations. The selection was slim: a local news channel out of Tortola, a propaganda video about Marsh's company, a video of nature scenes accompanied by bad elevator music and fake chirping, and The Weather Channel.

"Uh-oh."

It was the tropical update. They were showing a satellite image of the Atlantic Ocean and Caribbean Sea.

Ryder opened his eyes. "Dude, like, so what? Who cares about the weather right now? It's rainy and gray outside. I can tell you that."

"*Like, dude,* look again," Hugh mocked.

Tristan knew immediately what had Hugh concerned. After all, he lived in Florida. "I thought it was too early for hurricanes."

That got everyone's attention. A satellite image showed a lima-bean-shaped swatch of yellow and red, indicating a developing storm. Spiraling bands around it suggested the beginnings of rotation. It was still well to the south and east of the British Virgin Islands.

"It may be early, but that doesn't mean we can't get a storm," Meg told them. "It's just less likely."

Hugh increased the volume. "The storm is forecasted to intensify and reach hurricane status overnight. The models, however, are not in agreement about the track." An image of colored spaghetti lines going in different directions from the storm came on. "Some have it going west into the Caribbean Sea; other models suggest it will take a more northerly track toward the British Virgin Islands."

Tristan stared outside. The weather didn't seem much worse than before. A *hurricane*? That's all they needed. Wasn't being trapped and threatened by a drug-making nutcase bad enough?

"Even if the storm does head this way," Meg said, "Looks like we still have some time before it hits. Maybe we can even use it to our advantage. Let's focus on getting out of here."

"Hey, come look at this," Rosina urged.

Meg stayed on the couch with her foot raised, but the others joined Rosina at the sliding glass doors.

"What?" Ryder asked, looking around outside.

Rosina pointed to some birds circling over the cliffs to their right.

"Yeah, they're birds."

"Frigatebirds," she told them. "Maybe they can help us."

Ryder went back to the couch. "Like, how can *they* help?"

"Why don't we try to get their attention?" Sam suggested, turning to Rosina. "Maybe you can talk to them."

"Happen to have any fish for them to steal?" Tristan asked sarcastically.

They searched for something to use to attract the birds. Hugh picked up a pair of the white pajama pants Marsh had left for them.

"Pants? Dude, I don't think they wear pajamas," Ryder said.

"No, but maybe their eyesight's not great." Hugh pulled the drawstring out of the top of the pants. From his pocket, he withdrew a smaller version of the multi-use tool he had carried around last year. "The other one was too big and not waterproof. Mom got me this to bring to camp this year." He opened a small knife blade and cut off a short piece of the drawstring. He waved it in the air. "Kinda looks like a fish."

"Worth a shot," Tristan said.

Hugh handed it to Rosina. "Try it."

She took it hesitatingly. "That's pretty lame."

"Just try it," Sam urged.

In the drizzling rain out on the patio, Rosina began waving and flicking the white piece of drawstring in the air. The frigatebirds soared effortlessly over the cliffs. Staying high overhead, two glided closer to the teens.

"Look, they're looking down," Sam said.

Rosina kept waving the string as if it was a wriggling fish. One of the birds dipped its head and dropped so that it was hovering just above her head. She laughed awkwardly.

"What's so funny?" Tristan asked.

"It asked if we're crazy or just plain stupid. Says it doesn't look anything like a fish."

"Well, it got their attention," Hugh noted. "See if they can help us."

"Okay, give me a minute."

The bird continued to hover overhead, gently rising and falling. The other frigate flew over.

"They don't like Marsh. He built over their best nesting area and is ruining the fishing. They want to know how they can help."

"Maybe they can create a distraction so we can escape," Tristan suggested.

"Or they could carry a note to the ship for us," Sam added.

Rosina passed on the suggestions and the birds agreed to try the note idea. Inside the suite, Hugh

found a pen and piece of heavily scented yellow sta-
tionary. While nearly gagging on the overpowering
smell of vanilla, Meg wrote a note. They rolled it up
and tied it with another piece of pajama-pant drawstring. Rosina raised the note above her head and the
frigatebird grabbed it with its talons. Flapping its long
black wings, the bird rose high into the sky. In the
strong winds aloft, it soared swiftly out of sight.

"Hope some other frigate doesn't try to steal it,"
Tristan said.

They went back inside.

"Well, that's something at least," Meg told them.

There was a soft rapping of knuckles on the door.

When the door opened, the group was surprised to see
the doctor, Maria. An armed gorilla guy was with her.

"Mr. Marsh would like to run a few tests on you."

Meg hopped up. "Maria, how can you go along
with this? They're just kids. Help us get out of here
and come with us."

"You'll have to stay here, Meg, while the rest of us
go down to the lab. And don't try anything; the seda-
tive in the guards' guns is quick acting and potent. It's
based on the venom from a cone snail. One of my own
discoveries."

Tristan crossed his arms and planted his feet.
Clearly, he wasn't planning to go anywhere. Tristan

was scared, but his anger gave him courage. The other teens followed Tristan's lead and remained firmly planted where they were.

"Now, don't make this difficult. We could just shoot you and carry you down there unconscious," the doctor told them.

Another burly security guard entered the room to emphasize the point.

"Go ahead," Meg said to the teens. "It'll be okay."

The campers reluctantly followed the doctor out the door. Tristan was the last to leave. As he passed Meg, she secretly slipped something into his hand. He slid it into the pocket of his swimsuit as inconspicuously as possible.

21

A HUGH SURPRISE

THEY WERE MARCHED THROUGH THE MAIN HOUSE to an elevator. The guards stayed close by the entire time. One whole side of Marsh's mansion was built of glass and overlooked the ocean. Tristan had to admit it was impressive. On the other hand, the overdose of yellow, scented candles, fake chirping, and gurgling fountains made him feel like a cat with a giant hair ball—ready to gag.

Ryder stared at the sweeping view of the ocean and the mansion's fine furnishings. "You know, I could get used to living in a place like this."

The others glared at him murderously.

"Hey, I'm just saying, like, the lifestyle's not bad."

Once the group was inside, the elevator descended. After stopping, the doors slid open to a large laboratory. It was gleaming white and silver, the exception being the yellow lab coats worn by the half-dozen scientists working at long benches with high-powered microscopes, spectrometers, and other sophisticated instruments. Marsh's people glanced up only briefly when the teens were led in.

"This won't hurt a bit," the doctor told them.

"Speak for yourself," Rosina snarled.

With sufficient prodding by the armed guards, the doctor was able to weigh, measure, and stand each camper in front of a three-dimensional X-ray scanning system. She also drew samples of their blood. Tristan had always hated going to the doctor for checkups. Being Marsh's lab rat was *way* worse. He had an overwhelming urge to smash all the fancy equipment to the floor.

With his anger and frustration growing by the minute, Tristan watched the guards closely, looking for an opportunity to escape or do something. He prayed they wouldn't discover what was in his pocket. Luckily, it didn't show up on the X-ray. Hugh wasn't so fortunate. His multi-purpose tool was quickly taken away.

"I've seen the video," the doctor told them. "I know about the webbed feet. So, how does it work?"

Silence. The teens stared purposely at the doctor, tightened their lips, and said nothing.

"We have ways of getting it out of you, you know. It would be much better if you just cooperate. Besides, Marsh is a very generous employer."

They shook their heads.

"Well, you can't say I didn't try. Joseph, could you

please take them to the pools? I believe Mr. Marsh would like to show them to our guests personally."

One of the guards nodded and poked Sam in the back with his tranquilizer gun. The teens were then herded toward a set of metal double doors.

Two of the souped-up yellow golf carts were waiting for them in the cavern beneath Marsh's mansion. Tristan thought about trying to escape right then. He could dive into the water next to the black submersible. But he wasn't sure where the water led or that he could get away before being darted. And he didn't really want to go alone. Tristan decided to wait, hoping there would be another and better opportunity to get away. He felt for the small plastic bag in his pocket.

The carts sped through and out of the tunnel. The rain had stopped, but the weather outside was gloomy. Dark gray clouds filled the sky, and a strong breeze was blowing. They drove past a large white yacht alongside the dock. It hadn't been there earlier.

The carts stopped by a hot tub shaped like a scallop shell. Nearby was a swimming pool with a floating blow-up yellow raft and lounge chair. Tristan assumed those really were for relaxing. The guards got out and escorted the teens to a group of round pools a little farther away. These clearly weren't for chilling out in. One pool was empty. In each of the other three, a huge gray shark was circling. Two of the sharks had cameras mounted on their backs. A gate at the end of each pool separated it from a larger rectangular pool.

Tristan's attention was drawn to the far end of the bigger pool. He squinted, trying to better see what was there. It looked like a square opening of some sort, maybe the entrance to a tunnel. He turned to the connecting shark pools and then looked back at the opening. It had to be a tunnel so the sharks could swim out. Tristan nudged Sam and Hugh, who were standing beside him. He nodded toward the entrance to the tunnel. He then dramatically began gasping, pointing at the sharks, and backing into his friends—as if it was the scariest thing he'd ever seen. Tristan thought for sure he'd overdone the acting job, but the guards laughed at his feigned fright. Meanwhile, he had quietly slipped the plastic bag out of his pocket to show Sam and Hugh. "Meg," Tristan whispered.

Two more carts pulled up next to the pools. Marsh hopped out of one, but the men in the other vehicle remained seated, hidden from view behind the driver.

While the guards' attention was on their approaching boss, Sam whispered to Tristan and Hugh, "You should take them and go get help."

Hugh shook his head. "No, Sam, *you* go with Tristan."

Marsh was now too close for them to say anything more without being overheard.

"So, if you won't tell me how your unusual abilities work, maybe you'll demonstrate them for me and a few of my partners. And you can choose whichever pool you'd like." The man did his slurred Santa laugh.

"We can't just make it, like, happen," Ryder said.

The others glared at him, silently telling him to shut up.

"Thank you, young man. Then how does it work?"

"Don't say anything," Tristan said angrily. "And what did you do to the sharks?"

Marsh stared at Tristan as if deciding what to do next. "I'll tell you, if you tell me."

Tristan shook his head adamantly.

"I'll tell you anyway, because eventually *you will* tell me exactly what I want to know. A little drug intervention to relax the sharks, make them more pliable. We then enhance their electro-sensing capabilities, and with some electrodes embedded below the cameras— we can pretty much control where the sharks go and what they do."

"That's horrible," Sam said. "You're torturing them."

"They're just stupid sharks," Marsh responded.

Tristan imagined strangling Marsh and throwing him to the sharks.

"Look, dude, like I was saying," Ryder interjected. "We can't just will our feet to get webs."

Marsh turned to Ryder. "So how does it work, then?"

"What's in it for us?"

Sam shook her head. "No way, you can't tell."

Never in a million years did Tristan expect what happened next.

Hugh stepped forward. "Uh, sir. I'll . . . I'll show you."

The other teens stared at Hugh like he just said he loved swimming with sharks.

Hugh turned to Sam and Tristan so the others couldn't see him and winked. Tristan couldn't believe it. He seriously hoped Hugh knew what he was doing. Tristan decided to play along with whatever his friend had in mind.

"Don't listen to him," Hugh said, staring at Ryder. "If the pool is saltwater and I jump in, the webbing will come out."

"Hugh?" Rosina muttered.

Ryder stared at him, clearly baffled.

Tristan covertly slipped two red pills from the small plastic bag. "You can't tell him!" he shouted, lunging at Hugh. He pretended to stumble and bumped into Sam, secretly passing her a pill.

Hugh shook his head and stepped away from them, as if divorcing himself from their childish behavior.

"So glad one of you has finally come to your senses," Marsh said. "You will be well rewarded, son. But hold on, my partners will want to see this." He waved to the men in the cart.

As the men walked toward them, the teens' eyes grew wide. Tristan nearly choked. One man appeared to be your average well-to-do businessman in a suit and tie. The other man was short and thick around the middle, with a goatee, black beady eyes, and a head like a slightly hairy bowling ball—overall, very toad-like.

"Rickerton," Tristan muttered under his breath, letting his hair fall down to hide his face.

The other teens ducked their heads so he wouldn't see their faces, either.

"So nice to see you *again*," J.P. Rickerton offered, his voice laced with malice. "I'm so very sorry I didn't get to meet you personally, last summer, *in the Bahamas*. When I heard that my good friend and business associate here, Mr. Marsh, had discovered some teenagers with unusual swimming skills . . . well, you can just imagine how it piqued my interest."

Hugh was now visibly shaking. "So, do you want to see this or not?"

"Yes, young man, please go ahead," Marsh said. "Choose your pool." He laughed again. "I expect you'd like the one that is shark free."

"Yeah, thanks, that was going to be my choice." Hugh glanced briefly at Sam and Tristan, and then walked over to the empty pool. He stood staring at it and at the gate that separated it from the bigger pool and the ones with the sharks. Throwing off the towel from around his shoulders, Hugh took a deep breath. He then jumped into the water. Within seconds, he was back at the surface. "Okay, it might take a minute or two for, you know, the webbing to come out." Hugh stared directly at Tristan and Sam when he added, "I have to concentrate to make it happen."

Tristan then realized what he was going to do, or at least try to do, and got ready.

"Okay, watch closely." Hugh dove to the bottom of the pool. He then whipped off his swimsuit and flattened himself against the pool's white concrete base. Seconds later, Hugh simply disappeared.

"What the—!" Marsh exclaimed.

As Marsh, Rickerton, the other man, the guards, and even Ryder and Rosina ran to the side of the pool to look for Hugh, Tristan grabbed Sam's hand. "Now!"

They swallowed the pills and sprinted to the larger pool. Without stopping, they dove in and swam hard. Tristan prayed the pills would work quickly and that he was right about the square opening at the far end of the pool. They headed straight for it. Tristan let Sam enter first and then followed. It was just as he hoped; the entrance to a tunnel. The smooth-walled passageway swung right in a wide, sweeping turn. They kicked hard, racing to get away from Marsh and his goons.

By the time the dart-wielding security guards got to the tunnel entrance, Tristan and Sam were gone. The two muscle-bloated men stood helpless with a look of complete disbelief on their faces.

Hugh was only able to mimic the color and texture of the pool bottom for about thirty seconds. After that, he put his swimming shorts back on and popped to the surface. He raised his very normal hands to the men staring down at him. "Sorry, guess it didn't work."

Marsh scowled and ran to a poolside cottage, nearly tripping over his pajama pants. He opened the door, stepped inside, and came out holding some sort of computer tablet.

"You imbecile, those other two are getting away!" Rickerton shouted. "Get them!"

"No worries," Marsh responded calmly.

As Rosina helped Hugh out of the pool, Marsh tapped on the tablet screen. Two of the pool gates began to rise noisily.

Marsh tapped a few more times on the tablet and then ordered one of the security guards to radio the speedboat drivers. "Tell them to recover whatever's left after the sharks are through." Then he turned to Hugh, Rosina, and Ryder. "I don't really need all of you, anyway." He eyed Hugh. "That was a very interesting trick, something else we'll need to discuss."

"This changes the deal," Rickerton barked at Marsh.

"We'll just make an adjustment in the investment required."

The drizzle turned back to rain, and the men headed for the protection of the carts.

"Come along, kids," Marsh said. "Let's go have a little chat with your *professor*—Dr. Gladfell."

The security guards ushered the teens into a cart, staying even closer than before. As they drove back to the main facility, Rosina and Ryder stared at Hugh. He returned their gaze with an uncharacteristically mischievous and self-satisfied grin.

Inside the tunnel it was dim, and there was just a thin layer of air near the top. Tristan and Sam made it through the wide turn, popped up, and twisted their necks to get a breath. Just then, the sound of something mechanical reverberated through the water, like metal gears grinding. Tristan and Sam looked at one another, clearly thinking the same thing about the source of the noise. They dove, kicking their now-webbed feet even harder. They entered a long straight-away. Up ahead, it looked a little brighter. Tristan couldn't resist. He paused and glanced back. Then wished he hadn't. Something big and dark was in the tunnel, and it was swimming toward them, fast. He put on a burst of speed, swimming up to Sam and waving for her to go faster. Minutes later, they shot out of the tunnel into open blue water and made for the surface. He looked back. A camera-carrying bull shark was just exiting the tunnel. And it wasn't alone.

Tristan and Sam porpoised once for air and dove. They swam as fast as they could. Tristan looked for a place to hide, knowing they couldn't outswim the sharks. There were just a few scattered corals, some small rocks, and a big patch of sea grass. Making it a big zero for spots to hide from the we-want-to-eat-you sharks. As scared, angry, and freaked out as he was, Tristan tried to concentrate as he swam. He repeat-edly told the sharks that they were the good guys. He glanced back and again wished he hadn't. Coming straight for him was a giant mouthful of razor-sharp teeth. Tristan squeezed his eyes shut, thinking this was not the way "shark boy" should bite it.

He felt a rush of water at his toes and then waited for the searing pain that was sure to follow. Instead, Tristan heard a heavy thud. He stopped swimming and looked back. Toes—he still had toes. A flash of gray raced by. It was a dolphin. Then he saw another. Two dolphins were racing around and head-butting the sharks. Bolting for the surface, Tristan and Sam nearly ran headfirst into a gigantic black manta ray. Behind it were more rays. There were at least twenty manta and eagle rays swimming like a flock of giant under-water birds. They began to circle protectively around the teens.

Tristan heard the manta. *Hey, chap, stick with us. We've bloody well had enough of these blokes.*

"Tell the dolphins to hit the cameras," Tristan suggested to Sam. "Maybe they can break them off or something. That's what's controlling the sharks. I'll tell the rays to help by distracting them."

Sam communicated with the dolphins. One then hit the camera atop one of the sharks. It didn't move. The other dolphin charged in and hit the camera harder. Meanwhile, half of the manta and eagle rays swarmed around the other shark to keep it busy. The dolphins hit the camera again, and this time it slipped to the side. Soon the camera came loose, but it remained attached by wires embedded in the shark's back. The shark abruptly stopped swimming. It shook its head and its cloudy eyes cleared.

The dolphins then worked on the other shark's camera. It, too, came loose. Once free of Marsh's elec-troshock mind control, the sharks hung motionless in a daze. Tristan explained where they were and what had happened. If they could have turned red with anger, they would have been the first-ever scarlet-colored sharks. With blood seeping out from around the wires on their backs, the two bull sharks swam off, swearing to get even.

"Do you think they'll be okay?" Sam asked Tristan.

"Hope so. C'mon, let's get out of here."

The sound of an engine firing up echoed across the water.

"The dolphins say to follow them," Sam said.

"Rays say the same thing."

Led by the dolphins and surrounded by rays, the two teens swam away from Scar Island as fast as they could.

22

NEW ARRIVALS

Tristan and Sam were led south into the deeper water between Scar and Eustatia Islands. They stayed submerged as much as possible. When they did go to the surface, it was just a brief sea turtle head bob for air. At one point, Tristan paused to look back. Two speedboats were slowly motoring in a widening search pattern off Scar Island. One boat seemed to be headed in their direction.

Sam came up beside him. "C'mon let's keep going."

Tristan nodded, and the two of them rejoined their sea creature escorts. He waited until they were on the other side of Eustatia to again turn back. So far, neither of the speedboats had followed them around the island. The Bitter End Yacht Club wasn't too far away, but they had a new problem. Another boat was motoring slowly past Saba Rock toward them. Tristan could see the outlines of two people inside the small boat's covered cabin.

"Do you think it's more of Marsh's ape goons?" Sam whispered nervously.

"Different kind of boat, but could be. Let's swim around it just in case."

Right before diving down to go under and around the boat, Sam stopped. "Hang on." She stared at the boat as it slowly came closer. Minutes later, she began waving her arms. "It's Coach!"

The boat sped to the teens. Coach cut the engine. At the stern, someone climbed out to help Sam and Tristan onto a small dive platform. It was Mary, the owner of the Bitter End.

"Get in and stay down in case anyone is watching," Coach Fred ordered.

Mary handed them each a towel, staring at their hands and feet. "Oh my."

Coach did a U-turn and punched the throttle. Several rays and two dolphins jumped high out of the water. Tristan hadn't even had a chance to thank them for their help. Both Sam and Tristan began talking at once.

Coach Fred held up his hands. "Okay, okay. One at a time."

Tristan let Sam explain.

"Coach, that Marsh guy we saw last night, he's a total nutjob. We escaped, but he's still got the others. He's the one causing the fish kills, and he's torturing sharks. *And* he knows about the webs, and . . ."

Coach put up a hand to interrupt. "Okay, slow down and tell me exactly what happened starting from when you left the ship this morning."

After the two teens explained, Tristan wanted to immediately go back to Scar Island to get Hugh and the others. But Coach convinced him they needed a plan. He also told the teens about the unexpectedly large hole that had mysteriously appeared in the *Reef Runner's* hull. Captain Hank was furious. He made Charlie and Sarah bail while he and Coach built a temporary patch. Meanwhile, reports about the developing storm started coming in, and the teens were overdue from their swim. A search boat was sent out from the Bitter End. Coach also called Flash at camp to get the group's location based on the tracker bracelets. While he was on his cell phone, a frigatebird dropped a note, which strangely smelled like vanilla, right on top of Coach Fred's head. After that, the captain basically threw Coach off at the Bitter End and took the *Reef Runner* to an anchorage where they could make a more permanent repair and potentially ride out the developing storm. The captain told Coach and the others he didn't want anything more to do with them or the trouble that followed them around.

When the boat arrived back at the Bitter End, the group went quickly and quietly to Mary's home on the hill behind the office building.

Coach was grim. "My fault, guys. I should have pulled you out sooner."

"No way, Coach," Tristan told him. "We wanted to stay."

"Yeah," Sam said. "And now we have to get Hugh and the others out of there."

"And stop psycho pajama man from killing more animals," Tristan added.

"Don't worry. Director Davis is flying in with some senior campers and we're going to launch a rescue mission."

"What? Without us?" Tristan blurted out angrily. "You can't send us home *now*! No way, we want to go with you."

Sam nodded vigorously.

Coach's initial look was enough to make Tristan wish, once again, he'd kept his mouth shut, but then the man's expression softened. "Hunt, we're not sending you home. You've done well and proven that you can think on your feet. Besides, given the situation and the storm brewing, we'll need to make our move as quickly as possible, and you have intel and skills that will be critical to the operation."

Tristan sighed with relief. He wasn't going to have to leave or even fight to stay. He had to help save Hugh and the others, and stop Marsh—permanently.

"Mr. Coach?" Mary said.

"Yes?"

"Speaking of the storm. I've already notified my guests. They've started leaving. We can't take any chances. Boats are pulling out as well, heading to safer harbors."

"I understand," Coach Fred said. "However, the approaching storm could be just the distraction we need to get onto Scar Island and get our people out. Mary, if the storm does come this way, is there a safe place to ride it out?"

The woman pulled out a map of the Bitter End property. "If it's a category one or two, we should be fine; anything much stronger and no guarantees. Here, on the southwestern side of the property, we built a hurricane shelter about halfway up the hill."

Tristan decided that was about the only good news they'd had in days.

"Roger that. Good to know. So all we need to do is find a way onto Scar Island, get into Marsh's compound undetected, and then get the three campers and Meg out, preferably without anyone noticing."

"Is that all?" Tristan said sarcastically.

Coach gave him a withering look.

Exhausted, Tristan just shrugged. "Hey, I've had a really bad two days and my friends are stuck with a full-fledged nutcase with sleep guns."

A wall-mounted radio then squawked to life. "Bitter End, Bitter End. Hey, Mary, got your guests. We're approaching the dock."

Mary jumped up. "Looks like your friends have arrived. Please make yourselves comfortable. I've got to talk to the ferry captain and make sure the staff is preparing for the storm. Just let me know how I can help or what you need." She hurried out the door.

Coach Fred got up as well, turning to Tristan and Sam. "You two stay here. Get some rest. We'll be back shortly." He, too, ran out the door.

"Well, at least he didn't just tell us to *relax*," Tristan said to Sam.

A short time later, Coach Fred returned to Mary's home at the Bitter End. Following him were Director Davis and two senior campers—Mia and Luis. Tristan was surprised to see the two teens. They were the campers he'd searched for spies with earlier in the summer. The director went immediately to Sam and wrapped her in a big bear hug. He then patted Tristan heartily on the back. "Well done, campers. Tell me everything."

Sitting with the group around a small table, Tristan and Sam again recounted what had happened and everything they could remember about Scar Island and Marsh's facility. They even tried to draw a map of the place. Coach Fred and the director peppered them with questions about how many men there were, what sort of weapons they carried, how many boats they had, and where Meg, Hugh, Rosina, and Ryder were being held.

"Uh, director?" Tristan said hesitantly.

"Yes?"

"Do my parents know about the storm and everything?"

"I called all of the parents personally to tell them I was coming here to ensure your safety should the storm come this way. About the rest of it, I think it's best if we keep that to ourselves for now."

Tristan nodded. He figured eventually it would all come out, and this would undoubtedly be his first and last mission. But right now he just wanted to get Hugh and the others off Scar Island and stop Marsh. He'd worry about his parents later.

A weather update on the television attracted the group's attention.

"The storm is intensifying. It is expected to be at least a category one or two by morning. It's tracking north-northwest. It's still unclear if the British Virgin Islands will take a direct hit, but the islands are going to get strong winds and heavy rain starting overnight."

"Looks like it'll be a little rough out there tonight," the director said.

"Nothing we can't handle," Coach responded. "Right campers?"

"Right, Coach," Luis said.

"Yup," Mia added.

Sam and Tristan didn't say anything. They looked at Coach Fred and gave the slightest of nods. The rush of escaping from psycho pajama man Marsh and not being eaten by mind-controlled sharks had faded. Tristan was determined to help Hugh and the others, but he was also bone tired and had started thinking. Thinking about Marsh, his goons, Rickerton, and a hurricane that may be headed their way. Tristan didn't want to admit it, but he was scared. He also started to have doubts. Could they really rescue Hugh and the others? Was he good enough to be part of a rescue team at night in a storm? What if they all got caught? What if someone got hurt?

As if reading Tristan's mind, the director calmly put his hands together and spoke in a soft but confident tone. "Campers, it's okay to be scared. Fear is perfectly normal. It can actually help us be better prepared, take caution when needed, and grow stronger. As Luis and Mia can tell you, this is something the older teens work on at camp. You'll learn to control your fear and channel it to fuel your actions. And working together as a team, we are much stronger and smarter than any individual, no matter how powerful he or she may seem."

The director's speech made Tristan feel a little better. Besides, when he didn't think so much about what could go wrong, he did fine. Maybe that was the problem. Tristan decided he was thinking too much. He just had to believe in himself and the team.

"That's right, campers, we're a team," Coach Fred added cockily. "Together, we'll rescue the others and do away with the bad guy. Now, enough of the mushy stuff; time to come up with a plan." He looked at the chart they'd been using to mark the locations of the fish die-offs. Several sites on Scar Island had been highlighted. "We should leave as soon as it's fully dark."

Director Davis stood up and began pacing. "From what you've said, they'll probably be in either the guest suite of the mansion or in the laboratory. Luis can go in through the patio to check the suite."

"How?" Sam asked. "That cliff is wicked high and really steep."

"No problem," Luis answered. "I think you know

my little sister, Melissa. She's a Squid. We have similar talents."

Tristan thought back to their challenge at the lagoon. Melissa was the tree climber who squashed their chances of winning. She had sticky hands and feet like a sea star.

"Mia, Sam, and Tristan, you'll go with Coach Fred. Get some of our friends to help and then find the entrance to that cavern. If they're launching a submersible from there, it must be connected to the sea. We'll also need another distraction to keep Marsh's security team busy beyond just storm preparations."

Mia smiled. "I've got that one covered. Well, not really me, but, you know, one of the other *friends* we brought along." She explained to the others.

"What about Rickerton?" Tristan asked. "And they know about our webbed feet."

"Right now our priority is to get the others out of there safely," the director said. "Then we'll worry about Mr. Marsh and our old friend Rickerton."

Outside, the passing squalls became more frequent, hitting the Bitter End with strong, gusty winds and driving sheets of rain. Whitecaps topped the chop blowing across Gorda Sound. The last ferry of the evening departed, packed with guests leaving early. Boats were moved off their moorings in search of more sheltered coves, and the yacht club's staff stored or tied down anything that could become a flying projectile in hurricane-strength winds. As darkness fell at the Bitter End, another group was also preparing to depart.

23

HAMMER TIME

POWERED BY STRONG WINDS, THE SMALL MID-night-blue catamaran cut through the waves. It sailed silent and swift. If a gust hit the dark sails full on, the small sailboat could turtle, flipping over. Mary expertly worked the lines and rudder to avoid just such a mishap. She maneuvered around the reef off Eustatia Island and then tacked back and forth, heading stealthily toward Scar Island. Beside her, Luis reported the weather and sea conditions on a small waterproof radio. As they got closer, he noted the activity on the island—at least, as much as he could see.

Meanwhile, Coach Fred, Tristan, Mia, and Sam were in a small, black inflatable they borrowed from the Bitter End. They skirted the edge of Gorda Sound and tucked in behind Saba Rock, where it was still relatively calm. Coach put the engine into neutral, the teens each swallowed a red, rubbery pill, and Mia slid into the water. Mia was known at camp for two things. She could dive deep and communicate with almost any type of fish or invertebrate. Things with a shell seemed to take a particular liking to her. Tristan and Sam followed her in. Several enormous silver fish immediately surrounded them. Mary had tried to prepare them, but even so, Tristan was still unnerved. Regular happy-hour feedings at Saba Rock made for some seriously big tarpons. Each was at least five feet long and thick with muscle. They were intimidating even for a shark boy.

Mia had a quick conversation with the meaty tarpons. They agreed to act as guides in and just outside of the lagoon. But the tarpons wouldn't go too close to Scar Island. Most creatures stayed away from the place due to some ultra nasty sharks and rumors about what went on there.

The teens climbed back into the boat. Tristan was thankful for something else they'd borrowed from the Bitter End—black neoprene wetsuits. Along with providing warmth, the wetsuits would help them hide within the night's darkness. And now that they were out doing something, Tristan felt more confident. He just had to stay focused, keep busy, and remember not to think about what could go wrong.

"Okay, Coach," Mia said. "The tarpon are ready, and the sea turtles are getting into position."

"Excellent work, Miss Chen." Coach responded. He then looked to Sam and Tristan.

"Sorry, Coach, no sharks or rays around," Tristan said disappointedly.

"No dolphins, either."

"Okay, let's deploy the distraction team and then find the entrance to that cavern with the sub."

With the tarpons in front and a few sea turtles following behind, the black inflatable motored slowly through the lagoon. They stayed in the lee of Virgin Gorda and out of the strongest winds as much as possible. The tarpons led them to a narrow channel through a coral reef off Virgin Gorda. It was a shortcut to Scar Island. Coach steered carefully into the channel and passed the sharp coral.

Outside the reef, the rolling seas lifted, dropped, and rocked the boat. The teens held on tight and braced their legs against the boat's rubber sides. As they neared Scar Island, the tarpons departed. The wind and seas calmed. Coach slowed the boat to a quiet crawl, and they crouched down inside.

At the well-lit main dock, yellow carts wheeled back and forth from the yacht. Tristan figured they were preparing to leave because of the approaching storm.

"We need to stay out of that light," Coach whispered, slowing the engine further and swinging the boat well to the right of the docks. The teens ducked down even lower.

As they got closer, the island protected them more fully from the wind and waves. Coach cut the engine. The black inflatable glided silently forward, its momentum taking them nearer to the shore. Mia slid into the water to confirm the plan with the sea turtles and the many-legged hitchhiker aboard one of them.

"Coach, we're pretty close to the tunnel into those

pools. Can I swim in and try to get that last shark out?" Tristan whispered. "The one without a camera on it."

"Hunt, I know you'd like to, but it's not a good idea. Besides, how would you get the gate up?"

"I'll find a way."

Coach shook his head.

Mia climbed back aboard. "They're off."

"Bitter End, come in?" Coach said softly into the radio.

"Bitter End here, go ahead." The director had stayed behind to coordinate the rescue and give them real-time updates on the weather.

"We're ready for 'Hammer Time.'"

"Roger that. Good work. Hobie One's all set as well, and the next squall line should hit in about ten minutes."

"Roger, standing by, Dark Star out."

Tristan thought about their secret weapon. "How'd you get Hammer to come?"

"The mantis shrimp is from a reef around here," Coach whispered. "He gets to come home and take his anger out in a more productive way. Besides, Chen here has helped him deal with some of his issues." Mia nodded, acknowledging her skill in crustacean psychology.

Following Coach's lead, the teens rose up in the boat just enough to see the shore. A bouncing light was moving through the pool area.

"Must be a guard on patrol," Coach told them. "Everyone stay down."

The light bounced its way to the small docks and then swung toward one of the speedboats. In the reflection from the boat's white hull, they could see a man staring into the water. Tristan held his breath, hoping the guy didn't notice any unusual activity under the boat. The light swung out over the water in their direction. They ducked below the inflatable's black rubber sides. Abruptly, the light swung back, shining on another of the tied-up speedboats.

"Bet Hammer just did his thing," Coach said. "Stay low; we'll give it a few minutes and then motor slowly out and go around the docks to find that cavern entrance."

Just then, something big and heavy thumped into the inflatable, shoving them sideways. Tristan thought they must have hit a rock or run aground. He tentatively rose up and peered over the side. Two huge gray dorsal fins passed by, one behind the other. Tristan looked closer. Each of the sharks had a camera trailing from wires embedded in its back. They did a U-turn and nudged the inflatable with their snouts.

"What's going on?" Mia questioned nervously.

"It's the sharks that chased us earlier," Tristan said with relief. "Don't worry, they're on our side now. I bet they want to help. Sam, hold onto my legs."

Tristan leaned over the boat so that his head and shoulders were in the water. Sam grabbed his legs to hold him steady. He twisted around, looking for the sharks, thinking: *Hey, you guys want to help us get our friends? That psycho guy who tortured you has them.*

You bloody well believe it, a shark answered. *But our mate is still stuck in there.*

Hang on, Tristan told the sharks. As he sat back up, Tristan happened to glance toward the dock. A bunch of lights were converging around one of the speedboats.

"Looks like Hammer was a hit," Coach Fred told them. "A few high-speed whacks to crack the hull and that baby's going down." He then radioed the director to say that phase one of their plan was well underway. "Okay, we'll meet up with the turtles and Hammer on the way."

"Coach, the sharks want to help, but they want to free their mate in the pool first. Can I help them do it?"

"Me too," Sam offered. "Then we'll come find you. It'll be quick. Besides, we still have to wait to hear from Luis."

Coach hesitated. "Okay, you two go with the sharks, but be careful. Do not be seen and make it fast. If you can't get the gate up, leave immediately. Come find us; we'll need you two."

"Thanks, Coach."

Tristan slid into the water, followed by Sam.

Coach Fred started the engine, keeping it as slow and as quiet as possible. Tristan and Sam followed the two bull sharks toward the tunnel that led into Marsh's pools.

To the north, the small, dark catamaran sailed slowly
past Scar Island's steep northwestern cliffs. In the
rough seas, Mary couldn't bring the Hobie Cat to a
complete stop, so she slowed down just enough to let
Luis take a Sea Camp pill and jump off without breaking any bones. He swam close to shore and waited,
treading water. His timing had to be perfect or he'd be
brutally smashed against the rocks, definitely breaking
bones . . . or worse. The water began to rise as a wave
approached. Luis began kicking. He was lifted up with
the wave and then, just before it crashed ashore, Luis
jumped. He grabbed for the rocks with his sea-star-
sticky hands and feet. The wave hit and water cascaded
all around him. A powerful surge then tried to pull him
back into the ocean. But Luis stayed put, stuck to the
rocks. All that practice in the Wave Pool had paid off.

Luis crouched, waiting for the squall line to hit.
The strong winds would make the precarious climb
more difficult, but the rain would hide him from any
prying eyes or cameras. The black wetsuit helped there
as well. As the wind picked up, rain pelted his back.
Luis ducked his head and began to climb. He was even
better than his sister (or most mountain goats). Mon-
keys had nothing on him. His hands and feet clung to
the rocks, held by hundreds of miniature suction cups
tipped with sticky glue. In fact, if he lingered too long
in any one spot, Luis had to forcefully pull himself off
the rocks. Going faster was better. He swiftly scaled
the sheer cliff to the edge of a patio deck. Luis began to
pull himself up. From out of the dark, two giant black

birds dove for his head; each had a hooked bill, forked tail, and incredibly long, sharp talons.

Luis froze and muttered, "Hey! I'm one of the good guys."

The birds passed just inches from his face and then hovered menacingly over his head. One bird again lunged threateningly at him. Unfortunately, Luis couldn't talk bird. He glanced around desperately. The wind pounded his body, and rain pinged off his head. The giant black birds stayed overhead, seemingly at the ready to peck his eyes out. Luis scrambled to the left, keeping a close eye on the birds. There was another patio not too far away.

He hesitantly reached to pull himself up. The birds made no move to attack. Luis hauled himself onto the deck, staying as low as possible. A bird dove. He ducked. It brushed by his ear before assaulting a fixture on the mansion's outer wall. Luis looked closer—it was a security camera. He nodded his thanks to the bird and then crept to a set of sliding glass doors. Cupping his hands around his eyes, he put his nose up against the glass and peered in. It was dark, and the room looked empty. He tried the doors; they slid open. He went inside. Nobody home.

24

THE SHARK-MOBILE

BACK AT THE DOCKS, MEN IN FOUL WEATHER GEAR with flashlights swarmed around the speedboat that had inexplicably begun to take on water. Meanwhile, the dark inflatable had disappeared into the stormy night. And Sam and Tristan were heading for the tunnel into Marsh's pools.

At first, Sam hesitated. But once she saw Tristan do it, she was all in. Now each of them had hold of a shark's dorsal fin and were being pulled alongside the shark. The powerful bull sharks moved quickly, silently, and smoothly through the water. Periodically, they rose to the surface so Tristan and Sam could get a breath of air. For Tristan, it was the best mode of underwater transport ever. And with the sharks' night vision guiding them, Sam didn't even need to turn on the small dive light strapped to her wrist. At night, without lights, under shark power, and in their black wetsuits, the teens were practically invisible as they slipped into the tunnel.

The sharks slowed. The passageway was cramped and pitch black, darker even than the night. Tristan held on tightly to the shark's fin. Entering the sweeping curve, the sharks brought them up for air. Tristan and Sam hit their heads and twisted their necks to get a breath. A few minutes later, they exited the tunnel. The sharks took them directly to the closed gate of the one occupied pool.

"Now what?" Sam asked softly.

"The sharks think the controls to the gate are in one of the cottages by the pools."

The two teens popped up just enough to look around for any yellow-shirted ape-men guards with tranquilizer guns. Luckily, the security team was still crowded around the sabotaged speedboat. Sam took the dive light off her wrist and turned it on, using one hand to shield the beam. They quietly climbed out of the pool. Almost immediately, Tristan ran into a lounge chair. It slid, scraping loudly over the concrete. He froze, his heart once again hammering. Sam stopped and turned off the light. They stood very still, holding their breath. The security team's attention remained focused at the docks. Sam turned the light back on, and they crept more carefully to the nearest cottage. The door was unlocked. They went inside. Lying on the floor was a giant blow-up shark, a pile of buttercup-yellow pool noodles, and a matching raft with a drink holder and little flag on it. Tristan saw a pole with a sharp, pointy end. Figuring the raft was probably Marsh's favorite pool toy, he happily used the pole to pierce it. As the raft deflated, it made a very sad and satisfying blubbering sound.

"Come look at this," Sam whispered. She was standing next to a desk. On top of it was a large flat-screen computer monitor and keyboard. A small computer tablet lay nearby. Tristan picked up the tablet, hoping it controlled the pool's gates.

"Here, let me," Sam said. "A friend of mine has one just like that."

She turned on the tablet. Ten icons popped up. Sam tapped "Pools." A list appeared that included temperature, salinity, pH, jacuzzi, lights, and finally—gates. Her finger was shaking. Carefully avoiding "lights," she pressed "gates." An image of four pools came up. She tapped one. They heard a metallic grinding noise. Tristan and Sam cringed at the sound and peeked out toward the pools. An open gate was closing. Sam quickly tapped again, and the gate stopped moving. She took a deep breath and tried another icon. A gate began to rise. It was the pool with the shark. But the noise was much louder, and a green light started blinking on the flat screen on the desk.

"Uh-oh," Tristan groaned.

"C'mon," Sam urged, grabbing his arm to make a run for the pool.

"Hold on."

Tristan wasn't quite ready to leave. He smashed the

tablet on the ground and jumped on it several times. Then he swept the flat screen off the desk. He wasn't normally into vandalism, but, in this case, it felt really good. They sprinted for the pool.

Two bobbing flashlights raced toward them from the docks. Sam switched off her light and dove into the pool. Tristan was right behind her. The two bull sharks were leading the new escapee into the tunnel. The teens kicked hard to catch up, never looking back.

Up in the mansion, Luis informed the director about the empty guest suite using the small radio that had been strapped to his leg. He then climbed down the cliff under the watchful eyes of the frigatebirds still hovering overhead. At the water's edge, he dove in and swam away from the rocks. The rolling waves had grown to mini-mountains with white-capped peaks. Luis treaded water and turned on the tiny strobe light Mary had strapped to his arm. The bright light blinked rapidly on and off. Minutes later, the Hobie Cat was nearly on top of him. Mary tacked into the strengthening wind and threw Luis a knotted line. He struggled, but was able to pull himself in and climb aboard. She swiftly spun the watercraft around. The wind grabbed the sails, and they sped back toward the Bitter End. With the wind and sea growing, soon it would be too much for the small catamaran, even in Mary's expert hands.

In the dark inflatable, Coach Fred and Mia motored slowly in the opposite direction, toward the western tip of Scar Island. They were now well to the left of the brightly lit docks. But the night's darkness, combined with the intermittent rain and blasting wind, made it hard to see anything past the bow of the boat. They stared at the shore, straining to find the passage that led into the cavern beneath Marsh's mansion. Mia leaned out over the boat's rubber sides, peering ahead. Three large fins unexpectedly rose up right in front of her. She jumped back, startled. Coach put the engine into neutral. Tristan and Sam surfaced and grabbed onto the side of the inflatable.

"Welcome back, Snappers," Coach whispered. "Luis just reported in. The suite is empty."

"They're probably in the lab," Sam said.

"Campers, we need to get inside to see if they're there."

"Uh, Coach," Tristan said.

"Yes, Hunt?"

"I think they're going to know the shark got out."

"Did anyone see you?"

"Not exactly."

"Better hurry, then. Marten, can you tell where the entrance is by echolocating and lead—"

"The sharks," Tristan interrupted. "They say they know where it is and can take us there."

"Roger that. Chen, in the water you go. Be careful

and stay out of sight. If you don't find the entrance or don't see the others, come back. But hurry. The director says the storm is moving closer . . . and strengthening."

Tristan felt a surge of adrenaline as Mia slid into the water beside him. Their success in freeing the shark gave him both courage and confidence. They could and *would* do this. *They had to*. They had to save Hugh and the others and stop psycho-man Marsh. Tristan dove after the three bull sharks. A few other creatures had joined the team. The two sea turtles were back, one with Hammer on it. The attack shrimp held onto the front rim of the sea turtle's shell, riding cowboy style. Two octopus had also joined and were jetting alongside them. On the bottom, a slightly pudgy green moray eel slithered along. It looked familiar to Tristan. He thought maybe it was the green moray from the Rehab Center. Last year, when he first saw it, the moray was overweight and trying to get fit. Maybe helping out on the mission was part of its weight loss and fitness plan. Swimming just above the moray eel were four reef squid in a single file.

Not wanting to use any lights, the campers again depended on the sharks' navigation skills. Tristan grabbed hold of a dorsal fin and steeled himself for whatever might come next. The shark looked at him and said, *Climb aboard; it'll be easier and faster.*

Without a second thought, Tristan swung his leg over the shark and straddled it horseback style. He felt its powerful muscles flex and held tightly to its dorsal fin. Tristan immediately felt comfortable aboard the shark, and the closeness gave him strength. It made him feel like they were true partners, a real team. They went to the surface, and he told Sam and Mia to get on the other sharks. The teens looked at him like he was nuts. It took some convincing, but they too climbed aboard the sharks.

Swimming below the waves and whipping sea spray, the sharks were swift and quiet. Tristan loved riding the shark even more than being pulled alongside it. It was exhilarating, and he felt totally connected to the creature. Soon, a faint underwater glow ahead drew Tristan's attention. The sharks aimed for the light. They rose up for the teens to get a breath and then dove back down. As they got closer, the light got brighter. They swam on. The sharks went to the surface and stopped. The whistling of the wind had lessened, and the water around them was surprisingly calm. Tristan glanced to the side—a rough rock wall. The teens got off the sharks and treaded water. They were just inside the entrance to some sort of cave or tunnel.

"This has to be it," Tristan whispered. "The way in."

The sharks told Tristan they'd take the lead. Following the massive bull sharks, the team cautiously swam farther into and under Marsh's creepy psycho spa. Tristan felt a faint vibration in the water, and the light ahead got noticeably brighter. Suddenly, the sharks in front darted to the bottom. Tristan heard them shout: *To the side, mates, move!* He grabbed Sam and Mia, and yanked them against a rock wall.

The light was now nearly blinding and seemed to be moving directly toward them. It was Marsh's black submersible, and it was heading out. Tristan held his breath and stayed still, plastered against the rock. The sub cruised slowly by, missing him by what seemed like inches. As it passed, Tristan saw two men sitting in the acrylic bubble at the front. He prayed they wouldn't see him or the others flattened against the tunnel's walls and floor. He'd also noticed something else—at the sub's front was a cradle holding a metal barrel.

Tristan figured they were going on one last dumping run before the storm. More sea creatures would die. Tristan wanted to stop them, but then he thought of Hugh and the others still trapped inside. They'd have to let the goons go. Tristan cursed as the black sub disappeared into the dark. Hopefully, it would be the last of their nighttime pollute-the-sea cruises. The team swam on.

When they reached the dock in Marsh's hidden cavern, Tristan noticed something he hadn't seen before. He and the others stayed low and swam to it. Marsh had a second black sub tied up at the far end of the dock. They used it for cover and, as quietly as possible, rose to the surface. The open underground space was lit up like a football field ready for a nighttime game.

"Hey, have you seen Hammer?" Mia whispered. "He was going to be one of our scouts."

Sam and Tristan shook their heads; last they'd seen the mantis shrimp he had been riding rodeo-style on a sea turtle. Mia frowned and then gave the go-ahead to their other recon experts. They slithered silently out of the water. Almost instantly, the two octopus morphed into dock-lookalikes. One crawled onto a stack of crates and did a quick color change to match. Each octopus then raised its head up on eight arms like a living periscope in camouflage. A few minutes later they slipped quietly back into the water and jetted to Mia.

"Hugh and Rosina are inside the lab," Mia reported. "Looks like they're loading stuff into boxes or something. They didn't see Ryder or the woman scientist working with us."

A familiar deep voice, somewhat less calm and relaxed than before, boomed across the cavern. "Get moving. Make yourselves useful. We'll have our little talk once we're off the island. Of course, I could just leave you here in the storm, but honestly, you're too valuable a commodity to risk."

"Gee thanks."

It was Hugh's voice.

Tristan stayed low and peeked out from behind the submersible's black hull. Marsh stood with his hands on his hips. He wore a yellow foul weather jacket with matching pants. Tristan wondered if he had his pajamas on underneath. Marsh turned to two of his security men; their sleep guns were pointed into the lab. "Stay here and watch them. Whatever you do, don't let those kids anywhere near the water. We'll come back for the last load then take them out." In a hushed voice he added, "We'll leave the woman, don't need her. Make it look like a casualty of the storm."

Marsh jumped onto a cart with a few of his researchers and some supplies. They took off through the tunnel toward the docks. Tristan ducked back down behind the sub to talk to Mia and Sam.

"It's just the two goons left. Let's do it now."

"But what about the plan? What about going back to get Coach?" Mia whispered nervously.

"Might be too late," Tristan responded. "We've gotta do it now." Somehow he just knew it. He felt it in his gut. This was their best and maybe only chance. If they went back to get Coach Fred, the others would be gone by the time they got back.

Sam and Mia nodded less certainly. Mia dove under to communicate with the crew below.

"You ready, Sam?" Tristan asked.

"I . . . I think so. Are you?" she whispered.

The more Tristan thought about all that Marsh had done, the more ready he was. "Yeah, I'm sick of this creep and his pajamas. Let's get Hugh and the others outta there."

Mia came back to the surface and gave them the thumbs up. Tristan got ready. Sam struck her dive light on the side of the sub. A loud clanging rang out. The two security guards stepped closer to the dock's edge, curiously peering into the water around the sub. Then, unseen and unheard, numerous suckered arms slid out of the water and wrapped around the men's ankles. The two octopus pulled with the strength of eight of Marsh's big goons. One man fell face-first into the water. The other crashed onto his back on the dock, hitting his head. Tristan jumped out and grabbed the dart gun from the man lying stunned on the dock. Sam caught the other man's weapon as it flew across the water.

Tristan had never shot anything in his life—other than a big-blaster squirt gun. With only a slight hesitation he pulled the trigger, as did Sam. They both shot again, just to be sure. Luckily, they were too close to miss. Their darts hit their marks and both men took a quick trip to dreamland. The teens struggled to pull the one man out of the water, drowning him was not part of the plan—unless it was absolutely necessary.

Tristan and Sam sprinted for the lab. Hugh and Rosina were just running out. It was another head-on camper collision. Rosina fell to the ground, but this time she just bounded up and gave Tristan a tight hug. "You came back for us!"

"Of course, what'd you think we were going to do?" Tristan said, pushing her off him. "C'mon let's go."

Meg was sitting in a chair nearby. Her foot was still wrapped in bandages. "Well done."

Sam looked around. "Where's Ryder?"

Hugh shook his head. "He went to the yacht, *that traitor*. Said we never really appreciated his great talents. He's going to work with Marsh and Rickerton. Wants to live like the rich and famous."

Sam gasped. "No way."

"What?" Tristan exclaimed. He'd never been a big fan of Ryder's, but he couldn't believe the guy would actually betray them and work with those creeps. He'd give away all their secrets. This was bad on so many levels. Tristan suddenly felt sick to his stomach.

"Sorry 'bout that, guys," Meg said. "It's true. Let's just get out of here. What's the plan?"

"Coach is waiting outside in a boat," Tristan said, thinking about what he'd like to do to Ryder. His shark friends again came to mind.

"Can you swim?" Sam asked the scientist looking at her foot.

"Not really. But I have a better idea."

Meg got up, leaning on Hugh and Rosina for support. Mia was still in the water on lookout. When they approached, she put her finger to her lips and whispered, "There's a boat coming in through the tunnel."

The puttering of an engine echoed across the cavern's rock walls. While the others hid, Sam and Tristan readied the tranquilizer guns. Their hands trembled. The nose of a boat cruised into view. It was made of black rubber.

"Relax, it's just me," Coach said hurriedly. "Sorry, poor choice of words. Weather's gotten worse. It's too much for the inflatable out there now. No way we'd make it back without flipping."

He noticed the two ape-men sleeping like babies. "Excellent work, campers."

"Now what?" Rosina moaned.

"Coach, feel like taking a little submarine ride with me?" Meg asked. "Underwater, the wind and waves shouldn't be as bad."

Coach stared where she was pointing. "It would be my pleasure, Dr. Gladfell."

"Hey, what about us?" Hugh asked.

Climbing out of the inflatable, Coach pulled out two red pills. He passed one to Rosina and one to Hugh. "You'll be fine. Just follow us and stay submerged as much as possible. Everyone okay to swim back?"

Before they could answer, they heard the sound of a cart returning.

"No time for discussion," Coach ordered. "Help Meg into the sub. Sam, give me the dart gun."

Sam handed her dart gun to Coach Fred. The others helped the injured scientist into the submersible through a hatch at the top. The front of the yellow cart was just coming into view. Following Coach's lead, Tristan fired several darts at the approaching vehicle. He had no idea if he was anywhere close to hitting it, but the cart stopped and began backing up. That gave them the time they needed. Coach Fred climbed into the sub and closed the hatch. He and Meg sat side by side in the big see-through bug eye at the front. Tristan heard a low hum. He undid the lines securing the sub to the dock, threw the dart gun into the water, and dove in.

The sub moved slowly into the tunnel. It was led by three bull sharks, two octopus, a moray eel, and a couple of sea turtles. Four teens followed. Mia waved as they left.

Marsh and his driver entered the cavern cautiously. The rain of sleep darts had ended. Mia and the reef squid waited silently just below the surface. The cart stopped and the two men jumped out. They ran to the dock and leaned out over the water to shoot at the escaping teens. She signaled the squid. One by one the well-armed creatures swam up to the surface and shot a cloud of ink into the men's faces.

25

A CRAZY PLAN

COACH FRED AND MEG HAD TO LEARN HOW TO operate the sub on the fly. It was slow-going and more than once they banged into the tunnel walls. The rest of the team stayed close, hoping the damage wasn't catastrophic.

The group paused at the tunnel exit and stared out into the night. Storm winds drove the rain horizontally and spray flew off the white-capped waves. It was either the worst squall yet or the edge of the hurricane. As the submersible moved slowly away, it began to pitch. Coach Fred and Meg were tossed about as if inside a tin can rolling back and forth. They angled the sub down and dove toward the seafloor. The teens watched it go and then stared nervously into the dark, storm-whipped seas.

Mia suddenly popped up beside the others. "Inked 'em good. Should buy us some time."

"It looks rotten out there," Rosina groaned, backing away from the cavern exit.

"Stay underwater as much as possible," Tristan said encouragingly. "We can do this, especially with our friendly shark-mobiles. Just grab a fin and jump on. It's the best." After he said it, Tristan turned to Hugh. Tristan couldn't wait to get back on the shark, but then he remembered how Hugh felt about sharks. He might have a heart attack at just the thought of riding one—a big shark with lots of teeth.

"I'll take crap weather and a shark ride over that psycho Marsh guy any day," Hugh announced.

The others turned to him in shock, a look of complete disbelief on their faces.

Tristan grinned. "What kind of Kool-Aid have *you* been drinking?" He was stunned. Hugh's new adventurous spirit couldn't have come at a better time.

"C'mon. We should stay with the sub," Sam urged.

"I'll tell the sharks to follow it," Tristan added.

"Okay then, let's do this," Hugh said.

"Hey, wait," Mia said. "Anyone seen Hammer yet?"

They shook their heads and then dove into the stormy sea. Tristan ended up riding beside the sub on one shark. Sam and Hugh followed, riding together atop another. Mia hopped on the third shark and tried to help Rosina climb aboard. But Rosina was so nervous she swung onto the shark's back and then immediately slid off the other side. Tristan jumped briefly off his ride to help Rosina get more firmly situated aboard her and Mia's shark-mobile.

They stayed close to the small submersible. Its lights made it easy to follow and gave the campers some comfort—at least for the moment.

Once Marsh finished spitting out squid ink and wiping it from his eyes, he radioed for a speedboat. He also called the yacht's captain telling him to depart and that he'd catch up after he took care of a few last-minute annoyances.

"I'll just have to take care of this myself. After all, one cooperative study subject is all we really need."

When they were in the deeper water between Scar and Eustatia Islands, the submersible descended. The sharks and teens swam above it. Fortunately, the red pills seemed to have a useful side effect—they could somehow stay underwater longer than before. Still, every once in awhile they had to go up for air. But the surface was not a place anyone wanted to be. The waves and blasting wind made it like being inside a washing machine on the dark wash spin cycle. Getting a gulp of air meant sucking in seawater at the same time.

Tristan wished they could go faster, but the sub's top speed seemed to be at the pace of a slow walk. He was anxious and getting fidgety, wanting to speed ahead. Out of the corner of his eye, Tristan saw a brief flash. It was a reflection of the sub's light off something up ahead. He suggested to his shark transport they go check it out.

They approached warily. Tristan felt the shark tremble slightly and hesitate. He stroked it comfortingly and urged the shark on. They were literally on top of the thing before Tristan realized what it was— the other submersible. It was lying on the seafloor on its side and the acrylic bubble at the front was cracked and filled with seawater. The two men who had been inside were nowhere to be seen. On the sand in front of the sub was the metal barrel it had been carrying. Thankfully it was still sealed and didn't appear to be leaking. Seeing what was sitting on top of the submersible made Tristan smile so wide he nearly swallowed a bunch of seawater. Hammer was perched proudly atop the sub like a conquering and smashing hero. The attack shrimp jumped to the shark's snout and then crawled onto Tristan's leg. Tristan stopped smiling and prayed the mantis shrimp wouldn't decide to demonstrate the power of his punch. They went to rejoin the others.

As the team rounded Eustatia Island, the water began to get shallow. Tristan got off the shark and swam to the surface. He stared back toward Scar Island, but it was too dark and too rough to see much of anything. Then Tristan heard a distant, but familiar sound. The others let go of their rides and popped up nearby.

"Boat," Sam shouted over the wind, swiveling around.

The waves tossed the teens and the wind battered their heads, but they stayed at the surface, treading water, searching for the boat. They could hear it, but couldn't tell where it was or which direction it was headed. Tristan actually wished Ryder was there and could jump up to see better. He rose up higher and spun around, scanning the area. He thought he saw a glimmer of light—in the direction they came from. Then he heard another sound. It was the grinding screech of metal against sand and rock.

Tristan looked around and then down. "Oh no."

A little way ahead and not far below was the sub. To its right was a coral reef that rose steeply to the surface. Beside the reef was the sub—stuck in the sand with its top nearly poking out of the water. Tristan figured they must have seen the reef too late and turned into the sand while trying to avoid it. The campers tried to push the sub out. Coach Fred gunned its propellers. The small submersible was hard aground. And its lights were filtering up through and reflecting off the surrounding white sand making it resemble nothing less than a lit-up otherworldly spaceship.

Tristan went back to the surface. The noise of a boat engine was now distinctly louder. He turned toward the sound and could make out a light and a white dot—the hull of a boat speeding toward them.

He turned to warn the others and nearly ran face first into a dolphin. It bypassed Tristan and headed straight to Sam. Another dolphin appeared and the two of them began pushing Sam with their beaks. Moments later, Tristan felt something brush his leg. He turned— the manta ray.

"Speedboat heading this way," Sam shouted. "Not a friendly one."

With the sub all lit up, Tristan figured the people on the boat were homing in on it like a beacon. He immediately dove down and tried to tell Coach to turn off the lights. But from inside the sub's acrylic sphere, the man couldn't hear him or understand the crazy hand gestures Tristan was making. He went back to the surface. The boat was still pretty far away, but it was definitely headed their way, aiming directly for the sub at ramming speed.

The teens looked at each other and then to Tristan. He knew they had to do something and do it fast. Unfortunately, nothing came to mind. *C'mon, think,* Tristan said to himself—if only they had a rocket-launcher or a grenade-dropping frigatebird. The boat was getting closer. He could make out two people aboard and one held a powerful spotlight. They needed a distraction while they tried to free the sub, but what? Then he thought of something, but it was truly crazy, probably the worst plan he'd ever thought up.

Tristan explained his idea to the others; they all agreed it was ridiculous. Then again, it was the only thing anyone had come up with. The other teens made a few suggestions to add to the absurdity of the idea. Tristan then talked to the sharks and manta while Sam communicated with the dolphins. Hugh and Mia took care of the rest of the team.

Hugh and the two octopus dove to the sub. They began pulling armfuls of sand out from under its front end. Mia and the sea turtles went to the back. She directed each turtle to wiggle its way under the sub. Hunching up on their flippers, they began to slowly lift the sub up like undersea car jacks.

Meanwhile, Tristan and the others swam toward the racing speedboat. When they were as close as they dared, the dolphins dove. With a pump of their tails, they rose up under Sam and launched her into the air. She rocketed skyward, waving like a madwoman and yelling at the people on the boat to get their attention. But they had miscalculated. In the dark rolling seas and whistling wind, she was still too far away for them to see or hear her. Marsh and his driver hadn't changed direction in the slightest. They remained on a collision course with the sub. Tristan shook his head—even the first part of their crazy plan was a failure. He didn't know what else to do. In minutes, Coach Fred and Meg would be toast, crushed inside the sub.

Suddenly, something else jumped out of the water—literally leaping right in front of the speeding boat. It was large, had slightly webbed feet, and blonde surfer-dude hair. Tristan couldn't believe it. Sam and Rosina appeared equally shocked.

The boat swerved sharply and then slowed. Hugo

Marsh aimed the bright spotlight out over the water in search of the jumper. Staying out of the beam, Tristan nodded to Rosina. She looked scared, but determined and ready for the next part of their hare-brained scheme. The manta ray swam beneath her and she grabbed onto its wing-like fins. As the manta shot out of the water next to the boat, from its back Rosina flung a giant glob of mucus into the driver's eyes, shouting, "Take that!"

On the other side of the boat, a dolphin flung something else up and in. It resembled an overgrown thick green arrow and landed with a heavy thud on the deck. The moray eel slithered to the driver's ankle and clamped on with its super sharp teeth.

The driver was now slime-blinded with an eel clamped onto his leg. He dove from the controls and the boat swerved wildly. Marsh grabbed the wheel and cut the engines. The driver wrestled with the eel on the deck. But the moray's body was coated with slippery, slimy mucus, making it nearly impossible to hold on to. The boat came to a standstill and pitched violently in the stormy seas.

The next part of the teens' plan kicked in. A bull shark swam up to the boat and its club-armed hitch-hiker whacked the hull several times in rapid succession. A spider-web of cracks developed at the stern near the boat's heavy twin engines. Water began trickling in. Hammer whacked it again.

Marsh found a tranquilizer gun and began shooting wildly. He shot the moray eel and then aimed into the water at anything that moved. Tristan felt a dart whoosh by his head. One struck a shark and another just missed hitting Sam. Marsh then tried to restart the boat's engines. They roared to life, but Rosina had also filled the cooling water intakes with mucus. The engines began to smoke, sputter, and then, were silent. The stern began to sink. As water filled the boat, Marsh spun around in a panic trying to keep his balance. He was definitely not calm or relaxed.

With the help of its undersea road crew, the submersible was now free from the sand. Coach Fred steered it toward the sinking boat and the two men, who were now treading water, terrified. Enraged dolphins, furious rays, livid sharks, and angry campers surrounded the men.

The rain and wind began to let up. It was a lull in the storm. The teens gathered together trying to decide what to do next. Tristan was busy convincing the sharks not to kill Marsh. He told them the campers would see to it that the man got what he deserved and, besides, he would taste really bad; probably worse than most humans. The sharks grudgingly agreed not to fatally wound Marsh, but one shark did bite him solidly on the leg as a little remembrance of his time in the BVIs.

The sea creatures assured the teens they could lead them and the sub back to the Bitter End safely. Rosina held the unconscious green moray eel in her arms; they had an instinctual bond based on mutual mucus affection. She made sure that water passed in

through the sleeping eel's mouth and over its gills so
that it could breathe during its drug-induced nap. The
shark that had been hit was drowsy and acting kind
of loopy. The other sharks helped it, but at one point
it came close to giving Hugh a little love bite. Hugh
wasn't flattered by the shark's affections and tried to
climb on top of the sub to get away from it. His newfound confidence only went so far.

Ryder joined the group. "Their boat's just about on
the bottom. Let's just leave them here in the storm."

The others still looked stunned that he was even
there.

"Hey, I was, like, faking it. I wasn't going to work
for that dude. What a whacko."

"We can't just leave them here," Sam said. "That'd
make us just as bad as them."

"Let's leave them on the reef," Tristan suggested.

"But you just told the sharks not to kill Marsh?"
Hugh noted.

"It'll just rough 'em up a little. We can send a boat
out from the Bitter End to get them."

The others agreed. They towed the injured boat
driver and Marsh to the reef off Eustatia Island. It was
shallow enough for the two men to stand on.

"Hey, you can't just leave us here at night," Marsh
yelled. "I'm hurt and there's a hurricane coming."

Most of the teens simply turned and began swimming away. But Tristan couldn't resist a look. He
paused and watched the men. As waves struck and
blew across the reef, the two men fell over. When they

got up, they hopped around trying to avoid numerous black spiny sea urchins and the sharp coral. Then another wave hit. It looked as if they were walking over hot coals while being blasted by a fire hose. Tristan thought—*couldn't happen to nicer guys.*

He also couldn't resist shouting, "Just relax!"

The campers swam slowly alongside and behind the sub. The sea creatures led the way, navigating through a channel in the lagoon between Eustatia and Virgin Gorda. As soon as they passed behind Saba Rock, the wind and waves subsided even more and they saw a familiar boat cruising toward them.

The small, covered workboat glided to a stop next to the group and submersible. Director Davis and Luis leaned out. Alvin was at the helm. He nodded to them. The teens thanked the other members of their undersea rescue team, telling them they couldn't have escaped or survived without their help. The campers then climbed into the boat and gratefully wrapped themselves in dry, warm towels. Without wetsuits, Hugh, Rosina, and Ryder were shivering and their lips had turned an interesting shade of blue. Alvin drove the boat slowly back to the dock at the Bitter End. The sub followed. The teens helped Coach Fred and Meg out of the submersible and it was secured as well as possible. Alvin, Director Davis, and Coach Fred went back to get Marsh and his man. Coach Fred still had one of the tranquilizer guns. Luis led the others as they made a beeline for the hurricane shelter.

26

UNFINISHED BUSINESS

THE WORST OF THE STORM HAD YET TO HIT THE British Virgin Islands. The bad weather they'd been experiencing was just the outer bands of the still intensifying category one hurricane.

By midnight, everyone left at the Bitter End was huddled together, hunkered down in the hurricane shelter—except Marsh and his man. After they were rescued from the reef, Coach roughly patched up their wounds military style, and they were locked up in a concrete shed for the night. It would be safe and secure, but not the most comfortable place to ride out the storm.

Tristan and the others were now dry and warm, lying on cots, and trying to sleep. The noise outside the shelter was frightful. The wind continued to howl, and strong gusts rattled the roof. Debris periodically slammed against the small concrete building's walls. And although they were halfway up a high hill, they could still hear huge waves crashing ashore below. Other noises were harder to identify, but no less disturbing.

Rosina and Hugh were under their blankets with pillows over their heads. Sam was curled up in a ball on her cot, while Ryder lay on his back staring at the ceiling. Tristan was awake as well, wishing he could fall asleep. He wondered what he'd done to deserve this. Seriously, could one person be that unlucky? Especially after all they'd already been through and done. Trying to take his mind off the thought of being crushed inside the shelter as it blew apart or being impaled by flying debris, he turned to Ryder. "So, how'd you get off the yacht, anyway?"

Since no one was able to sleep, the other teens either sat up or rolled over to hear the answer.

"Like, I can't believe you all thought I joined up with the pajama dude and toad guy."

"That's what you said when you left with them," Hugh explained.

"Yeah, well, I decided to go after I saw what you did in the pool, Hugh. Cool move dude, except for, like, losing the shorts. Didn't need to see that."

After a few snickers, Ryder continued, "I figured I could fake it too and maybe find a way to radio for help or escape or something."

"Really?" Tristan said.

"Dude, c'mon. Anyway, once I agreed to work with them and tell them about you guys, they let me roam around the yacht. Fed me whatever I wanted. It was pretty sweet."

The teens shook their heads and rolled their eyes at him.

"I'm just saying. Once we left the dock, I overheard on a guy's radio that you got away. So when nobody was looking, I went to the side and, like, just dove off."

"How'd you find us after that?" Sam asked.

"Well, kinda turns out I can talk to sea turtles. Ran into one and it led me to you. I didn't have full webs or anything. But after a while a little came out, leftover from the pill I think."

"Not bad, Jones," added Coach Fred, who'd been listening from a nearby cot. "Any idea where the yacht was headed? Did you overhear anything that might help us locate it?"

Ryder grinned. "I did better than that, Coach. Right before I got on the yacht, I took the robo-jelly that was still in Meg's mesh bag from when we swam out to the reef. It was sitting in Marsh's lab. Took it out of the case and hid it in my pocket. By the way, will it, like, work in freshwater?"

Coach looked at him questioningly. "That's an affirmative. Why?"

"I stashed it on the yacht—but I'm not sure if it's in fresh or saltwater."

"Where'd you put it?" Tristan asked curiously.

Ryder smiled even broader. "In the toilet."

Even Coach smiled. "Excellent job, Jones."

Tristan was impressed. Maybe he'd been wrong about Ryder—maybe he wasn't such a bad guy after all.

The director had also been listening in. "As soon as I can, I'll let Flash know. We should be able to use the signal from the robo-jelly to track the yacht. I'll also notify the authorities. Hopefully the men aboard the yacht won't discover too quickly what's in one of their toilets."

Nearby, Mary had her ear to a battery-operated radio. "The storm has taken a jog to the west. That's good news for us."

By about three in the morning, the hurricane had passed to their south into the Caribbean Sea, and conditions began to slowly improve. As quiet descended outside, the people inside the shelter got some much-needed sleep.

Mary and her husband were the first to wake up. They held hands and nervously tried the shelter door. Debris was jammed in at the base. Using all their weight, they pushed the door open. Sunlight streamed in, along with air still heavy with moisture. Coach, the director, Meg, and Alvin soon joined the Bitter End's owners as they surveyed the damage. From what they could see, trees were down and debris was scattered about. A few buildings appeared to have sustained minor damage.

"Doesn't look too bad," Mary noted.

"Nowhere near as bad as a few years back during Hugo—the hurricane that is," her husband added.

"Speaking of Hugo," Director Davis said. "I suppose we'd better go check on our overnight guests in the shed."

"I'll join you," Coach offered. "Think I'll take that last dart gun with me, just in case."

"Sounds good. We'll let the campers get some well-deserved rest."

The adults headed down the trail, clearing debris as they went.

When Tristan woke up, he thought for a moment he was back in Marsh's psycho spa. It was a huge relief to realize that he was at the Bitter End and that the shelter was still standing and intact. He rose groggily to his feet and promptly tripped over Hugh lying on a cot nearby. He landed on Rosina, who woke up with a start. Seeing the look on her face, Tristan leapt to his feet and went for the door. "Hey, check it out. The storm's over."

"Yeah, I'll check you out," Rosina said with smirk. Ever since Tristan had helped her in the boulder pool and then returned to get them from Marsh's lair, she'd been acting strangely nice toward him, even joking with him. It was a bit unsettling.

Sam got up and joined Tristan staring out at the blue sky. "Today's got to be better than the last couple of days."

"You can say that again," Tristan added. "But, what a mess. Imagine if the hurricane had come right over us."

Alvin arrived back at the shelter with a scarily large machete in hand.

"Its nots toos bad," he told them. "Justs a few days of works. Ms. Marys and the others are downs at the office. Says you should goes down theres."

After rousting Ryder, Mia, and Luis, the teens followed Alvin down the trail to the road. He used the machete to help clear the path as needed. Leaves, branches, and palm fronds were strewn about and piled high by the wind. The shoreline road had been flooded and then drained, leaving several inches of sand behind. One of the long docks was torn up and the sports shack had no roof and one wall was missing. Several small sailboats had also been washed off their moorings. They'd collided and run aground in front of the office building.

The teens tossed debris to the side and picked their way over slabs of wood, pieces of roof, and plant material. On the patio outside the office building, a makeshift breakfast had been set out. It included some fruit, orange juice, coffee, and an assortment of day-old muffins. Alvin left as Director Davis and Coach Fred joined the group.

"Where's creep-man Marsh?" Tristan asked through a muffin-filled mouth. He was so hungry the stale muffin tasted better than a hot-out-of-the-oven chocolate chip cookie. And that was saying a lot.

"No worries," Coach responded, holding up the dart gun. "He and his pal are taking a little nap till the local authorities get here."

Mia stared at the two sailboats piled up against the dock. "Are we stranded here? Is the place ruined?"

Director Davis smiled. "No, Mia, the place just needs some cleaning up. We were lucky not to get a direct hit by the storm, so the damage is pretty superficial. We expect communications to be up and running later this morning. But we probably won't be able to get out of the islands for a day or two. As soon as I can, I'll let your parents know everyone's alright and that we'll be headed back to Florida soon."

"What about the yacht?" Ryder asked.

"No word yet. But once communications are up, we'll get right on it. We're setting up a command post for cleanup and we'll get you all set up in a couple of cottages for the night."

Coach pulled out a jug of Sea Camp water. "They could use our help in the cleanup and there are some tasks that you all are especially well-suited for. So, campers, fuel up and let's get to work!"

"No rest for the weary," Hugh moaned.

"You can sleep when you get old," Coach Fred responded.

Once they'd eaten something, the campers perked up. They went out on an inflatable with Coach Fred and Meg to find the other submersible and the metal drum it was carrying. Since Tristan had seen it the night before, he led them to the general area where he thought it might be, assuming it hadn't moved too much in the storm. The teens jumped in and began searching. Using her echolocation, Sam quickly found the sub. It had rolled over several times during the night, but was still basically in intact.

Meg handed the teens a yellow marker buoy and line. "Tie this to the sub so we can recover it. Any sign of the metal drum they were carrying?"

The teens shook their heads. It was nowhere to be seen and Sam couldn't locate it.

"Okay, start a search pattern. Work as a team and make your way out from the sub," Coach instructed.

The campers began swimming in a widening circle out from the damaged sub. A cloud of sediment billowing up from the bottom caught Tristan's eye. He swam closer. In the midst of the roiling sand was a large gray stingray. It was flapping its body while blowing sand out from openings just below its eyes. Tristan hovered over the creature, staying safely away from the barbed spine on its tail. He tried to read its thoughts.

Dumping wastes in our home. Hope the shark bit that nutter good. Gotta get rid of this thing too.

With one powerful flap of its broad body, the stingray rose off the bottom and swam away. Its digging had exposed the top of the metal barrel. The drum had been buried by the storm. Tristan waved the others over. Meg recorded where the metal drum was relative to the submersible so they could remove it later and safely dispose of the chemicals inside.

"Okay, now let's head back and clear some of the debris from the coral reef off Eustatia," Coach instructed.

The teens climbed into the inflatable. They sped back toward the reef where they had stranded Marsh and his man. Old fishing line, some rope, and a few palm fronds were now tangled in the coral.

"Hop on out," Coach instructed. "But watch yourself on the coral."

"And stay well away from the *Diadema*—those dang black spiny sea urchins," Meg added.

They spent about an hour carefully swimming around the reef, clearing debris off, and piling it in the inflatable.

"One last job for you before lunch," Coach said after they'd climbed aboard the boat.

"C'mon, Coach, give us a break. We could use a rest," Rosina said wearily.

The others nodded in agreement.

"Just one more task. It won't take too long or be *too* painful for you."

They rolled their eyes and sighed in tired acceptance.

Coach Fred drove the inflatable into the rectangular swimming area at the Bitter End. Along the way they pulled more debris out of the water. He beached the boat on the sand. Sitting nearby was the giant blow-up trampoline. It had been deflated and stored for the storm. Alvin stood next to it with a scuba tank. He had just re-inflated the trampoline.

"Thought you alls mights want to helps us puts this backs out and tests to be sure its working okays," Alvin said, grinning.

Coach gave them one of his rare smiles.

The teens dragged the huge blow-up trampoline out into the swimming area and connected its anchor line to a large cement block on the bottom. Ryder tried to be the first to climb on, but with Luis's sea star hands and feet, he scrambled on quicker than seemed possible. Ryder followed, along with Sam, Tristan, Mia, and Rosina. While the others jumped up and down, crashed into each other and laughed, Hugh treaded water nearby looking up at them anxiously.

"Climb on, Hugh!" Tristan shouted as he bounced into Sam and she went flying off. "Hey!"

"C'mon," Sam said to Hugh as she climbed back on. "After what you did at Marsh's you can't be scared of this!"

Hugh shook his head. "I'm not scared. It's just that, well, with everything that's happened the past few days, I think I've lost some weight. My shorts are kinda loose. One bounce and . . ."

Ryder laughed. "Don't worry, dude. Like, we've seen all of that before."

The others laughed and Hugh shrugged his shoulders good-naturedly. Tristan helped him up onto the trampoline. The campers spent the next hour bouncing, jumping off, and pushing each other into the water. Tristan swallowed a ton of seawater, twisted his ankle, smacked his head on the side of the trampoline, and hadn't had so much fun in what seemed like years!

A little while later, the seven of them lay on their backs on the trampoline staring up at the wispy clouds drifting by.

"Is this how all missions go?" Tristan asked Luis and Mia.

"No," Luis answered. "You guys have just had rotten luck. I mean, usually things go pretty smoothly."

"Yeah," Sam added. "I'm sure our next mission will be easier, you know less *life-threatening*."

"That would be good," Tristan said, though once his parents found out about this one, he didn't think he'd be going on any more missions.

They heard the director calling from shore, announcing that lunch was served. They were about to jump into the water, when a wave nearly knocked them all off. The teens spun around curiously looking to see what had caused it. A large manta ray leapt up and splashed them on landing. Two dolphins and three sharks then swam by, creating another wave that rocked the trampoline and, again, nearly knocked them off.

"Very funny," Rosina said, wiping the water from her face and trying to regain her balance.

"That was pretty good," Sam laughed.

They jumped in and swam with the creatures. Tristan thanked the sharks and rays, and they did likewise. He also told them that Meg said she would bring in an expert to remove the wires from their backs. Sam thanked the dolphins and they told her all the fish in the area appreciated what they did to stop Hugo Marsh. They also reported that Hammer was back in his reef and already causing trouble. But, periodically, a new neighbor, a slightly pudgy green moray eel, came by to keep him in line. The teens said good-bye and swam to the beach. After drying off, they walked with the director to the restaurant for lunch.

"So, did you reach Sea Camp and our folks?"

"How about the yacht? Did you, like, find it and Rickerton?"

"Yeah, what about Marsh? Did the police arrest him?"

The director held up his hands. "Hold on, one question at a time. Yes, communications are back up and I've spoken to Ms. Sanchez at camp and she is calling your parents. We're arranging a phone call for each of you this evening. No word on the yacht yet, but we're tracking its location. And yes, the police came and took Mr. Marsh and his beefy friend into custody."

The teens were scheduled to leave first thing the next morning, but after lunch they had one last important task to take care of. It was unclear whether Marsh had been emptying the harmful chemicals out of each barrel or just dumping the drums. They needed to be sure there weren't any barrels left in the water still leaking. The campers split up into two boats and spent several hours searching. By late afternoon, they found one additional metal drum and marked it for removal. Meg would continue the search after they left. They decided, however, to release their remaining robo-jellies, hoping that if there were still leaking barrels out there, the drifters would help by detecting any unusual chemical concentrations.

"So what's going to happen to Scar Island and the lab?" Tristan asked Meg on their way back to the Bitter End.

"Not sure. Maybe we can do a little remodeling and make it an ocean research and education center for the BVIs. A place where we can help the local community learn about the sea and how to protect it for the future."

"What about the submersibles?" Hugh asked.

"I'm hoping we'll be able to take the working one back to our institute. Hey, anyone want to do a little driving?"

Sam had driven the inflatable before so Hugh hesitantly volunteered to give it a shot. After he nearly ran them straight into a rock, it was Tristan's turn. He grasped the twist throttle on the stick-like handle of the outboard engine. Giving it a little gas, Tristan tested the steering. He pushed the handle forward and the small boat turned left. When he pulled it closer to him, they went right.

"Okay now," Meg told him. "Steady it up and head for that first empty mooring ball up ahead."

Tristan nodded and pulled the handle toward him to veer left and line up with the ball. But he pulled too hard and they swerved sharply.

"Nice job," Ryder shouted from the other inflatable that was just speeding past.

"Yeah, yeah," Tristan muttered, trying to straighten them out. He pushed the engine handle forward. But he overcompensated and they swung too far right.

"You better jump for it!" Ryder shouted back to them.

"Oh shut up," Sam yelled. "It's not like you could do any better." She then put her hand lightly over Tristan's and twisted the throttle a little. "You'll have more control if you go a little faster. My dad taught me when I was little. With some speed, just small movements are needed to steer straight."

Tristan blushed at Sam's touch. It was almost like they were holding hands. He suddenly felt light-headed and was so flustered he could hardly understand what she was saying. Hugh stared at Tristan and then down at Sam's hand and grinned. Sam saw Hugh and quickly took her hand away.

"Uh, okay. I got it," Tristan said.

With some coaching from Meg, Tristan drove most of the way back to the Bitter End. Meg took over when they neared the dock. They made it back just in time for their calls home. Each of the teens assured their parents they were fine and that the storm hadn't been all that bad. The director asked them not to say anything, at least yet, about everything else.

Dinner that night was a true test of the teens' endurance. Not because of the wait for food or an overly long and boring conversation. The campers were just so tired. It was all they could do to stay awake for dessert. They retired to their assigned cottages and were asleep in minutes.

The next morning, the teens packed their backpacks and readied to leave. A boat would take them to Beef Island where they'd head to the airport and board Sea Camp's jet. They said their good-byes. Mary and Meg hugged each and every one of them and told them anytime they wanted to come back they were always welcome.

On the plane ride home, the campers once again sank into the cozy, plush leather seats. Tristan began to nod off, but a couple of things were still bothering him. For one, why did Sam putting her hand on his while he was driving the inflatable make him feel so weird? It's not like they were actually holding hands or anything. That would be too weird; Sam and Hugh were his best friends. Tristan decided maybe it had been a lack of food or he'd been dehydrated. He then undid his seatbelt. Tristan walked forward to the cockpit where Director Davis sat in the copilot's seat.

"Uh, Director?"

"Yes, Tristan?"

"What happened to the yacht? I mean, did you find Rickerton? Because he knows about us and the webbing."

Director Davis got up and led Tristan back to his seat, sitting nearby. "Yes, we located the yacht in Tortola. The authorities have taken Mr. Marsh's people into custody, but by the time they got there, Rickerton was gone."

"What does that mean for camp? And us?" Tristan asked nervously.

"We've been discussing that ourselves." He looked

to where Coach sat piloting the plane. "At Sea Camp, we've always worked on a reactionary basis. That is—when things happen, we react and send a team out to investigate. But in this case, I think we're going to have to try a different tactic. This time we're going to go on the offensive. Luckily, some of our friends in the government have agreed to help us with that. Rickerton's on the run right now and we plan to keep it that way."

"But do you think he'll come after us again?"

"No, we'll be keeping him way too busy for that. But in the meantime, we may have to cut camp a little short this summer. Just to be safe."

"What?" Rosina said, sitting nearby. "But . . . but, what if we don't, I mean, what if we don't want to go *home*?"

The director looked at her warmly. "Don't worry, Rosina. I am well aware of your situation. We'll work something out. Come talk to me once we're back at camp."

Tristan wondered what that was all about. "What about next summer? And more missions?"

"Oh, we haven't given up on you or our missions. But right now we need to put Rickerton out of business and keep him off our tail. Don't worry. We'll take care of him. By the way, Tristan, you and the other Snappers did a great job back there. What did I tell you? Teamwork is a powerful thing. Relying on your friends—both human and in the sea—will help tame your fears and make you stronger."

Tristan thought back to riding on the shark and

how safe and connected he had felt. And when they were all working together—even in the middle of the storm—he thought less about his own fear.

The director got up and hit him playfully on the head. "Now enough with the questions. Get some rest and we'll talk more back at camp."

As it turned out, that was the last conversation Tristan would have with Director Davis for quite a while. After they landed, the man rushed off and was only seen a few more times over the next few days. Coach Fred and Ms. Sanchez spoke to the camp as a whole and explained that due to circumstances beyond their control, the teens would have to go home early this year. Of course, rumors had already spread about what had happened in the British Virgin Islands.

None of the campers wanted to leave early. Many of the teens blamed the Snappers for the abbreviated camp season. When Tristan ran into Brianna at the Conch Café, she avoided even looking at him. Anthony Price, the Squid who always looked at Tristan a little funny, now openly sneered at him. Tristan didn't understand. Given all that had happened in the British Virgin Islands, he thought they'd done incredibly well—performed almost heroically. He was glad when he went to pack and the only other person in the room was Hugh.

"I can't believe everyone is blaming us!" Tristan said angrily. "It's not like any of it was our fault."

"Yeah, this is crazy," Hugh said. "It's like they hate us because camp is being cut short this summer."

"What do you think is going to happen? Do you think we'll even get to come back next summer?"

"I don't know."

"Hugh, let's go talk to Sam and the others. This is so totally unfair. After all we went through and did, we should be treated like heroes. We have to do something. If what the director said is true, and he's going after Rickerton, maybe we can help. We're good at this stuff. You know, like he said, go on the offensive."

With one eyebrow raised, the newly adventurous Hugh replied, "What did you have in mind?"

NOTE FROM
THE AUTHOR

I HOPE YOU'VE ENJOYED ANOTHER TRISTAN HUNT and the Sea Guardians adventure. The story and characters are pure fiction, but once again many of the locations, ocean habitats, issues, and creatures portrayed in the book are based on real places, real problems, and real marine organisms, along with some of my own experiences in, on, and under the ocean.

In the 1980s, I sailed through the British Virgin Islands (BVIs) aboard a bareboat charter (no, we were not naked) with fellow students from a marine lab in St. Croix and have returned several times since. It is a fantastic place! As described in the book, the BVIs have a history as a hideout for plundering pirates and supposed buried treasure. Numerous islands, small coves, and specific sites really are named after pirates or things related to their infamous ways. (Yes, there is even a Cockroach Island.)

The Bitter End Yacht Club is a gorgeous resort on the northwest coast of Virgin Gorda. During a recent visit, I stayed in a hillside cottage on the northern side of the property. I went on several early morning swims and made it across the lagoon to Eustatia Island, having to swim across a boat channel, over piles of black spiny sea urchins, and around a very shallow and long reef (I ran aground on it during my first attempt to swim across). By the way, getting stuck by *Diadema* spines is a very unpleasant experience, and while some people say to pee on it—I personally don't recommend the practice.

While in the BVIs, I dove in a cave with a swirling school of silver spoon-sized fish and had a nurse shark spot me and sink to the bottom where I swear it pretended to be still as a statue to go unseen. There was a fish-filled rock hot tub near a small cove off Mosquito Island and I swam on scuba through a narrow, V-shaped chute between giant rocks at a spot called The Chimney. The rock walls looked just like brightly colored abstract paintings, covered with splatters and splotches of pink and purple coralline algae, along with orange cup coral and red and yellow sponges. I also hiked through the towering piles of giant granite boulders and swam at The Baths. (It is just as wondrous and unique as described.) Saba Rock exists as in the story and they really do feed the tarpon at happy hour—those are some fat and happy fish.

While I was there, I saw plenty of sea turtles, jumping manta rays, eagle rays, and an odd fish that looks
very much like a serving platter. It is the scrawled file-
fish—look it up. Scientists aren't sure why manta and
eagle rays jump. Theories include that it is to get rid of
parasites, to avoid something chasing them, some form
of communication, or simply their idea of fun.

While diving in the BVIs, I waved my hand by the
fuzzy tentacles of a pillar coral and found an octopus
sitting camouflaged on a giant block of rock. I didn't
see any green moray eels, but they're there and are,
in fact, coated with mucus to protect their skin (no
scales). There are also probably stomatopods, aka
mantis shrimp, living in the reefs in the region, though
I wasn't fortunate enough to observe any. They live in
burrows under rocks or in the sand. Mantis shrimp
are truly bizarre-looking creatures and have one of
the fastest, most powerful strikes in the animal kingdom. Stomatopods with club shaped legs really are
called smashers and those with sword-shaped legs are
referred to as spearers. And they have super freaky
looking stalked eyes that provide excellent vision.

I also mentioned pufferfish and squirrelfish in the
book. Do you know what the yellow coin-shaped fish
are or the multicolored striped fish? The small spiraling creatures that Tristan saw on a brain coral that
withdraw into tubes are called Christmas tree worms.
The algae that looks like a green paintbrush is *Penicil-
lus*. *Halimeda* is one of my favorite algae and I choose
green cornflakes for its cereal lookalike. And squid

really can squirt ink as a means of defense to escape from predators.

Lionfish, which are native to the Indian and Pacific Oceans, can now be found in the BVIs and throughout the Caribbean and the Bahamas, off Florida, and in the Gulf of Mexico. These non-native invaders eat tons of small reef fish and crustaceans, reproduce quickly, and have no natural predators in these regions. The ecological impact of invading lionfish is not yet fully understood, but we do know that it won't be good. But, they are tasty. Just be sure to carefully cut off the poisonous spines before cooking them.

Scientists use robotic sensors that drift in the sea and go to the surface to relay their data by satellites, but I'm not sure any of them look like a jellyfish or have all the capabilities of my robo-jellies. I have a colleague/friend who builds small submersibles. I was fortunate enough to go down 300 feet on a test dive in one (tritonsubs.com). What a great ride! And researchers across the world are studying how chemicals found in marine organisms might be used to fight disease or better understand human physiology. Organisms in coral reefs, such as sponge, are of particular interest because many do, in fact, use chemicals in defense against predators. The venom from the cone snail has already been used to create a new and powerful painkiller.

Unfortunately, overfishing is a real and serious problem in the BVIs and elsewhere. One of the problems in this region is potfishing. It is a fishing method that uses baited wire traps that are set on or near coral reefs. Everything that gets in (including small reef fish) is collected and sometimes thrown into a pot to cook—hence the name *potfishing*. This form of fishing does terrible damage to the fish population and the reefs. I'm not against fishing, but just against fishing in ways that cause harm or are destructive and/or unsustainable.

Worldwide, pollution in the ocean is also a very serious problem. Trash, oil, chemicals, and other wastes are washed or swept off the land and flow into the ocean. Marine debris and plastics kill tens of thousands of fish, sea lions, sea birds, turtles, whales, and more every year. Unfortunately, sea turtles really do eat plastic bags. In the ocean, the bags resemble one of their favorite foods—jellyfish. When I swim or kayak in Miami, I am continually collecting these bags from the water. Please ask your parents to use recyclable bags at the grocery store and always, always recycle or dispose of your trash properly.

If you want to learn more about me, the ocean, and the science mentioned in this book, go to www.tristan-hunt.com or visit our fan page on Facebook. And send me a message—I love hearing from readers. Tell me what your favorite sea creature or ocean habitat is. Maybe I'll put it in the next Tristan Hunt and the Sea Guardians adventure. And, as always, get out there and dive in!

ACKNOWLEDGEMENTS

To all my family and friends who are endless sources of moral support, encouragement, and humor, I thank you with all my heart. Kathy—thanks for always being ready to lend an ear for a sisterly vent and to give great advice. Mom and Dad, I swear I'll tell you what happens in book three soon. Buzz, your friendship, laughter, and support are hugely appreciated. Thanks also to all my other early morning swimming pals that put up with my silly sea creature stories and help me pick up trash at the beach (Ugh!). I am also grateful to my test readers who continue to give their time and provide excellent feedback. To the readers of book one, *The Shark Whisperer*, who wrote fantastic reviews, sent me fun tweets, posted on Facebook, or e-mailed me—thank you. You inspire me to keep writing and make all the hard work well worth it. Thanks to Sandra Grisham-Clothier and the others at the Bitter End Yacht Club who made my stay in the British Virgin Islands so lovely, productive, and fun. I'd also like to recognize and say a big thank you to Carl and the others at The Safina Center. Their support in travel, writing, and speaking engagements has been invaluable. Great appreciation also goes to my agent, Janell Agyeman, and all the folks at Mighty Media Press for their hard work, attention, and support. Special thanks to Nancy Tuminelly, Josh Plattner, Sara Lien, Sammy Bosch, Chris Long, Anders Hanson, and editor Karen Latchana Kenney. And once again, admiration and thanks to Antonio Javier Caparo, who continues to surprise and amaze me with his superb illustrations for the maps and cover.

A SNEAK PEEK
FROM THE PAGES OF
STINGRAY CITY ...

TRISTAN HUNT AND THE SEA GUARDIANS

RYDER STOPPED AND STARED ACROSS THE STREET
at a small park and, beyond it, the dark waters of Monterey Bay. He raised an eyebrow mischievously. "Hey, let's go for a swim."

The other teens turned to where he was looking.

"Now? Out there in the dark? Are you crazy?" Hugh said. "Besides, Pete said to go back to the house."

"Exactly. Like, do you always do what people tell you to?" Ryder jeered. "Are you scared, Hugh?" He turned to Tristan. "How about you? Are you afraid too, shark boy?"

"No. I'm not afraid."

"C'mon then. Heard great whites swim around here," Ryder taunted. "I dare you."

"We've been in the ocean at night before," Tristan countered. "And it was during a wicked storm."

"Then it shouldn't be a problem. Or are you *afraid of the dark*?"

The other teens watched Tristan, waiting for his response.

Hugh whispered, "Don't do it."

"Wimp!" Ryder exclaimed. "I'm going in." He jogged across the street.

Tristan hesitated and then chased after him. He could only take so much of Ryder's bluster. Besides, he didn't want the others to think he was scared or anything. With the exception of Ryder, they looked to him for leadership. And if Tristan was going to be a good leader, he needed to be brave. Besides, he could just jump in, swim a little way out, and then get out. It was dark down by the water, so no one would see them, and if a shark came by, he'd just talk to it. He'd gotten pretty good at this swimming-fast-and-talking-to-sharks thing. What could go wrong?

The other teens followed as the two boys ran through the small park to a flight of stairs that led to a sandy beach. It was nestled between rocky outcrops at the base of a waterfront hotel and a restaurant on Cannery Row. The teens stayed in the shadows as much as possible.

As the group gathered at the ocean's edge, Ryder sat down on a rock and began taking off his sneakers. "So, who's going in?"

Hugh and Rosina shook their heads.

Tristan began to undo his laces. "C'mon. We'll just jump in, swim a ways out, and come back. No big deal."

Sam nodded and started to take off her shoes. "I'll go with you, Tristan."

Rosina felt the water. "Nope, no way."

"Wuss!" Ryder announced.

"You'd better take one of these," Hugh said, shaking his head and handing Tristan, Ryder, and Sam each a red, rubbery pill from a plastic bag in his backpack.

Tristan and Ryder began pulling off their jeans. Rosina snickered. Sam had gone silent, obviously realizing she was going to have to strip down to her underwear too if she was really going in.

Minutes later, Sam, Tristan, and Ryder stood on the beach staring at the dark water, shivering. The air was cool and smelled of seaweed. Small waves lapped the shore. It was a calm night with almost no moon, even darker than usual. And except for a periodic loud laugh or the distant noise of people on Cannery Row, it was quiet.

"Chickening out?" Ryder asked.

Tristan turned to him. "No. Are you?"

"Like, no way."

Together they raced into the cold, dark water.

"I have a feeling I'm going to regret this," Sam said, before running to dive in behind them.

Almost immediately, their feet became webbed. Tristan put his hands out front and zoomed ahead. He was still the fastest swimmer. But the water was so dark he could hardly see his outstretched hands. Worried about ramming into something headfirst at high speed, Tristan slowed. He surfaced and stopped to look back. The beach was already a good distance away. Tristan treaded water and waited for the others. It was freezing compared to the water in Florida, and his heart was hammering. Ryder and Sam popped up nearby.

"Okay, we did it," Sam said, her teeth chattering. "Let's go back."

"Nah, let's go farther out," Ryder insisted, staring at Tristan in a silent dare.

"You are seriously twisted," Sam countered, starting to turn back toward shore. She paused. "Hey, what's that?" She pointed to a dim, blue-green glow some twenty yards farther offshore and a little to the left.

"Let's go check it out," Ryder suggested, taking off.

Tristan and Sam looked at one another, shrugged their shoulders, and followed. As he swam, Tristan began to warm up. His eyes also began adjusting to the night's darkness, and he could see a little farther ahead.

Whatever the glowing thing was, it was about ten feet down and sort of spherical. The three teens dove and hovered close to the shimmering orb. Tristan watched as Sam reached out to gently touch the jellyfish's bell, staying well away from its hanging strings of sting. The bell sparkled blue-green. As she pulled her hand away, Tristan realized that it, too, gave off a faint, luminous, blue-green glow. He looked at his own hands. They were shimmering too. He swam to the surface.

"What's going on with our hands?" Sam asked, looking at her glimmering hands. Then they looked at their legs, which had also begun glowing blue-green.

"Whoa!" exclaimed Tristan. "We're bioluminescent."

"Like, awesome," Ryder added.

"Let's go back and show the others," Sam suggested. "Must be another effect of the new pills. Very cool."

"Nah, let's stay out here," Ryder said. "It's not even that cold."

"Yeah, actually, that's strange," Sam noted. "We should be freezing by now without wetsuits."

"I'm liking these new pills more and more," Tristan said, thinking that must be why he had warmed up so quickly.

Sam ducked underwater. Tristan heard a sort of clicking noise. Seconds later, Sam popped back up and pointed seaward. "The kelp is kinda messing with my echolocation, but I think there's something out there."

Tristan squinted, trying to see where she was pointing. "Where and what kind of something?"

"Something kinda big," Sam answered. "I think it's tangled up in the kelp."

Tristan was now feeling warm and more confident. "Let's go check it out." Without waiting to see what the others would say, he swam toward the forest of kelp that lay offshore.

Ryder followed. Sam paused, but soon she, too, headed farther out into the darkness.

As Tristan got closer to the kelp, he could see that something pretty big was caught up in it, about fifteen feet down. Whatever it was, it was wrapped up tight in a tangle of the rubbery seaweed and struggling to get out. Tristan dove, pushed a few pieces of kelp out of the way, and held up his hands. The faint glow from his skin provided just enough light to see what was there. But what was a scuba diver doing alone at night in the kelp forest—and without a light? Tristan waved his hands at the diver, trying to get his or her attention. But the diver was too busy trying to get free of the seaweed to notice. Tristan reached out and tried to grasp one of the long pieces of kelp encircling the diver. The seaweed was slick and slimy, making it hard to hold onto. Tristan felt the kelp brush against his legs. He kicked at it while trying to pull at the kelp trapping the diver. Seaweed encircled Tristan's knees. Another piece began to wrap around his neck. Tristan's pulse quickened. He stopped trying to help the diver and began pushing at the kelp now wrapped around him. But it only seemed to make it worse. The more he fought, the more tangled up he became.

Will Tristan escape the kelp forest and rescue the diver? Find out in *Stingray City*!